"...ant to go on a date?"

"Sure, why not?" Sean gave Jess a gentle shove on the arm. "I get company and you get a chance to remember what it's like to be dating. Kind of a practice run. Courage, remember, Jess?"

"Oh, well, but...I couldn't..." she stumbled. Her fingers went to her mouth and she bit a fingernail before seeming to realize what she was doing and clasping her hands firmly in her lap.

"Come on, what are you scared of?"

"I'm not scared."

Suddenly, Sean saw his chance. "Bo-oo-ook, bok, bok." He did his best chicken imitation, complete with flapping elbows.

Jess rolled her eyes in an expression he was now familiar with.

"I'm not scared," she repeated.

Sean did a few more "boks" for good measure.

She shook her head and smiled. "You're being stupid."

"I'm not the only one."

Dear Reader,

I hope you enjoy reading this book half as much I enjoyed writing it! There was so much fun research involved.

To start with, a very friendly and helpful neighborhood vet kindly assisted me with some of the veterinary details to help me make Jess's world feel real. As did many of my dog-loving friends, who took delight in sharing their pets' tales of misadventure. I have to say researching the world of injured dogs and dog shelters was less fun (and occasionally tear-inducing), but there were many positive, wonderful happy endings there, too.

Building Sean's world was a little like stepping into a parallel dimension—one I'm very glad to have discovered. It wasn't exactly hard work, going to conventions and playing on Twitter to see how Sean might interact with his fans and build his following. And once again I met some lovely people, willing to share their passions and experiences. But I do have to admit, it wasn't like I *really* needed to do much research: I've soaked up plenty of fan-style experience in my years as an eager fan girl of all sorts of things from pop music to TV shows. It's great fun being a fan of something and part of the community it generates.

Jess and Sean are at very different stages in their lives when they meet, but they're both in need of something only the other can give them. I hope you like the journey they go through that involves dogs, Twitter, comic books, cosplay and one very red vintage muscle car called Desdemona.

I'd love to hear from you. Visit me at www.emmiedark.com.

Cheers,

Emmie Dark

Just for Today...

EMMIE DARK

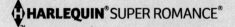

HARLEQUIN® SUPER ROMANCE®

Recycling programs
for this product may
not exist in your area.

ISBN-13: 978-0-373-60783-9

JUST FOR TODAY…

Copyright © 2013 by Melissa Dark

Printed in U.S.A.

ABOUT THE AUTHOR

After years of writing press releases, employee news-letters and speeches for CEOs and politicians—none of which included any kind of kissing—Emmie Dark finally took to her laptop to write what she wanted to write. She was both amazed and delighted to discover that what came out were sexy, noble heroes who found themselves crossing paths with strong, but perhaps slightly damaged, heroines. And plenty of kissing. Emmie lives in Melbourne, Australia, and she likes red lipstick, chardonnay, sunshine, driving fast, rose-scented soap and a really good cup of tea.

Books by Emmie Dark

HARLEQUIN SUPERROMANCE

Other titles by this author available in ebook format.

To my wonderfully loving, encouraging and patient family: Mum, Dad, Chris and Georgina, and Neil, Kerryn, Steve, Gemma, Stephanie, Michelle, Nick and Oliver. Love you all.

CHAPTER ONE

"YOU PROMISED ME SEX."

Sean Paterson lounged against the wall, crossing his arms as he surveyed the room.

Despite the refinement of the five-star-hotel ballroom, the party was beginning to get out of hand. It was late, and the volume had risen in direct proportion to the consumption of alcohol. The dance floor was heaving. Women's shoes had been abandoned, men's coats left hanging limply on satin-covered chairs. On a nearby table, an overturned glass created a slowly spreading stain in the crisp, expensive linen cloth.

As weddings went, Sean figured this one would go down as a success.

"I did *nossuch* thing," his brother slurred. Rob was looking flushed, but whether it was from champagne or the untold dizziness of his newlywed status, Sean wasn't sure. Either way, he took big-brother pride in his little brother's happiness, while also being simultaneously suspicious and—strangely—a tiny bit jealous of it.

He raised his eyebrows as he turned to Rob. "Yes, dear brother, you did. When you asked me to be your best man, I declined for all the sensible reasons we both understand all too well. But then you told me the ladies go gaga over a guy in a tux and the bridesmaids would be desperate to get in my pants, so I reluctantly capitulated. What you didn't tell me was that, of said bridesmaids, one would be about-to-pop pregnant and the other would be jailbait."

Rob swayed a little. "Yeah. Maybe I did. Sorry 'bout that."

Sean straightened and slapped his brother on the arm. "Might want to take it easy on the grog, mate. Don't want to disappoint your bride on her wedding night."

Rob laughed. "Look at her. As if she isn't going to pass out as soon as she hits the sheets." There was an unmistakably fond warmth in his voice as he gestured to the dance floor, where Hailey was dancing with her friends. The flowers pinned in her hair were about to fall out and her frilly skirts were hitched up in her arms so she could show off all her steps to the '80s retro hits the DJ had insisted on playing all night. If anything, she was drunker than Rob.

"Besides," Rob said, awkwardly peeling off his black jacket, "when've I ever had to help you score? You do just fine on your own."

Sean inclined his head in acknowledgment. Although he and Rob were close, they'd taken very different paths in life.

Rob and Hailey had met in their senior years of high school and there'd never been any question that they'd marry—it was just a matter of *when.* Sean knew that Rob had only slept with one other girl in his life—when he and Hailey had broken up for a few months during their university years—and Sean wasn't sure if he approved of that. Surely it wasn't right for a guy to commit himself to one girl—forever—without sampling more of what the world had to offer. But Rob insisted he knew what he wanted, and what he wanted was Hailey.

Sean's life, in comparison was...different. Very different. Much to the despair of their parents. But despite all the family difficulties, they were still brothers, and so here he was. For Rob, he'd do just about anything—even face his mother's frown and his father's scowl and the general disapproving air from the rest of the snotty Paterson clan.

He scanned the room again. Weddings were *so* not his thing—family or otherwise. But there was—

"Who's that?" Sean asked. He'd noticed the woman before, at the ceremony, but lost sight of her when he'd had to go with the wedding party and pose for a ridiculous series of photographs in ever-more-unlikely locations: the bustling kitchen of a Chinese restaurant, and on the tram tracks in the middle of one of Melbourne's busiest city streets. For the couple of hours they'd been under the photographer's control, Sean hadn't been sure if she'd been trying to photograph them or get them killed.

"Who?" Rob asked.

Sean pointed with his chin across the room. She was hard to miss. Sitting at a table by herself, trying to look okay with that fact, but failing badly.

Bronzed brunette hair hung in waves down her back. Her burgundy evening dress was cut low in front and swept across her hips to fall in soft folds around her legs. They were great legs—Sean had noticed when she'd sat down in the church. From his vantage point, he'd had a great view of the generous split up the front that had parted and almost revealed all her assets before she'd primly pulled the two halves of the skirt together and covered herself from his sight.

It was one of those moments that Sean always noticed—a moment his writer's brain took in and preserved for future character-revealing traits. Her little maneuver told him a lot about her: she'd worn an unmistakably sexy dress, and yet wasn't quite comfortable in it. *Intriguing.*

"Oh, the brunette?"

Sean nodded.

"Yeah, that's Hailey's boss."

"The vet?"

Rob nodded, his head bouncing as though it was attached to his neck by a spring. "Uh-huh."

"Who's she here with?"

"Oh, uh, I think she came on her own." Rob was distracted by someone calling out to him from the other side of the room.

Sean stopped himself from rubbing his hands together. "Nice," he said under his breath.

Rob heard and his attention abruptly returned to their conversation. "Sean, she's Hailey's boss."

Sean didn't miss the warning. "I'll behave," he said.

Before Rob could say anything more, the room was filled with the sound of cutlery clinking on glasses—a tradition that demanded the newlyweds kiss before the noise would stop.

"Oh, jeez, again?" Rob groaned.

The guests had been taking great delight in forcing Rob and Hailey to kiss as often as possible—and usually when they were on opposite ends of the room.

Sean gave Rob a shove toward the dance floor. "Better go do your husbandly duty."

"Yeah, I guess." Rob's words were flat but his expression showed he was nothing less than thrilled about another chance to kiss his bride. He took a step toward the dance floor, but then paused and turned back. "Hey, man?" Rob settled a serious look on his brother. "Thanks. You know? Really. I know how much this sucked for you. I'm just glad you could be here."

Rob grabbed Sean in a drunken embrace, and Sean found himself stepping into it, clasping his brother in return, slapping his back hard, then just hanging on. He'd had a key role in the wedding, but this was the first time they'd had the chance for a brotherly moment—every other minute of the day had been packed with tasks, obligations, and with Sean taking great care to avoid being alone with either or both of their parents.

Rob stepped back, blinking suspiciously.

Sean wasn't about to get *that* soppy. Besides, unlike Rob, he hadn't had much to drink—he'd learned from hard-won experience it was better to keep his wits about him when surrounded by his family.

He gave Rob another slap on the arm. "You're welcome. Now go be a husband."

Rob grimaced, but Sean watched his face transform as he headed to his bride, the frown turning into a goofy smile when Hailey did a clumsy pirouette and began to dance in his direction.

Poor sucker.

Sean turned his attention back to the room, scanning it before his gaze once again settled on the brunette. Hailey's boss—she owned and ran the small vet clinic where Hailey was working while she finished her veterinary studies. Rob hadn't told him her name. Oh, well, at least that gave him his opening.

JESS'S FEET WERE TWITCHING in their uncomfortable heels, and she hoped most people would mistake it as an urge to dance. Actually, it was an urge to get the hell out of here.

It had been a lovely gesture for Hailey, her veterinary nurse, to invite her to the wedding. It was wonderful to see Hailey looking so beautiful and so happy; she and Rob were the picture-book bridal couple. Jess had listened to all the wedding planning and prewedding nerves over the past few months, so it was nice to be here to see it all come together—especially knowing how much the whole thing cost. There'd even been a photographer in attendance from one of the glossy magazines—apparently a Paterson family wedding was a bigger deal than she'd thought. She also better understood some of Hailey's bridezilla-style hysterics now, having met the indomitable Mr. and Mrs. Paterson, who presided over the event like a stern king and queen.

But at the moment, Jess wished she'd been able to find an excuse not to come. When Margie, the clinic receptionist and third team member of their tiny practice, had realized she wouldn't be able to attend the wedding because it clashed with the Pacific-island cruise she'd booked with her husband, it had been too late for Jess to retract her acceptance.

At least if Margie had been here, Jess would have known *someone.* It wasn't that she was a wallflower, really. It was just hard being the odd man out, so to speak, in a room full of people who otherwise all knew each other.

Unfortunately, she'd been seated at the table with Hailey and Rob's university friends. Jess could understand the logic—a lot of them were single, too, and they weren't family. But they were all Hailey's and Rob's age—making them at least ten to twelve years younger than Jess—and that made her feel like the grown-up who'd been seated at the kids' table. While they'd made occasional polite attempts to include her, they'd spent most of the night getting very drunk and reminiscing about their shared history and university high jinks and pranks. It had been fun, at first, but it was only possible to stay enthusiastically interested in such things for so long.

Especially when she was sober.

How early could you politely leave a wedding

reception, anyway? Weren't you supposed to wait until after the bride and groom left?

She stifled a yawn as she watched the happy couple grooving on the dance floor. Didn't look as though they were in any hurry.

The thought of her bed had never been more appealing.

Jeez, when had she turned into such an old, boring grump?

"You look like you could use one of these."

A misty glass of champagne appeared in front of her and Jess looked up to see mischievous green eyes twinkling down at her with a predatory grin beneath.

"I, uh…" Her hand took the proffered glass more out of reflex than anything else, but her temporary wine waiter took that as encouragement and sat down beside her, placing his own glass on the table.

"I'm Sean Paterson. Best man. And you are?" he asked.

It was such a smoothly delivered line Jess's instant reaction was to shoot him down, but he was the first person who'd approached her since her tablemates had all moved to the smoking area outside. At least with someone sitting with her, she wouldn't look like such a loser.

Not to mention that *he* was the man she'd been trying hard not to stare at all afternoon. In this instance the term *best man* was more than a job description.

His short, rich brown spiky hair had been artfully arranged; his jaw showed the shadow of a beard that held more than a hint of ginger. Those mossy-green eyes had flecks of gold in them, making them look as if they were constantly sparkling—as if there was some joke going on that only he knew about. He was tall but not freakishly so—only just making it to six feet Jess would guess—a good thing because very tall men always made her feel uncomfortable about her own five-feet-four-on-a-good-day. His tuxedo fitted him perfectly; tailored to suit his broad shoulders and narrow waist.

He was, in short, devastatingly gorgeous.

And he was Hailey's husband's brother.

Jess knew all about him. She'd known his name was Sean before he introduced himself. He was a writer of comic books or schlock horror novels, or something like that, and a nomad, apparently, of no fixed address. The black sheep of the Paterson clan—the one they didn't like to talk about at family gatherings. He'd dropped out of his accounting degree at university and run away. There had been, according to Hailey, a massive fight over Rob's insistence on having his older brother as his best man.

He was also—*what were the words Hailey had used? Oh, yeah*—irresponsible and reckless and immature. Hailey said they were the adjectives his own mother invoked.

Sean was the center of most of Hailey's more extreme hysterics about all the things that could go wrong on her wedding day. Sean would forget the rings. Sean would refuse to wear the suit properly. Sean would bring a hooker as his date. Sean would simply not turn up.

Jess had listened patiently to Hailey's rants. Listened, while secretly thinking that Sean sounded kind of thrilling, only to silently chastise herself immediately. She had appalling taste in men. Her attraction to Hailey's brother-in-law-to-be, just from a description of his faults and the potential chaos he could cause, was yet further proof of that.

When she'd seen him standing at the front of the church next to Rob, she'd inwardly sighed. Of course he was the most attractive man she'd seen in years. Of course that would be how it worked.

He was hot. And so off-limits it wasn't funny. Not that anything like that was likely. It just wasn't something she did these days.

Yep. Somehow, when she hadn't been paying attention, she'd turned into a miserable old spinster who preferred to be at home in her slippers than dancing the night away in heels.

What a depressing thought.

"I'm driving," she said, putting the glass he'd handed her on the table. But she twisted a little in her seat to face him. It would be rude to ignore him, after all, and there was no harm in talking. "Thank you anyway."

"Strange name."

"Sorry?"

"'I'm driving.' It's a strange name."

He was teasing her because she hadn't answered his question. She thought for a moment for a witty comeback but nothing sprang to mind. "Jess. Jess

Alexander," she said in the end. *Really sparkling repartee there, Jess.*

"What kind of car?" he asked, putting his own champagne down on the table untouched.

"Huh?"

"What kind of car do you drive?"

"Oh, a Subaru. Station wagon." A sensible car that was large enough to transport animals occasionally but not too large to maneuver in the city.

He nodded, looking as if he was waiting for something. Finally Jess caught on.

"What kind of car do you have?" she asked politely.

"My car was used for the wedding."

"Ah. Yes, of course." Jess remembered that particular conversation with Hailey now. It was the one thing that Rob had insisted on for the wedding—apart from having his brother as best man. He'd been adamant that they use his brother's pride and joy as the bridal car. Hailey had cried buckets because she'd wanted white limousines, not a red '70s vintage muscle car with black stripes down the hood.

It had been Jess who had suggested that perhaps the groom should have just *one* thing in his own wedding that he'd decided upon. Jess had tried—gently—to advise Hailey that a great deal of marriage was about compromise. But then her own marriage had not exactly been a shining example to hold up for comparison, so once the irony of the conversation had occurred to her, she'd shut up and kept her advice to herself.

Something of that conversation must have penetrated Hailey's wedding-addled mind, though, because in the end, Rob had been given final say over the wedding cars. And truly, Jess had thought the car was a fun and quirky touch this afternoon as the happy couple had climbed into it outside the church.

"It's a nice car," Jess said, as she knew she was expected to.

He looked pleased, and Jess steeled herself for a conversation about carburetors and horsepower. The guy was too good-looking not to be totally self-absorbed. But he surprised her by asking instead, "So, do you know many people here?"

He sat sideways in the chair, resting his arm over the back. It made his jacket gape, revealing the crisp white of his shirt, and sending a ribbon of his scent in Jess's direction. Something spicy and forbidden, rich and romantic. Something unique and penetrating among all the clamoring smells in the room: food, wine, flowers, the suffocating perfume of the older woman at the table beside them.

"Not a soul," Jess admitted.

"Me, either." He leaned forward and said it in a whisper, as if he were confessing a sin.

"But what about your family?"

He gave a twisted smile that hid as much as it revealed. "Well, I know Mom and Dad of course. Be a bit strange if I didn't. But I'm not really... Well, Rob's the one who's good at keeping up with all the *rellies.* Wouldn't know my great-aunt Sally if I fell over her."

As if to prove his point, a ruddy-faced portly man clapped him on the shoulder as he walked past. "Sean!"

Sean gave Jess a highly amusing "uh-oh" look before tilting his head up to the man. "Uncle Stuart."

"Good to see you."

"You look well."

"You, too, son. You still off doing those funny books or have you got a proper job now?"

"Uh—"

Uncle Stuart didn't give Sean a chance to answer. "No, that's what I thought. When are you going to get your head into gear and go back and finish that accounting degree so you can join Paterson Associates?" His tone was jocular, but there was no missing the fact that Uncle Stuart wasn't joking.

A flash of something crossed Sean's face, too quick for Jess to really analyze it, but if she'd had to guess she'd call it anger. And it was totally understandable. Uncle Stuart was being incredibly rude.

But then Sean was smiling that carefree, easy smile again. "How's Auntie Laura?" he asked pleasantly.

"She's good, good. And you are?" Uncle Stuart leered at Jess, sending a puff of foul breath over her along with his lecherous gaze.

"I'm Jess, Jessica Alexander." She introduced herself for the second time in as many minutes.

"Jess is Hailey's boss. She's a vet," Sean added.

Jess started with surprise. He knew who she was? Why had he asked her name?

"Well, you just be careful with this one then, Sean."
Uncle Stuart gave a wink that made Jess want to
cringe, and she saw that dangerous flash pass through
Sean's eyes again. "Don't need Hailey to find she
doesn't have a job when she gets back from her honeymoon!" Uncle Stuart chuckled as if he was the
most amusing man in the room before stumbling off
to share his halitosis with others.

Sean blinked a couple of times, as if mentally eras-
ing the incident from his memory. "Where were we?"
he asked.

Jess found herself tilting forward. She told herself
it was just to move away from the pungent aroma
Uncle Stuart had left behind, but that wasn't true.
She felt as if Sean was somehow magnetic, and like
an iron filing she couldn't help but draw close to him.

It wasn't as if anything was going to happen, so
taking a deeper whiff of him couldn't hurt.

"I think we were talking about cars."

"Really? I'd much rather talk about you."

Again with the cheesy line. Somehow, he managed
to carry it off. Maybe it was his seemingly unshakable confidence.

"I'm not that interesting," Jess said, as flippantly
as she could manage. She was enjoying flirting with
him. It felt fun and kind of dangerous. Things she
hadn't let herself feel in far too long.

"Now, I think that's a lie."

"Really?" She raised an eyebrow and twisted in her
seat to echo his posture. Like exercising a long-atro-
phied muscle, something inside her began to warm up.

"Really. You're certainly the most interesting woman in this room."

Jess managed to stop herself rolling her eyes. But only just. "And what makes you so sure of that?"

"Because you're the only person here I want to talk to."

He managed to sound so sincere when he said it that it didn't even sound like a line. Jess was rapidly realizing Sean deserved the reputation Hailey had reported. He clearly worked hard for it. The polar opposite to his responsible, down-to-earth younger brother, who'd joined the family accounting firm and married his high school sweetheart. Sean had a woman in every town—in every suburb, if Hailey was to be believed.

He'd be good in bed, then.

The thought sent a wave of heat through her body. It had been a while. Too long, really.

She shook it away. "And why's that?" she countered.

"Everyone else is incredibly dull. I know. I've pretty much worked the entire room. Not an original thought to be found."

"So I'm just the best of a bad lot? Hmm, that's *very* flattering." Jess stroked a lock of hair behind her ear before she realized what she was doing.

The side of his mouth quirked and she watched his eyes follow the movement of her hair before returning to meet her gaze. "You could see it that way, I suppose." He leaned back languidly, one hand toying with a crumpled menu card on the table. "Or you could see it as an opportunity."

Jess gave him an exaggerated quizzical look. "An opportunity? An opportunity for what?" She ran her fingers around the misty stem of the glass of champagne on the table. *Oh, how easily the old moves came back!*

"To get to know me better."

That was too much; Jess couldn't hold in her laughter.

Sean pouted, faking a hurt look. "My lady, you wound me." He clapped one palm to his chest, over his heart.

His chest would be firm, she'd bet. Hairy or not? His high collar and bow tie allowed for no hints, and the shirt was fastened with those special tuxedo studs that matched his cuff links. Jess had never played with those before. A wicked impulse came from nowhere. It made her fingers itch to undo that tie and open the shirt, button by button, to reveal his skin and satisfy her curiosity.

She raised her eyes to his and realized some of her thoughts must have been painted on her face. The green of his eyes had turned forest-at-dusk dark, and his body was poised with a careful stillness.

The stillness of a predator about to strike.

A sudden jolt of nerves shot through her belly. *Be careful, Jess.* It was all very well to play games, but when you had no intentions of following through, the line in the sand had to be very clear. "I, uh," Jess began, not entirely sure what she was going to say.

He leaned forward, a fraction, and his hand reached for hers, peeling her grip from the stem of the wine-glass and taking her hand lightly. He didn't clasp it tightly, just let her fingers loosely sit in his palm. His own fingers moved almost imperceptibly to stroke the inside of her wrist.

Jess felt the touch echo throughout her body, reso-nating loudest in the parts that had been empty for too long. Her breath caught and a slow burn of arousal lit deep inside her.

Oh, it had definitely been *far* too long. A thrill of anxiety went through her—nerves and excitement all wound up together. Was it time to remedy that? Could she possibly let something like that happen?

From everything Jess had heard from Hailey, Sean was the epitome of the love-'em-and-leave-'em type. No permanent address, he'd been dragged to town for the wedding and would be disappearing again as soon as he could—much to Hailey's relief.

If a girl wanted some casual, no-strings-attached sex, Sean Paterson was probably the perfect choice. But he *was* Hailey's brother-in-law, and Jess didn't want her sex life—or lack thereof—to be workplace gossip.

Excuses, excuses, the wicked impulse from within tutted. *You want to be alone the rest of your life? You really want to be defined by failure forever? You've got to start somewhere....*

Jess took a quick glance at the dance floor where Hailey and Rob were drunkenly clutching each other as they swayed to the music. *It wasn't as if they would notice.* And she doubted Sean was the kiss-and-tell kind.

But there was one more thing. Sean was Rob's older brother, she knew that, but he still had to be significantly younger than her. It just wasn't...*proper.*

The fact that all this *thinking* was required had to be a sign, too.

She managed a strangled-sounding laugh as she extracted her hand from his, feeling her cheeks heat and hoping her flush wasn't too obvious.

"If I only wounded you, clearly my sword isn't as sharp as it used to be," she said.

"Perhaps you just need more practice." He didn't seem deterred in the slightest.

"At fighting?"

"If that's what's on offer, I'll take it." He gave her a lopsided smile, the kind of charming, disarming look that had undoubtedly broken hearts all across the country.

Jess was afraid it was about to be her undoing, as well.

She licked her lips, wondering if there was any lipstick left on them. "You should be more careful. You don't know much about your opponent."

"True. But I like what I've seen so far."

This time Jess *did* roll her eyes. A girl had her limits. "Does this shtick really work for you?"

His expression turned suddenly serious and he shifted forward, elbows on his knees, fingers interlaced, his face mere inches from hers. She could feel the heat of his legs where they bracketed her own.

He'd well and truly invaded her personal space, and Jess would have edged away, but her back was right against the chair and there was nowhere to go.

"What would you prefer?" he asked, eyes boring into hers.

"What? In terms of a seduction?" She held his gaze when she said it, just to see if he flinched. He didn't.

"Is that what this is?"

"Isn't it?"

He seemed to give the matter some thought. "I'd probably call it flirting, but, yeah, I guess if we break it down, *seduction* probably better expresses my eventual goal."

There was something incredibly appealing about confidence like that. In any other circumstances, it would be annoying as hell, but right here, right now, it was definitely working for him. And for her—despite the butterflies tangoing in her belly.

She couldn't help but smile. "You're pretty sure of yourself, aren't you?"

He shrugged one shoulder. "I can be. When the moment calls for it."

"How old are you?"

A quick frown creased his forehead. "Twenty-eight. Why?"

"I'm thirty-five."

"And?"

"And?" He was incredible. "I'm seven years older than you."

"So?"

"Do you even remember when this song came

out?" Jess gestured to the dance floor where wedding guests were bopping away to a song Jess fondly remembered from her high school days.

"I prefer classic rock from the sixties and seventies. This pop stuff is giving me a headache."

Jess sighed. He didn't get it.

A woman called out Sean's name from the other side of the room. Jess looked over and saw her wave and head their way—Rob and Sean's mother in an imposing teal-green suit. Her hair was a solid helmet of hairspray and not a strand of it moved as she strode toward them. The chunks of diamonds in each ear and around her throat sparkled almost blindingly.

"Isn't that your mother? Does she want to talk to you?"

Sean glanced up and a pained expression crossed his face. "Not now, Mom," he called out to the woman who was still three table lengths away.

"But, Sean—"

"Later." He dismissed her with a careless wave.

Mrs. Paterson stopped with an expression so wounded, Jess almost wanted to make Sean apologize. But then she shot her son a look that would curdle milk and threw up her hands in exasperation. She mouthed the word *typical* and rolled her eyes before turning back the way she'd come. Sean didn't see any of that, Jess noted; his gaze was back on her, and it was as if the interruption had never happened.

"Let's dance."

"Huh?"

"Come on."

Jess wasn't quite sure how it happened, but a moment later she found herself being pulled to the dance floor, her hand clasped firmly in Sean's. He found a small clearing and let her go, turning to face her. He shuffled his feet, clearly uncomfortable, and raised his hands in a halfhearted accompaniment. Jess began swaying her hips, just as the boppy pop song came to a close. They were left standing, facing each other, as the strains of one of her favorite Madonna ballads began. The floor began to clear around them, hot and sweaty dancers muttering how they were grateful for a break, leaving behind couples happy to enjoy a slow dance together.

"Well, this is awkward," she muttered.

"Sorry, I'm a crappy dancer." He didn't sound especially broken up by that fact. Was his confidence really *that* unshakable?

"It was your idea."

"I know. Here."

There were still a few other couples dancing, and Sean seemed to look around for inspiration before pulling Jess close, his hands resting on her lower back. Jess had no choice but to put her hands on his shoulders—solid and warm, even through the padding of his jacket.

As dances went, it wasn't going to score them any points in a competition. But they found an easy rhythm and no one seemed to be commenting on their ineptitude.

Jess found herself staring at the shiny tuxedo

buttons on his shirt, her thoughts running a million miles a minute with ideas that she had no business entertaining.

Hailey's brother-in-law.

She should definitely *not* be thinking about seeing him naked. Or about what kind of kisser he'd be. Certainly not about how good he smelled, or how, if she just stepped a little closer, she'd be pressed full-length against his body. Definitely not about how his fingers were stroking her back gently through her dress, and the touch was sending ripples of sensation to other, needy, parts of her.

Until this moment she hadn't realized how much she missed being touched.

Sean said something, but she missed the words, feeling the rumble of them instead. She looked up. "Sorry?" Luckily she'd started to speak before her eyes met his, because once they did, her breath seemed to stop somewhere halfway in her throat. He was wearing that half grin again, eyes sparkling mischievously.

"I said, you look very serious."

"This is a serious song."

"I guess." He dismissed her comment with all the gravity it deserved—none—before nudging Jess's knee with one of his own. "Come on, let's get out of here."

"What? We can't leave. They haven't cut the cake yet." As much as she'd spent the past two hours desperate to get out of here, Sean's offer of escape made her stomach flip unpleasantly at the same time as that little voice in her head cheered her on.

"Oh, like anyone's going to notice."

"You're the best man."

"Yeah, but my job's done for the day. Get the groom to the wedding, check. Hand over the rings, check. Make the speech at dinner, check. That's it."

"It was a very good speech," Jess said. Sean had spoken easily and confidently—no surprises there. He'd given a couple of the requisite humorous tales from Rob's past and done a lovely job of sincerely wishing the happy couple a bright future. As he'd taken the microphone and begun to speak, the apprehensive and then relieved looks on the entire wedding party's faces had to have been obvious to the whole room.

He dismissed her praise with a wave. "Thanks. So, ready to go?"

Those green eyes were staring down at her, half daring, half asking. The dare part appealed to the reckless streak that Jess mostly kept hidden—and that had certainly not seen the light of day in recent times. It was an impulse that had given her, among other things, a tattoo of a tiny star on her butt, a scar under her chin from a fall down a flight of stairs in a nightclub in Amsterdam and an occasional back twinge that hadn't been there before she'd bungee jumped over a river in New Zealand.

"Go where?" she asked.

He dropped his hands from around her and Jess stepped back, her body already mourning the loss of contact. Sean reached into his pocket. "For a drive," he said. His hand emerged and he threw a set of keys in the air before catching them again in one hand.

He took a step toward the exit, arm outstretched, one eyebrow arched in question. His eyes glinted with challenge.

Jess hesitated. "Just a drive?"

"Just a drive," he confirmed.

She thought for a moment. But only a moment. Then she reached for his hand.

"I have a feeling I'm going to regret this," she said under her breath.

Sean laughed and pulled her toward the door.

CHAPTER TWO

"WE CAN'T TAKE the bridal car!"

"Of course we can—it's my car." Sean pulled on Jess's hand until they stood on the apron of the curved hotel drive. His GT had clearly been parked by someone who appreciated that this was a car worth showing off.

But he'd forgotten about the freaking ribbons.

Someone had put ribbons on Dezzie. Ribbons! Sean crouched down in front of the car only to find the stupid stuff had been threaded through and tied tight around the front grille. He needed a knife, but bloody Rob had refused to let him wear one in his tux.

"Sorry, baby," he murmured as he stood. He stroked the hood of the car to try to make her feel better about the ignominy.

"Sean, seriously, we can't take this car."

He nodded. "Yes, we can. Rob and Hailey are staying here at the hotel tonight." He gestured to the tall building behind them. "Honeymoon suite." He winked.

"Are you sure?"

"Positive. I, uh, did a few things to make the room

ready for their wedding night." Sean opened the passenger door and reached for Jess's hand.

She hesitated. "Oh. *Oh*." She gave him a look of distaste. "What, lots of condoms and sex toys and stuff? Nothing too gross I hope."

"Nothing too gross, I promise. Just…being helpful."

Jess shook her head, but a smile played around her lips. He wanted to kiss her, to see if those lips were as soft and sweet-tasting as they looked. But she had something of the easily startled lamb about her and Sean figured he needed to work up to that. Reading people was one of his talents—a talent he was proud of—and that contributed to his success as an author. And he was sure he was reading Miss Jessica Alexander correctly. She wasn't going to easily succumb to his charms.

Just as well, he'd always enjoyed a challenge.

"Where are we going?" she asked, but she put her hand in his and allowed him to help her into the car. Sean blessed the designer of her dress as the split in her skirt once again fell open, revealing a length of creamy thigh. He swallowed hard as his body tightened, and he gave himself a silent lecture about restraint as he closed the door and walked around to the driver's side.

He settled into the familiar seat and smiled as the car started up with a welcoming rumble. Desdemona was more than a car. She was a friend, a shelter, a partner in crime, a symbol of his achievement.

Occasionally, even, a home. Dezzie meant more to him than most human beings of his acquaintance.

Tonight, she was an escape vehicle. Sean felt a weight lift as he maneuvered the car out of the hotel and away from the Paterson family, as if he'd been wearing a lead cloak that he'd finally managed to shrug off.

"Would you like me to leave you two alone?"

Sean was startled from his reflection by Jess's amused tone. "Huh?"

"The way you're stroking the steering wheel. It's almost…obscene." She laughed, a warm, rich sound.

Sean didn't rise to the bait. Jess wasn't the first person to comment on the close relationship he had with his car. And frankly, he didn't care what other people thought. Not about Dezzie, anyway.

"She's been through a lot today," Sean said. "Not the least of which was Rob driving her from the church. He's my brother, and I love him, but the guy has no idea how to work a clutch."

"Go on, give me the specs."

"Seriously?"

"Tell me as if I don't know anything about cars."

"Because you don't know anything about cars."

"Exactly."

Sean ran a hand over the dash as he spoke. "Dezzie is a Ford XY Falcon GTHO Phase III, affectionately called the Hoey. One of only three hundred made. This model won Bathurst in 1971 with Allan Moffat driving."

"Dezzie?"

"Yeah, short for Desdemona—the woman who elopes with Othello. Most of the other cars that are still around today are in showrooms or collections."

"But you like to drive it—I mean, *her,* Dezzie."

Sean smiled, pleased with Jess's correction. "Yeah. It'd be kind of like keeping a wild bird in a cage. She was born to be on the road."

Jess nodded with a surprisingly understanding look on her face. "I get what you mean. So, gonna show me what she can do?"

He flicked Jess his best wicked look. "I thought you'd never ask."

The speed limit on city streets was disappointingly low, so Sean headed for the closest freeway he could find—then he could at least let Dezzie off the leash a little. When he reached the on-ramp and accelerated hard, Jess let out a yelp, but he backed off as soon as he reached the limit. Well, just over the limit. Dezzie's top speed neared two hundred and fifty kilometers an hour, but Sean hadn't let her rip like that for a while. He needed to wait until he'd earned back a few more points on his license.

"That was fun," Jess said.

"It's better when you get out on a racetrack."

"I can imagine." She twisted and looked around into the backseat. Her dress gaped as she did, revealing to him that she wasn't wearing a bra. Sean did his best to be gentlemanly about it, but the sight of her breast almost down to her nipple had his mind fogging over. He couldn't remember the last time he'd felt such an instant attraction to a woman. And he didn't for the life of him understand how she could have been left sitting alone at the wedding. She should have been slapping off come-ons like flies.

"She's very clean. Did you have to get her detailed for the wedding?"

Sean struggled to focus on her question. "Dezzie's always pretty clean, but yeah, she did get a spruce up."

"And ribbons." There was no mistaking the tease in her voice.

"Yeah. And ribbons," he grumped.

He glanced over and Jess met his eyes. She was smiling, more than a trace of amusement in her expression over his fondness for his car. But it was kindly meant—and after a day with his family, Sean definitely knew the difference.

"You're a writer, huh?"

"Yep." She was the first person all day to ask him about his work. It was probably just as well, as the big news he wanted to share wasn't nearly final enough to make public. When he finally did make his announcement, he wanted it to be a big occasion—he wanted to be there to lord his triumph over his parents, see the recognition of his achievement light up in their eyes.

"What kind of books do you write?"

"This and that." He'd learned it was better to be vague with most people. Unless they understood his genre, they tended to be dismissive, if not insulting. Better not to get into it at all. "What's your favorite animal?"

"Huh?"

"Being a vet and all, I figure you must have one."

"Not really. I like all animals."

"What's your least favorite then?"

She paused a moment before answering. "I guess I'm less keen on reptiles. I'm more of a dog and cat person. But at my clinic I look after all kinds of house pets, and that occasionally includes snakes and lizards and the like."

"What happens when you get a snake and a pet mouse in to see you at the same time? Do you have a dividing wall in the waiting room or something?"

"Generally people don't just bring their snakes in and sit them on their lap," she said drily.

"But surely the potential is there for chaos."

"Not in my waiting room."

No. He could see that. She'd accused him of being overly confident, but there was a strength to her that he could see just from the brief interaction they'd had so far. She seemed very "together," compared to other women he knew.

He glanced across at her and their eyes met and held.

One of her eyebrows arched. "Shouldn't you be watching the road?"

"Probably." But it took him another few moments before he pulled his eyes from hers and turned back to face the windscreen. Jessica Alexander was seriously hot. And making him feel the same. He dearly wished he'd thought to remove his tux jacket before he'd gotten in the car.

Jess shifted in her seat and from the corner of his eye, Sean watched her skirt fall open again. She wasn't wearing stockings or panty hose—the bare skin of her legs was a pale pinky-gold that he just knew would feel like silk. Her fingers grabbed the fabric and she tugged on it to pull it back into place.

"Don't." Sean covered her hand with his. The contact sent a warm thrill through him. He wanted to touch her all over. The arousal that had been echoing faintly through his body became an ache at the thought.

Jess halted and looked down at their hands and her bared thighs before sending a smile his way. "Hmm. You sure I won't distract you from driving, sitting here like this?"

Sean tapped his fingers on the steering wheel, doing some quick mental navigation. "We're only ten minutes from where I'm staying."

"And that's where we're going, is it?"

"Well, it would solve the distraction problem."

"Hmm, I see what you mean."

It wasn't much of an answer. "Unless you have another suggestion?" Sean took his eyes off the road for a moment to get a quick read on Jess. He wanted to end this evening with those gorgeous legs wrapped around him—he very much hoped she wanted the same thing. And, in addition to that seductive image, she was right. Her bare skin, her soft floral fragrance, the ideas that were circulating through his head— none of it contributed to totally focused driving.

"How long are you in Melbourne for?"

He frowned at the question. "Not long. Why?"

One shoulder lifted and then dropped in a nonanswer. "Hailey said you don't stick around anywhere for very long. Where to next?"

"Sydney. I'm probably heading there tomorrow or Monday." He had to be somewhere with a solid internet connection by Monday evening. For one of the most important meetings of his life. It'd make sense to set off on the ten-hour drive the next day; stop overnight somewhere halfway so he was fresh when he arrived.

"Is that a problem?" he asked when Jess remained silent. It was better she understood now that this wasn't the beginning of something more than he could offer.

"No, no, it's not a problem." Her voice was a little faint.

Sean steered onto an off-ramp and turned into a side road. As soon as he could, he pulled the car over to stop on a low embankment. He turned to face her and, before she could protest, lowered his lips to hers.

It was a gentle kiss, just lips and breath and the warm rich scent of her skin. Their noses and chins rubbed together as Sean kissed either side of her mouth, before settling on her lips again to just barely caress them.

He pulled back just far enough to watch as her eyes drifted back open, her expression dazed.

"Wow," she whispered.

"Yeah." He grinned, knowing it would be goofy, but that one kiss had been enough to make him absolutely positive about what he wanted next. He cupped her chin with one hand. "Jess? I really like you. I'd like to spend the night with you—if you'd like to spend it with me."

Jess wet her lips nervously but her eyes didn't move from his. "That was direct."

He gave a small shrug. "Best to be up front about these things, I've found."

Jess didn't answer. Her eyes were round and her porcelain skin pale in the sulfuric glow of the street-light.

"You look a little scared."

She gave a weak laugh, shifting in the seat to pull away from him. Sean dropped his hand to rest on her thigh.

"I'm not scared," she said. She met his eyes, a curious determination visible in them.

"If you don't want to, that's cool. Seriously. We'll head back to the reception now." It was the right thing to say, but he hoped to hell she wasn't going to take him up on it.

She still looked nervous, but the smile she gave him was sure. "No, I was over the wedding anyway. Let's go."

"I THOUGHT WE were going to your hotel?" Jess asked as Sean turned onto a suburban street. She had a sudden sinking feeling about exactly where they *were* headed. And her nerves sang. He'd accused her of being scared—he was way off the mark. *Terrified* was more like it.

And that was why she had to go through with it. That and the urgent ache low in her belly that his kiss had only magnified.

"I said we were going to where I was staying."

"And you're staying at Hailey and Rob's place?" Her voice went up at the end, betraying her discomfort.

"Just for tonight. The house sitter doesn't arrive till tomorrow, and someone has to feed the dog in the morning. Does it make a difference?"

Well, yes. One-night-stand sex—with a guy seven years younger than her who also happened to be Hailey's brother-in-law—in a hotel room was fine, *mostly.* Doing it in Hailey and Rob's bed? Not so much. "Uh, well, I..."

"We won't turn any lights on. You can pretend to be anywhere." Sean pulled up on the street in front of a large '60s brick veneer house and its carefully tended row of roses along the fence line. It wasn't a mansion, but it was certainly a decent step-up from a typical newlyweds' first home—Jess knew the Paterson family had bought it, in full, for the couple as an engagement/wedding present.

Sean killed the ignition and the sudden silence made Jess aware of the pulsing of blood in her ears.

His hand reached for hers where they were clasped in her lap. She knew it wasn't by accident that his fingertips brushed against her inner thigh as he took her hand in his. The simple touch sent a bolt of heat straight to her core.

Damn.

She'd never been so turned-on by a guy so easily. Was it a hormonal thing? Didn't they say that women reached their sexual peak in their thirties, men in their twenties? Was that why the chemistry between them was smoking hot?

"Jess?"

She'd never be able to come here for one of Hailey's regular summer barbecues again if she did this.

There was a click and the shushing sound of Sean's seat belt retracting. Then his other hand was on her cheek, turning her to him. He was inches away, a stripe of color from the streetlight highlighting one side of his face. She blinked and her heart rate picked up as if he'd changed her gears as smoothly as Dezzie's.

Oh, who cared about barbecues, anyway?

It took less than a second for Jess to lean forward and banish the distance between them, her lips meeting his. Just like before, they were firm, but soft, and his hand slid across her cheek and into her hair, curling around the nape of her neck. Then he was in control of the kiss, tilting her head to meet his, parting his lips to gently swipe his tongue along her bottom lip. The hand that still held hers, in her lap, had stretched out, and his fingertips were stroking her thigh.

Jess melted into the seat. Any rational concerns she'd had—sex with someone she barely knew, the ramifications of Hailey finding out, the weirdness of doing it in Hailey's house—had vanished. All she knew was that the past couple of years had been hard, and lonely, and celibate. If she didn't deserve this, she didn't know who did.

Sean leaned a little more into her. Somewhere along the way Jess had forgotten to breathe. Her head was spinning, need spiraling deep inside her. She wanted him with a ferocity that astonished her. Her tongue met his, sliding against it with warm, wet heat. She prayed for his hand to climb higher, parted her legs in invitation.

But something held her back from reaching around him, pulling him over her, feeling his heat and heaviness resting on top of her.... *Damn seat belt.*

"How 'bout we get out of here?" He whispered the words against her lips, retreating from their kiss just far enough to speak.

"Yes, yes." Did she sound desperate? If so, she didn't care. The idea that she wouldn't see him again, that Sean would soon be moving on to his next destination, meant she didn't have to worry what he thought of her. She just had to get him to satisfy the raging need he'd stoked to a firestorm inside her. Nothing else mattered. It was incredibly freeing— she wondered why she'd never found the courage to do something like this before.

Something about this situation was different, though. Perhaps it had something to do with Sean's overwhelming confidence. Most guys who'd approached her in recent memory had given up in the face of her hesitation. Her divorce had left her with scars that usually took more than a sexy smile and a wink to overcome. Usually.

Jess fumbled with the seat belt for a moment and then had to scramble for her clutch purse on the floor. By the time she'd found it and untangled herself from the seat belt, Sean was at the door, opening it for her and offering a helping hand. She took it, grateful for his steadying grip. Her knees were feeling unreliable.

The cool night air was almost enough to sober her. Almost. She cast her eyes around the neighborhood, wondering if anyone was watching out of a chink in their curtains. Divorcée Jess Alexander, about to vanish inside with a man practically half her age, after making out in the car with him. It was indecent!

But no. Maybe she was overreacting a little. As nice a street as this was, it was still the city. And neighbors didn't really care what went on next door as long as it wasn't too noisy and it didn't affect the resale value of their property.

Jess had a feeling it might get noisy, but she figured the resale values were safe.

"Whoa, hey, girl," Sean said as they stood on the porch and he tried to push the door open. For a confusing moment, Jess thought he was talking to her, but then Hailey and Rob's aging golden retriever, Suzie, woofed an excited greeting. Jess could hear her tail banging against the wall inside.

"Come on, Suz, you've got to stand back so I can get inside," Sean said with a fond tone. He muttered from the side of his mouth, "Gorgeous dog, but certainly not the smartest one in the litter."

"Uh-huh." Jess was more than familiar with Suzie's goofy smile. She usually wore it when Hailey

brought her into the clinic with yet another accidental injury. Suzie had perfected the "Whoops! Look
what I did" look.

The dog was bouncing around excitedly, and Sean
was doing his best to control her as they stepped
inside the house and closed the door behind them.
"The neighbors walked her today," Sean said as Suzie
jumped up, her paws landing in his gut and making
him *oomph*. "Not that you can tell." He was laughing
and patting her and saying, "Down, girl," not using a
tone the dog would recognize as a command.

"Suzie, down," Jess ordered. The dog dropped to
the floor and turned her interest to Jess instead. "Sit."
Suzie sat. "Good girl," she praised, giving her ears
a scratch.

Sean looked at her with wide eyes. "You're like,
Doctor Dolittle or something."

"Not quite." Jess smiled. "Suzie and I know each
other, that's all. I've bandaged her tail more times
than I can count."

"Really?"

"She's the most accident-prone dog I've ever met."

"That sounds like Suzie." Sean took over patting
the dog, crouching down to rough up her fur and
scratch under her chin as he muttered in a silly tone,
"Who's the most accident-prone dog in the world?
You, huh?"

Jess could only watch as Suzie drooled with pleasure.

It was ridiculous to be jealous of a dog.

But as much as Jess loved animals, it was time

for this dog to go to her kennel and leave the human beings to indulge in a little primal behavior of their own.

Sean seemed to read her mind, because he straightened up and gave Suzie one last pat. "Suzie, go to bed," he ordered, pointing to the back of the house.

Suzie pouted at them for a moment, pulling a puppy-dog-eyes look, before turning away and obeying the command, tail between her legs.

"She thinks she's done something wrong," Jess observed.

"I'll make it up to her in the morning."

Dogs don't work that way, Jess almost said. But then tonight wasn't about that. Suzie would be fine. Jess on the other hand was feeling a little chilled. Goose bumps skated up her arms as Sean turned to face her, his eyes dark with promise.

Then, suddenly, the intent in his eyes faded. "You're right," he said. "I need to take care of her. Don't move. I'll be back in a second."

Jess barely had time to realize what was happening before Sean was back at her side.

"I gave Suzie one of those disgusting liver treats she loves so much. She's happy now."

"That's good." *He's kind to animals.* That gave Sean an automatic big tick in Jess's book.

And that delicious sparkle was back. "Let's go in here," he said.

He grabbed Jess's hand and led her into the living room, turning on one lamp in the corner to bring a soft peachy glow to the room. Hailey's housekeeping was immaculate, not a spot of dust to be seen anywhere.

"I've been dying to get this off since about five minutes after I put it on," he said, shrugging out of his tuxedo jacket and draping it over the back of a chair. He kicked off his shoes and tore off his socks at the same time.

"It suits you," Jess said. She took a few steps back, bumping against the end of the solid timber dining table that dominated this end of the open-plan living/dining room. Sean stood between her and the doorway, and her nerves suddenly came back to life with a vengeance. She wasn't trapped exactly—she knew, without knowing why, that if she changed her mind, he'd let her go without a problem. But part of her anxiety was realizing that she didn't *want* to change her mind—and she didn't want him to, either.

"Nah, the formal look's not me," he said, batting away her compliment. "But that dress, on the other hand... You look gorgeous."

He gave her an admiring full-length assessment that sent more chills through her. Then he worked at the cuffs of his shirt, frowning at them in concentration, pulling out the cuff links and tossing them carelessly on the table before turning the sleeves back to reveal strong, bony wrists, lightly dusted with hair.

Jess's stomach flipped. Maybe she couldn't go through with this after all. Maybe she just wasn't ready. "Sean? I—" She broke off and licked her lips nervously.

"Can you help me with this thing?" He stepped closer to her, tugging ineffectually at his bow tie. "I've got no idea how it works—Rob did it for me. I'll probably strangle myself, left to my own devices."

Jess sucked in a breath as she raised shaking hands to his collar. Her breath brought with it a lungful of his scent, as spicy and exotic as she'd thought when he'd sat down beside her back in the hotel ballroom. Only all the more powerful now that it was just the two of them.

Jess understood how scent worked in the animal kingdom. Pheromones were chemical communication signals that many animals used to let the opposite sex know they were ready to mate. She wondered what scent her own body was giving off. Would it reflect the turmoil of desire, confusion and fear that she was feeling right now?

It took only a couple of tugs on the tie to loosen it, and then it was hanging free. Having her untie it was clearly a ruse, but it had brought them closer together. Jess was backed against the table—nowhere to go. Sean was in front of her, looking down at her with an intense expression in his darkened eyes.

Those fancy tuxedo studs glinted at her, and Jess recalled her urge to find out how they worked. Before she knew it, before she'd made a conscious decision to do so, she found her fingers at the top one, working it free.

"I, uh, haven't come across these buttons before," she said. *Looked as though she was committed now.*

Some of her nervousness disappeared simply at having made the decision. But her fingers still shook.

"You'll work it out."

She could feel the vibration of his voice as she worked the stud free, unhooking it from the button on the shirt flap below. Her hand brushed the bare skin of his chest as she parted the fabric, and his breath snagged.

His skin was smooth and lightly tanned, a sparse sprinkling of hair in the center of his chest revealed when she undid the second button. Sean helped her by reaching behind himself to unhook his cummerbund, letting it drop to the floor and then tugging his shirt free of his trousers.

Finally, his shirt was hanging open, and Jess held out her hand, the four tuxedo studs sitting in her palm.

"Here you go." Her trembling was obvious, but Jess figured that was entirely understandable. He was standing there, right in front of her, like something out of a *GQ* celebrity photo shoot—bare feet, black pants, bared chest, white shirt hanging open, undone bow tie dangling around his neck. Jess half wished she could stop and take a photo, because this was a sight worth preserving.

"Thanks." He took the studs and tossed them on the table, barely even glancing at them.

"How complicated is your dress?" he asked.

Jess frowned. "What do you mean?"

He gave a little wave at her neck. "I mean, is it like

my tux? Do we need to begin preparations to remove it now? Or does it just unzip?"

Oh. That.

Jess had a sudden surge of memory, of what it had felt like when she'd been standing on that platform over a river in New Zealand, the safety people double-checking the rigging before she launched herself off into empty space.

She shook her head. "Nope. It's simple. It lifts up over my head." Leaving her in nothing but a skimpy thong. The dress clung to every curve, so she'd worn no bra and had done her best to minimize any VPL.

He gave her a slow smile. "Excellent."

Thinking in a situation like this was only going to lead to trouble, Jess rationalized. Therefore, the only suitable choice was to halt all logic and proceed purely on sensation. And as far as sensation went, kissing Sean Paterson was pretty darned magical.

Jess reached up to cup his cheek. The prickle of his stubble scraped her palm. With him in bare feet and her still in heels it was a simple matter of leaning forward, tilting her chin up slightly and bringing her lips to his. She kept the touch light, a mere brushing of her mouth against his. He returned her light caress, bracketing her lower lip between his, pulling on it slightly before doing the same again with her top lip. His hands came to rest gently on her waist and his thumbs spanned her belly, rubbing the curve of her stomach in soft, gentle strokes.

Once again, Jess wondered if her knees were going to support her. A dart of desire, so sharp it almost hurt, stabbed through her body. She knew men often had issues with "holding on"—her ex-husband was a case in point. But she'd never before wondered if she might have the same problem. Sean had barely touched her, and she was on the edge, already.

He deepened the kiss, opening his mouth, teasing her with his tongue. Jess wasn't sure whether to be embarrassed or proud of the low groan that came from her throat as she opened to him, welcoming him, meeting his desire with her own.

His fingers tightened on her waist and then one hand slid slowly upward until he cupped her breast, weighing it in his palm before he skated around to the low neckline of her dress and slipped inside. Skin against skin. He unerringly found her nipple and rubbed it between his thumb and forefinger.

Jess collapsed against the table, her head falling back as Sean traced her jaw with his mouth, stopping to nibble on the skin under her ear.

"Please," she murmured, although she wasn't entirely sure what she wanted. She just wanted more and wasn't too proud to beg.

Sean seemed to know before she did—the hand on her waist skirted her hip, trailing heat over her skin as he traced her thigh, finding the split in her dress and breaching it. A moment later his fingertips brushed the lace panel at the front of her thong, sending ripples of pleasure through her entire body.

He sucked her earlobe into his mouth, diamond earring stud and all, before pulling back with a pop. "Do you want me to touch you here?" he whispered in her ear, pressing his fingers against her core. "Is that what you want?"

Jess's first attempt at speech was a wordless gasp that seemed to please him; she felt his lips curve into a smile against her ear.

"Yeah?" he asked again.

"Yes." She finally managed to form the word. Her fingers dug into his shoulders, the solid resistance of muscle against her hands almost as arousing as his touch.

He slipped inside the lace barrier and then he was touching her, teasing and rubbing and slipping against her. He was still kissing her neck, light teasing nibbles that weren't enough, weren't what she wanted. She wanted to be taken, to be overwhelmed. Jess sought his mouth again, kissing him with punishing abandon, groaning when he caught up with what she wanted and returned the kiss, forceful and demanding. His tongue plunged into her mouth as his fingers tormented her, and the winding coil of desire inside her reached the point of no return.

"Sean," she gasped.

"Yes, baby."

Jess's breath caught, her body stiffened and every nerve sang with the power of his touch. Her last logical thought was that it had been far, far too long since someone had brought her to the edge of reason like this, and then there was no more room for logic, only sensation—exquisite sensation that made her thighs tighten, her toes curl and her fingernails dig deep into Sean's skin.

She cried out as she shattered, and he swallowed her cry with a kiss that went on and on, anchoring her through the shudders that racked her body.

Finally, dragging in a breath that sounded like a sob, Jess collapsed, her forehead sagging to his shoulder, her knees almost buckling. If not for the table behind her and the man in front of her, she would have fallen to a puddle on the floor.

Sean's arms went around her, half an embrace, half to support her, as she tried to regain her breath. She was very aware of the heat of him, her cheek rested against his still-shirt-covered shoulder, but the body beneath was hot, and she wished her dress was gone so she could press herself against him and feel that warmth directly against her skin.

"Hey, are you okay?" he asked gently, his hands rubbing circles over her back.

Jess managed a strangled-sounding laugh. "I'm awesome," she said, her voice breathy and strained.

He chuckled, too, low and a little raspy. "Glad to hear it."

As she regained some strength in her pleasure-weakened body, she straightened slightly to put a little distance between them. Just enough to see his face, watch him flinch slightly as her hands spread across his chest. A muscle ticked in his jaw, the only outward sign of his self-restraint.

His eyes were almost entirely black in the dim light of the room.

It took only a moment to slide her hands across his chest to his shoulders, pushing the shirt with her. He flexed his arms and the shirt slipped down and off, baring his chest and surprisingly muscled arms to her hungry gaze.

"You're so hot," she said, her hands tracing the heated skin and rounded muscle of his shoulders, across his collarbone, trailing a fingernail down to where the fine thatch of hair spread outward from his sternum. Too late she realized what she'd said had two meanings.

A deep laugh vibrated through his chest.

A blush heated her cheeks, but she shrugged. "I meant it both ways," she said, darting a glance to his twinkling eyes.

"Well, then, thank you, I guess."

Jess let her fingers continue their journey south, tracing a path from his chest, down his firm stomach to the waistband of his tuxedo trousers. The muscles of his belly jumped as she skated over them, looking for the button or catch.

After a brief search she gave up, her hands falling by her sides.

"I'll do you a deal," she said, giving him what she hoped was a sexy smile. "You get rid of the pants, I'll get rid of my dress."

He didn't hesitate, rewarding her with a wide grin. "Done."

As Jess pulled her dress over her head, she saw him remove his pants and briefs, walk over to where his jacket was and throw the pants over the same chair. She wondered for a moment about this display of neatness when he picked up his jacket and fished in the inside pocket for a moment, pulling out his wallet.

Ah. It really had been too long if Jess had almost entirely forgotten about that side of things.

Anticipation for what was to come next made her fingers shake as she removed her shoes and scrap of underwear, looking up to find Sean's gaze on her, any trace of humor in his expression vanished.

He stood there, a few paces away, proudly, defiantly naked. Fully aroused, his chest visibly rose and fell with rapid breaths. The sight alone was enough to send tremors of desire threading through her. Combined with the aftershocks of her recent climax, it was a potent mix.

A few confident strides brought him to her side. He paused, taking a moment to scan her naked body, an assessing, all-encompassing look that made Jess want to grab her dress and pull it on again. Instead she forced herself to stand still, hands by her sides, her fingernails digging into her palms as she fought her discomfort. Age had brought with it a certain measure of acceptance of her body—it was what it was, and it was hers, for better or worse. Now that she no longer had her ex-husband around, telling her that she wasn't good enough—proving it by making her second best in his life—it was easier to be more objective. But that was all well and good when she was alone, giving herself a critical review in the mirror. It was an entirely different thing to be standing in front of Sean's careful gaze. In front of a man in the prime of his youth—strong and firm and no doubt used to women who were the same.

"Keep in mind that I'm a few years older than you."

Sean's hand flicked in dismissal. "I don't care."

She bit her lip to stop herself from saying any further self-denigrating comments and instead turned them inward. Her breasts weren't as perky as they used to be, and it didn't seem to matter how many sit-ups she did at the gym, she couldn't shift the plump pad of fat under her navel that curved her belly outwards. And she wished—as she'd wished since she was a teen—that she was a few inches taller. If she could just stretch everything *up* a bit, she'd be more willowy than hourglass, and everything would be more balanced.

His eyes finally came back to meet hers. "You're gorgeous," he said.

Her first instinct was to deny the compliment, to point out her imperfections. But that wasn't what this night was all about.

"You're not too bad yourself," she said instead.

He took one more step, a step that brought him close, so close that Jess could simply sway forward and her nipples would brush his chest.

But he didn't touch her; instead, keeping his eyes locked with hers, he lowered his head until his eyelashes fluttered shut and his lips connected with hers.

She expected a hungry kiss, a demanding and passion-filled approach. But instead he nibbled gently at her lips, seducing her all over again. It was a kiss designed to mesmerize, to ignite and inflame, and oh,

God, was it working. It took her to the edge of her patience—beyond—and Jess could no longer wait. She opened her mouth to him, stepping forward into his body at the same time, moaning as her breasts met the hot, damp skin of his chest and his tongue surged to meet hers.

"Oh, Jess," he groaned.

Before she knew what was happening, Sean had reached down and swept one arm under her knees, scooping her into his arms. He kissed her again, silencing her protest, taking her several steps away from the light, into the darker end of Hailey and Rob's living room. He deposited her on the modern, modular sofa, one end of which extended into a chaise-longue-style arrangement, almost long enough and wide enough to be a bed.

Jess didn't want to think about whether Hailey had had something like this in mind when she'd chosen the furniture. Jess didn't want to think about anything except Sean as he knelt over her, his head lowering to her breast. Then her nipple was in his mouth, between his teeth, and whether or not Jess wanted to think was a moot point—she couldn't.

He made love to her thoroughly, patiently, as if he hadn't already brought her the ultimate pleasure. He was driving her mad, teasing, touching, tasting, drawing her to the brink and then halting, before beginning the exquisite torture all over again.

Jess did her best to touch him as he worked over her—his firm, fine body, hard planes of muscle and silky bronzed skin were impossible to resist.

Finally, when she was about to go out of her mind, he reached for the package he'd recovered from his wallet and tucked under a sofa cushion while they played. It took only a moment for him to ready himself, and then he was poised above her, his eyes boring deep into hers, the golden sparkle she'd noticed earlier completely gone in the heat and demand of his gaze.

She nodded, as if he was waiting for permission. "Yes, Sean. Now."

Jess tilted her hips and wrapped her legs around his thighs, drawing him to her, taking control as he seemed to hesitate.

Then he was sliding inside her and they both groaned. Jess arched her neck and Sean kissed her collarbone, his lips nibbling until he reached the pulse point at the base of her throat, nuzzling her, his tongue flicking against her skin.

Jess could only hold on as he built the rhythm, working her body expertly, taking her to the edge of reason once again.

"Jess, you…" he gasped. His arms trembled as they supported his weight over her.

"Yes," was all she could manage to say, not sure if it was the right answer, not sure of anything except the burning, building ache inside her, spiraling higher, deeper, harder, and then she cried out as she broke apart, feeling his shudders as he followed her into the light.

CHAPTER THREE

SEAN COLLAPSED ON top of her and Jess welcomed his
weight. She let her hands explore his broad, powerful back, sweeping over the curves of muscle and the
bony protrusions of his spine.

He sucked in a deep breath, then raised his head
to drop a kiss on her nose.

"Don't move," he whispered.

"Why?"

"Just…don't. Okay?"

Jess shrugged her agreement but regretted it as he
moved away from her, withdrawing from her body and
her embrace.

"I'll be right back."

He disappeared with the flash of a grin, retreating
into the darkened corridor. *Of course*. Jess remembered the condom. Inconvenient things.

Her naked, perspiring body felt suddenly chilled
without the furnace of Sean's presence nearby. And
with that chill came a creeping sense of mortification. She'd met him, what, less than an hour ago?
She'd begged for his touch, run her hands all over
his body and—if she was perfectly honest—would
love to do it all again.

But the idea of waiting for him, of cuddling with him on the sofa, enjoying the afterglow? It was all a little too...*intimate*. A strange thing to think, given what they'd just done.

Suddenly, all the fears and hesitations she'd successfully suppressed earlier in the evening came back in a wave. A cold, horrible wave.

Get out of here. Now.

Jess scrambled to her feet and found her dress. It took a moment to sort out the folds of fabric—she'd removed it in haste and left it in a pool on the floor—but once she'd found the hem, she pulled it over her head and was smoothing it down her body when Sean returned to the room.

"I thought you might like—" His words cut off abruptly when he saw she was dressed. He was still naked—still astoundingly, eye-wateringly gorgeous—and he held a bottle of wine and two glasses in one hand.

The man was sex on legs. What was she doing? Jess knew a strong, clenching feeling of regret at the thought she'd not get to experience being with him again, but the more solid certainty that she needed to leave won out.

"Sorry." She gave him a smile. "I have to get going."

"But..." He trailed off.

Jess had the definite impression that women didn't walk out on Sean Paterson very often.

"Thanks, though," she said, gesturing to the wine. She could feel a muscle in her cheek twitch with the forced smile she'd plastered on her face. Her breath was coming a little too fast and she forced herself to slow it down.

"Oh." Sean dumped the bottle and glasses with a clatter on the table. "How will you get home?" he asked. "Do you want me to drive you?"

"No," Jess said too quickly. It was absurd to be disappointed that he hadn't tried to object to her leaving. "It's late. I'll get a cab."

"I'll call one for you." He took a step toward his discarded suit, presumably to seek out a phone.

Jess put a hand on his arm to halt him. Oh, so hard and so velvet soft all at the same time. *Really, Jess, would it be too much to ask to hang around for more?* She shook the annoying inner voice away.

"It's fine. I've caught cabs from here before. There's no point calling one at this time on a Saturday night, it'll take hours. I'll just walk up the street to the main road and hail one."

He blew out a breath and Jess wondered for a moment if he was going to argue or finally get around to asking her not to go. But then he shrugged. "Okay. Give me a minute to put some clothes on and I'll walk with you."

"No!" It came out louder and more forceful than she'd intended. "I mean," she said, modulating her voice, "I'll be fine on my own. I've done it hundreds of times." A slight exaggeration. Maybe twice.

He gave her a look that made him seem older than his years. "Jess, forget it." His tone brooked no protest. "I'm either driving you home, walking with you to hail a cab, or we call one and you wait for it here.

I'm not letting you head off into the night by yourself. It's just not happening."

His commanding tone made Jess bristle. "I'm a grown woman. Old enough to look after myself. Older than you, remember?" He probably usually slept with nineteen-year-old airheads who'd get into a stranger's car when offered candy, Jess thought, knowing she was being more than a little ridiculous. But the strange feeling of panic was growing, and her every instinct was yelling at her to escape.

Sean muttered something under his breath, then reached for his clothes. Jess told herself not to watch, but it was impossible. He pulled on his suit trousers without bothering with underwear and zipped them up in front of her, seemingly unconcerned by her close observation.

"What's it to be?" he asked, ignoring her protest.

The quickest option would be to have him drive her home. Waiting for a cab at this time of night could, literally, take hours. It was impossible to know how long waiting for one on the street would take. From previous experience, Jess knew it could be minutes—or not.

All the options meant spending more time in close company with Sean. And Jess wasn't sure what was going on, but her gut was screaming at her to get away from him. She didn't know why. She needed to be alone to work out *why* she needed to be alone.

Her indecision must have shown on her face, because Sean reached out and took her hand.

"Look," he began with an exaggerated air of patience, "I'm not sure why you're freaking out like this, but—"

"I am *not* freaking out—"

He talked over her protest. "But everything's fine, okay? You're good, I'm good and we just had a helluva lot of fun." He grinned. "I was kinda hoping you'd hang around a little longer so we could do it again, but I get that you might've had enough. And that's okay. You only need to tell me how you want to get home."

Faced with his sensible, emotionless dissection of the situation, Jess's reaction felt like hysteria. A colder, more unpleasant feeling settled in her belly. If she didn't know better, she'd call it *disappointment*.

"I'd like for you to drive me home," she said after a moment. Logic won out. Of all the options, it meant getting home fastest. "If that's okay."

He squeezed her hand and then let it go. "That's fine. Just give me a sec to grab a T-shirt."

Jess had put on her shoes but still hadn't located her underwear by the time he returned, wearing sneakers, a tight gray T-shirt that hugged his shoulders and chest, and his tuxedo pants. It should have looked silly, but instead he looked effortlessly sexy and it made Jess's resolve weaken. Would there really be anything *terribly* wrong with staying a little longer? Maybe even sleeping over till the morning? If it had been a long time since her last sexual experience, it had been even longer since she'd slept with a man's arms around her. Jess liked that feeling. Missed it.

Yeah, right. Sean had said he wanted her to stay so

they could enjoy round two—nothing about breakfast in the morning. She was sure that after round two was done, he'd be the one bundling her into his car or calling for a taxi. All she was doing was speeding up that eventual outcome. And in doing so, staying in control of the situation. That was what was important.

"Ready?" he asked.

Jess opened her mouth to say something about her missing underwear, but the idea of going on a search for it seemed too...*undignified.*

"Sure, let's go."

SEAN THOUGHT HE'D encountered pretty much every postcoital reaction womankind was capable of. This was a new one on him, though. He'd seen tears. Giggling. Snoring. Even one unfortunate episode of throwing up, but they'd both been very drunk and it had been a long time ago.

He'd never seen ruthless *efficiency.* He wasn't sure what else to call the reaction from Jess Alexander. It was a pity, because he hadn't been finished with her—not by a long shot.

She'd barely said a word since they'd left the house, just brief directions on how to get to her home. She shifted uncomfortably in her seat, the silence in the car magnifying the soft rustle of her dress. The silence reminded him uncomfortably of the final weeks of the one-and-only long-term relationship he'd attempted.

Ten months—it hadn't been a bad effort considering ten days was pretty much his usual limit. If you didn't count the last month when they'd pretty much stopped talking to each other. There was still a minor ache somewhere hidden deeply away when he thought about that. He'd actually thought he'd been in love, when in reality he'd just been young and stupid.

"Crap," Jess said suddenly.

"What?"

"My car. It's parked at the hotel. I totally forgot."

Sean backed off the accelerator. "Do you want me to take you there instead?"

"No... No, I'll get it in the morning."

"Sure?"

She nodded. "Positive."

He thought about offering to pick her up in the morning, but after the argument about driving her home, he figured it was an offer extremely unlikely to be accepted, so he kept his mouth shut.

She shifted in the seat again, discomfort written all over her face.

"Are you okay?" he asked as she squirmed once more. He hadn't hurt her somehow, had he? "You look like you have ants in your pants."

"I, uh, couldn't find my underwear."

"Huh?" It took him a moment to realize what she'd said.

"I couldn't find my underwear," she said again.

He couldn't help but laugh, even when she shot him a look designed to wither. "Is that why you're twitching around over there?"

"It feels weird," she said, not bothering to hide her annoyance.

"So you don't make a habit of going commando, then?"

"No, I don't. When you get back, turn the lights on and find my thong, okay? I don't want Hailey and Rob coming back and finding it under a chair or something. I don't even want to *imagine* Hailey trying to return them at work one day." She shuddered.

"She wouldn't know they were yours. Unless you write your name in your panties or something?"

Sean didn't have to look to know that she was rolling her eyes at him. She seemed to like dismissing him like that.

"No. I imagine having you stay at their house means they're fully expecting to have to go through it and remove discarded women's underwear in every room before they unpack."

Ouch. That one was designed to wound. And it did. Sean wasn't sure why—it wasn't too far from the truth. Hailey had been clear that if—*when*—Sean brought female company home while he was staying, he was only to use the spare bedroom he'd been assigned. Rob had later said that all Hailey was concerned about was Sean having sex in their bed and Sean hadn't found it hard to promise that he wouldn't do that. And he'd once again marveled at his brother's ability to settle down with one woman for the rest of his life.

"Yeah, there's bound to be piles of the stuff," he

said agreeably. It was pure instinct to respond to a hurtful barb with a quip.

Jess didn't come back with the expected rejoinder. Instead she stiffened in her seat.

Sean pulled up to a stop at a red light and turned to look at her. Her mouth was a thin line.

"I *was* joking," he said, beginning to feel annoyed. She was just like his family—just like everyone else—expecting the worst from him.

She folded her hands primly in her lap, facing forward. "Of course. The light's green," she added.

Sean took off. They were only moments from Jess's home, according to her directions. If the traffic was bad, it could take up to twenty to thirty minutes to get there from Rob and Hailey's. But at this time of night, it was going to be little more than ten. Probably for the best.

Two blocks later, he pulled up in front of a series of modern town houses, and Jess directed him down the driveway to the third one back from the street— perhaps anticipating that he wasn't going to settle for anything less than seeing her right to her door.

"Here's fine," she said, her fingers already playing with the door handle.

"Jess, wait."

She paused for a moment and turned her head to face him.

Sean cut the engine, noting the flare in her eyes as he did so. His annoyance faded. What was she so scared of?

"Don't worry, I'm not coming in. I just didn't want

to disturb the neighbors." Sean found Dezzie's low rumble comforting, but he knew not everyone shared his fondness for the powerful engine, especially not in the dead of night.

"Oh, that's…nice. Okay, well, thank—"

"Jess?" He cut her off. Sean had always been fascinated by human behavior and psychology. It was, according to his agent and publisher and various reviewers over the years, what made his books stand out from the rest. Yes, he might write about vampires and demons and all kinds of strange and wonderful creatures, but what made his books different was… the word they used was *relatable.* Although the world of *Sebastian Douglas, Demon Warrior* was make-believe, Sebastian, his assistant, Robert—a shout-out to his brother—and the people they encountered on their adventures were *real.* Well, as real as Sean could make them. And the situations they faced, although perhaps not everyday in reality, echoed some of the most common themes of life: hope, duty, loss, friendship, loyalty.

It was one of the qualities that made Sean so good at reading other people.

He wondered if Elvire, the vampire queen who not-so-secretly lusted after Sebastian, would behave the way Jess was right now, if Sean ever let Sebastian and Elvire do the deed. It was something his fans were very keen on—they were very fussy about who Sebastian was paired with and nothing provoked a storm of fan correspondence than a new love interest for his unexpectedly sex-symbol-status hero.

Especially since double-agent Elvire had been hanging around since book two, waiting in the background for Sebastian to notice her. And not stake her. Well, not in *that* way, anyway.

"Hmm?" Jess said, feigning politeness. Sean could see her fingers already clutched around the door handle.

What did he want to say? As a writer, words were supposed to be his forte. Right now he was the superhero whose mortal enemy had flung his trusty weapon from his hands.

"Just...thanks," he ended up saying lamely.

Her mouth curved almost imperceptibly in the echo of a smile. "Ditto."

Then she was gone. The door creaked before she banged it shut—*must get that fixed*—and then in a flash of red from the exterior light hitting her dress, she was inside and hidden from sight.

A strange emptiness followed him home. And while Rob and Hailey's place had always felt welcoming to him, as he reentered it he couldn't shake a feeling of displacement.

Calling Suzie inside and pouring himself a glass of wine, Sean grabbed his laptop and threw himself on the sofa that just minutes before had held so much promise for the night ahead. It still smelled of her, of their lovemaking. Only now the body curled up beside his was furry, slightly stinky and already snoring. He opened his laptop. It was time to ramp up the sexual tension between Sebastian and Elvire. The fans were gonna love it—even if he was only teasing them. Happy endings didn't exist in Sean's world—not in fiction or in reality.

SEAN WOKE UP—still on the sofa—with a headache and dry mouth. He'd taken to the red wine a little too enthusiastically after driving Jess home. He'd also written an entire chapter—although he couldn't help wondering how much of it he would end up keeping. His inebriated writing was often pure drivel, but occasionally it contained a nugget of pure gold—a gift from Bacchus.

Hmm, Bacchus. Sean let his scrambled morning thoughts meander. The god could be an awesome villain, causing havoc by making everyone party orgiastically until they died of exhaustion. Just the kind of enemy to pit against Sebastian. And it could tie in the story line between Sebastian and Elvire that he'd started to write last night, a reason for them to—

An annoying noise—the sound that had woken him—interrupted his train of thought, and it was a moment before he identified it as the phone. Rob and Hailey's landline, not his mobile.

Whoever was calling was keen to get an answer. The answering machine kicked in but the caller hung up. Then as soon as the answering machine disconnected, the phone started ringing again.

"Yeah?" Sean managed to stumble from the sofa to the phone, but a polite "hello" was beyond him.

"Man! Where have you been? I've been calling your mobile for the past hour!" Rob's voice was equal parts annoyed and frantic.

Sean's phone was on silent. He'd changed the setting when he'd entered the house with Jess, because he hadn't wanted to be disturbed. That was too much to explain, though. "What's up?"

Rob swore. "Stupid Lucy. She's pulled out."

"Huh?" *Lucy?*

"The house sitter—Hailey's cousin. She's a university student and she's met some guy who lives on the opposite side of town so she's decided she doesn't want to look after the house and Suzie anymore."

"Oh."

"Our flight leaves in a couple of hours."

Sean scratched his stubbled jaw. He now deeply regretted the impulse to finish the bottle of red. If only he'd left it at one or two glasses. But the way things had ended with Jess had left him with a weirdly unsettled feeling—as if he'd somehow done something wrong. He hadn't wanted to think too much about that, and diving deep into the cabernet sauvignon pool had seemed like a good idea at the time.

"That sucks," Sean said, trying to sound sincere. His thoughts hustled to catch up.

"So we need your help."

Ah. Right. There was the reason he needed his brain right now.

"Can you stay a couple more days?" Rob asked. "Just long enough to organize a kennel for Suzie? If you need help, Hailey's boss, Jess, could probably give you some advice—there's a fridge magnet in the kitchen with her clinic details. We thought about asking her to take Suzie, but it's a big imposition for six weeks. Lucy has agreed she'll come and collect the mail once a week, and that should be enough—"

Rob broke off as a muffled voice spoke in the background—Hailey. Sean couldn't make out what she was saying.

"Yes, yes," Rob said, annoyance strong in his voice. He then clearly passed on what it was Hailey had said. "And don't forget to take the garbage out when you leave, because otherwise it will sit there."

It prickled that his brother—his *younger* brother—didn't trust him enough to know to take the garbage out. It prickled even more that they hadn't even thought to ask if he would step in and look after the house for them. It was just assumed that he wouldn't accept the responsibility.

Just like Jess with her quip about the women's underwear—Sean hated that people always expected the worst from him.

Especially his family.

Just because he loved words and pictures more than numbers, his family of accountants figured he wasn't capable of any kind of logic.

Story of his life.

"I was planning to be in Sydney for a meeting I have on Monday," Sean began.

"I know." Rob sighed, a heavy, put-upon sound. "Okay, well maybe we'll just have to ask Jess to pick up Suzie and organize the kennel."

Hailey's voice was shrill in the background. Sean was sure he heard the words *told you so* in there somewhere.

"Listen, mate," Sean said, raising his voice, his hurt transforming into irritation. He might prefer a more freewheeling life than his tradition-following brother, but that didn't mean he was incapable of being responsible when the occasion called for it.

"Would you just shut up for a second and let me talk? I was going to say, I have a meeting in Sydney but I can arrange to do it by teleconference. Why don't you just leave it all with me? I'll stay here and take care of things for you. I have to be back in Melbourne in two weeks for a convention anyway."

There was a moment of silence.

Did his brother really mistrust him that much?

Sean jumped in, quick to give Rob the out he so clearly needed. "If you don't think I can do it, that's fine…."

"Dude, it's not that at all." There was a pause as Rob seemed to choose his words. "I didn't want to ask, because I know it's not your scene. But if you were up for it, I'd be grateful. We both would."

Sean doubted that Hailey would be all that thrilled with Sean's presence in the house for more than the couple of nights he'd originally been allocated, but he was prepared to take his brother at his word.

"Then just forget about it all. Get your things together and head out to the airport. It's all cool."

"Yeah? Seriously? Are you sure?"

"Seriously. Just go…have fun. I'll work things out. If there are any problems, I'll call."

"Just a sec." There was the muffled sound of a

hand covering the phone and an indecipherable conversation. Sean just bet it was Rob convincing Hailey to go along with the plan. Then Rob returned to the call. "Thanks, mate. I owe you one. First the wedding and now this. I owe you big-time."

"Yeah, yeah. Name your firstborn after me."

Rob laughed. "Sure. I'll get started on that right away."

Sean heard Hailey's voice in the background, asking what they were talking about.

"You'll be waiting awhile," he heard her yell out after Rob explained the request.

Sean smiled to himself at her vehemence. "I bloody hope so," he said to Rob.

"We'll need to discuss this further. It could get awkward if it's a girl."

"There's always Shauna."

Rob laughed again, and Sean found himself joining in. "Just don't tell Mom and Dad I'm here, okay? The last thing I need is for them to discover I'm a sitting duck."

"Deal."

They said their farewells and Sean hung up the call and looked around the room. His suit was still lying over the chair, his shirt a crumpled pile on the floor. Under the table, near the wall, was a scrap of black lace he was just betting was Jess's thong.

"Home," he muttered to himself. His home for six whole weeks. His stomach tightened, but the thought wasn't nearly as scary as it should have been.

DEALING WITH A potential outbreak of Q fever for one of her regular clients—a breeder of Cavalier King Charles spaniels—was just the kind of Monday morning Jess needed to distract herself from the weekend. Following through to notify anyone who could have been exposed, reporting it to the department of health for further investigation and then moving on with her usual roster of patients—a couple of minor injuries, the usual canine and feline parasite infestations, an infected paw on a gorgeous Irish setter—it was easy to feel as if nothing out of the ordinary had happened. While animals and their anxious owners were in front of her, she was focused.

But any moment of downtime, left to her own thoughts, her stomach would slowly turn flip-flops. Her cheeks still burned when she recalled the knowing look she was sure she'd seen in the car park attendant's eyes yesterday when he'd processed her ticket, clearly time-stamped from the night before.

Ridiculous. In this day and age, it wasn't as if a one-night stand was particularly remarkable or even that noteworthy. It wasn't even the first she'd ever had—although the other one had been back in university days when life had been different. Before she'd grown more cautious, more careful. Before she'd been hurt enough to know to protect herself.

And she'd been much better at handling the situation without, as Sean had put it, "freaking out." His words from last night were, much as she'd protested them at the time, a pretty accurate summation of her reaction. She'd totally embarrassed herself in front of him.

Thank God she'd never see him again. Not that she was ashamed of what she'd done—not really. She just wished she'd managed her exit more gracefully. Without betraying how much the whole thing had meant in the scheme of her life.

The milestone it had become.

She and Mark had been divorced for more than six months now, and had been separated a year longer than that. Jess didn't want to change things, not at all. It had taken a while, but with the benefit of hindsight she could see just how destructive her marriage had become.

It was just… Sean was the first man she'd slept with since Mark, since the disastrous failure of her marriage.

Jess wasn't used to failing—at anything. Not at school, at work or in life. Mark should have been the perfect partner. He came from a good family, had a good job, spent his leisure time sailing and had a group of friends at the yacht club. He also had a problem with controlling his temper, a perfectionist streak a mile wider even than Jess's own and a vastly different understanding of what the word *monogamy* meant than most of the world.

"Jess? I'm going to pack up if that's okay."

Jess's temporary vet nurse, Andrea, interrupted her train of thoughts and stirred her back into action. "Of course. What time is it?"

"Almost six."

"Okay, sure. If you clean up in here, I'll go out and finish up at the front desk."

Jess straightened her navy tunic top, embroidered with the clinic's logo on the top left pocket, and headed out to the reception area. She straightened up the display of cat food that sat on the desk and headed for the computer. It was going to be a busy few weeks until Margie returned from her cruise. Why she'd let her two staff members take leave at the same time was a mystery explained entirely by the fact that she was a complete soft touch as a boss.

At least once Margie was back the administration side of things would be out of Jess's hands again— that had never been her strong suit. But it was going to be a long six weeks until Hailey returned from her honeymoon. Andrea was good, but Hailey was better. Besides, Hailey was a friend. Even if her only topic of conversation for the past few weeks had been the wedding, Jess was going to miss her.

It took half an hour to close out the register and the credit card machine—mostly because Jess wasn't entirely sure whether she was doing it right. In that time Andrea had mopped the floors and packed away the surgery ready for the morning. A little too quick for Jess's liking, and she made a mental note to come in early and check that it had been done to her satisfaction. Jess was used to Hailey's level of perfection; she never left so much as a stray hair behind. Right now, though, Jess just wanted to get home—she was too tired to think straight. It hadn't been an especially busy day workwise, but the emotional workout she'd been putting herself through had taken its toll.

"See you tomorrow?" Andrea appeared in front of her, purse already over her shoulder.

Jess gave a tight smile. "See you tomorrow. Can you lock the front door behind you when you leave? I'm going out the back."

"Sure. Bye."

The bell over the door jangled loudly as Andrea shut the door firmly behind her. She'd certainly made a fast exit tonight. Maybe she had something important to do. Maybe she had *someone* important to get home to. Jess wasn't sure if she missed that feeling or not.

She had only just left reception when a loud knock at the front door drew her back. "Is that you, Andrea?" she called out. "Did you forget something?"

She unlocked the dead bolt in the door and opened it, expecting to see Andrea's face.

What she found instead made her trip over her own feet.

If she hadn't been holding the door, she'd have ended up on her ass...in front of him.

Sean Paterson.

Just as gorgeous as she remembered.

Only instead of his winning smile and twinkling eyes, today his brow was creased and his mouth tight. His hair was flat and mussed—no product in it to style it into the spikes he'd worn on Saturday.

But his harried appearance and worried expression

didn't stop her stomach from ending up somewhere near her throat.

"What are you doing here?" she blurted, shock getting the better of her. One-night-stand-Sean was supposed to be long gone by now. Moved on to a new city and a new conquest. That was the thought that had been sustaining her each time she relived how badly she'd handled things on Saturday night. *At least I never have to see him again.*

"Jess, I'm sorry. I didn't know what else to do. Suzie chewed a pack of headache pills."

Beside him, Hailey and Rob's golden retriever woofed happily at Jess. The dog's tail banged against the window as she tried to stuff herself inside the door, past the man blocking the way. She had to be the only dog in the world that actually *wanted* to go to the vet.

Jess stepped back and opened the door wider, ignoring the leap in her pulse. "Well, then, you'd better come in."

CHAPTER FOUR

"How many pills did she swallow, do you know?"
Jess led the way back into the surgery. If she focused
on Suzie, she could forget the cold, sick mortification
that was seeping into every inch of her body, making
her shiver. *Couldn't she?*

For her part, Suzie trotted along happily, comfortable in familiar surroundings.

"I don't know for sure." His voice was strained,
such a difference from the charming, unshakably
confident man from the wedding. "I brought the pack
with me. There were only two missing when she got
at it, otherwise it was full."

Sean fished in his canvas jacket pocket and pulled
out a well-chewed cardboard box and two blister
packs.

Jess grimaced.

"Is it bad? It's bad, isn't it? Oh, God."

"It's not great, but let's not jump to conclusions just
yet." It was easy to slip into her well-rehearsed pet-
owner-reassuring tone. Thank goodness she'd had
years of practice. "Okay, let's take a look."

"You want me to lift Suzie up on the table?"

"No, let's take a look at the pack first, see if we

can work out how many she might have ingested."
Jess refilled a bowl of water that had been cleaned
and put away and set it down for the dog. "Here you
go, Suzie. Have a big drink."

Sean spread out the damaged pack and a crumpled
paper towel on the stainless-steel table in the center
of the room.

"These are what I managed to get out of her
mouth." He gestured to the paper towel and Jess
leaned closer to see a couple of chewed capsules inside.

"Good," she said. Not everyone was brave enough
to reach into a dog's mouth and pull out whatever it
was chewing—even with a dog as placid as Suzie.
She had to give him credit for that. "Okay, let's see
what the damage is."

Together they carefully took apart the soggy pack-
aging, counting the pierced blister pack, piecing together the chewed remains in the paper towel. By the
time they'd finished their stock taking, it appeared
the still-cheerful dog—now happily sniffing her way
around the surgery—had likely only swallowed two
full pills.

"You're lucky," Jess said with a genuine sigh of relief. "In a dog Suzie's size, two isn't likely to cause
any serious effects. They should clear her system
overnight."

"Thank God," Sean said. He blew out a breath and
leaned heavily on the table before letting out a nasty
expletive. "Stupid dog. What kind of animal thinks
a green-and-white cardboard box is edible?"

Jess didn't pay much attention to his anger—it was a pretty common response. "Most dogs will test out just about anything as food. And some medical capsules have a slightly sweet coating to help people swallow them, so I don't know—maybe they tasted good to her. Suzie isn't the first dog to give them a try, unfortunately." Jess found Suzie thoroughly sniffing out a corner of the surgery. She crouched down to the dog's level and checked her vitals, although Suzie was more interested in licking Jess's face.

"Okay, okay," Jess said with a laugh, backing away. "Thanks for the tongue-bath, Suzie. I think she's going to be fine." She wiped her face with the back of her hand.

"Now what?" asked Sean.

"You just need to observe her closely for the next few hours." Jess scratched Suzie behind the ears. "Keep an eye on her, and if she begins to show any signs of sluggishness, starts vomiting or seems wobbly on her legs, you'll need to take her straight to the twenty-four-hour animal hospital in Caulfield. That's the closest to Hailey and Rob's place."

"Oh."

Something about the tone of his voice made her glance up. As she did, a memory from Saturday night washed over her—the naked bunch of muscle in Sean's arm as he'd leaned over her, body poised to kiss her intimately. The scarlet heat of a blush started somewhere near her toes, but reached her hairline in mere seconds.

Thankfully he seemed too busy fiddling with getting his phone out of his pocket to notice.

"I don't suppose," he said, frowning at whatever his phone was telling him, "you could keep her here for observation?"

"What, do you have a date?"

Jess would have given anything to take the words back, to collect them from the air and stop them from ever being said. But no, they were out there, for better or worse.

"What?" He looked confused for a moment, but then that confident, slightly smug expression was back, complete with the almost smile that tugged at the corner of his mouth and had to make any mortal woman weak at the knees. "A date? Now, why would you ask that?"

Jess stood and moved to the other side of the table, putting distance between them as she fought to regain her composure. She didn't want Suzie to be sick, but if the dog could fake a fainting spell right now, she'd be everlastingly grateful.

"I just meant, you must have plans. If you can't look after Suzie." *Lame, lame, lame.*

"I have things to do," he said.

She knew he was being deliberately vague, just to taunt her. Frustration at his carefree nonchalance finally won out over her embarrassment. "Well, *things* will have to wait," she said sharply. "I don't have the facilities to keep animals here overnight."

The smile was gone. Sean looked once again

strained and unhappy. "I should have known this wouldn't work," he muttered.

"What wouldn't work?"

"Me, dog-sitting."

"Huh?" *Sean dog-sitting?* In fact, what was he even doing here? Wasn't he supposed to be in Sydney by now? "Why *are* you dog-sitting? Why isn't Hailey's cousin looking after Suzie while she house-sits?"

"Ah, you missed the last-minute change of plans. The cousin dropped out. I'm the house sitter."

"You're looking after Hailey and Rob's house? For six weeks?" Her voice rose and she heard the shrill note. What had happened to fly-by-night Sean, here and gone again before she knew it?

"I know." His shoulders fell, and Jess would have sworn he looked somehow defeated. "I should have known it was a bad idea. I already had to get a plumber in to fix the dishwasher this morning."

If Hailey and Rob had been stupid enough to leave him in charge of their home and their dog, they probably deserved to come home to a ruined house, women's underwear scattered everywhere and a sick pet. But as much as the thought was satisfying, she also knew she couldn't let it happen—she loved Suzie too much for a start.

"Well, then, you're just going to have to put on your big-boy pants and adapt to the responsibility." Jess put her hands on her hips, preparing herself for a lecture. "If Rob and Hailey trusted you to—"

"God, not you, too!" Sean threw his hands in the

air. "Do you think I didn't get enough of that shit at the wedding?"

Jess didn't want to feel sorry for him. Between that sexy smile and those puppy-dog eyes, she was pretty sure Sean never had to try very hard to achieve anything in life. People must just cave to his wishes all the time. But right now? Right now he looked stressed and slightly panicked, like a cornered dog in an unfamiliar environment.

"Look, Sean," she tried again, with a more conciliatory tone this time. "It's not a big deal. All you have to do is stay home tonight and keep a close eye on Suzie for the next four hours or so. If she hasn't shown any symptoms by then, you can rest easy." She nearly said "go to bed easy" but stopped herself just in time. She didn't want to put *bed* and *Sean* in the same sentence, even in her head.

Sean scrubbed his face with both hands, his palms against his stubble making a rasping noise. "It's just..."

He looked at her then, his green-and-gold eyes piercing. "I have a meeting, a teleconference, that's going to take a couple of hours. It's a pretty important one and I need to concentrate. I can't change it, but I don't want to leave Suzie unsupervised. There's no one else I can call on.... Help me out, please."

Jess wasn't sure if it was the pleading tone in his voice or the bewitching spell of his eyes, but she believed him. She was probably just a sucker. Mark had used similar tactics to protest his innocence and she'd believed him, too—the first couple of times, anyway. After that, the deception had been on both sides—Mark deceiving her, Jess deceiving herself.

She didn't want to give in, but she already knew she was going to.

"I don't… Okay," she said finally with a sigh that she hoped communicated the fact that she wasn't necessarily happy about it. "I'll watch Suzie."

The lines between his brows eased as his eyebrows lifted in surprise. "You will?"

Jess rolled her eyes. As if he didn't fully expect everyone to capitulate to his every whim. "Yes. I'm a chump, but I will. I'm only doing this for Suzie, though. You'd better—"

"Thank you!" Sean leaped around the table, grasped her face in both hands and planted a kiss right on her lips. Before Jess had even comprehended what he'd done, he'd pulled away again and was crouched down in front of where Suzie sat, rubbing her sides. "Oh, Suzie, Suzie, Suzie. You are a daft dog."

Jess managed to stop herself from pressing her fingers to her tingling lips. But only just.

She knew she should say something, but for a moment all she could do was watch as Sean made funny faces at Suzie. He tickled her chin. "But even if you are dippy, I'm growing kinda fond of you." Then he grabbed the dog's head and pressed his lips to her cheek with a loud smacking noise.

That was how much his kiss meant.

"Don't cause any trouble for the lovely Jess, will you?" He stood up and checked his watch—one of those oversize, expensive, diving kinds. "Crap, I'll only just make it. Thanks, Jess, you're a lifesaver. I'll pick up Suzie as soon as I'm done. From your place?"

Jess nodded dumbly.

"Cool. Thanks again. See you later."

The bell on the front door rang loudly as he made his exit, the building strangely silent for a beat afterward. As if he'd taken some kind of vital energy out the door with him.

Jess stood still, her brain taking a moment to catch up with everything.

"So, Suzie," she finally said into the silent room, "I'm not sure which of us gets the medal for biggest idiot tonight."

The dog banged her tail on the floor, recognizing her name. She looked up questioningly, as if asking for an explanation of what had just happened.

"Don't look at me like that. He...he has superpowers of some kind." He must—it was the only way to explain how she'd not only ended up taking on his responsibility for Suzie, but would also end up seeing him *again*. On the plus side, he hadn't said anything about her embarrassing departure on Saturday night. Not that the opportunity to do so had really arisen.

"All right, come on then." Suzie got up and followed obediently as Jess locked up the surgery again and headed out to the back alley behind the building where she parked her car. It was dark, but the security light she'd had installed clicked on as soon as she stepped away from the door.

"Don't get too excited," Jess warned as Suzie

jumped into the backseat and settled down as if she'd been in there a hundred times. "If you start to look any less cheerful, I'm going to make you vomit." She waggled a finger at the dog as she closed the door. "That's what you get for indulging yourself without thinking first."

Jess didn't know what her own punishment was going to be for the same crime, but a perverse, contradictory part of her was almost looking forward to it.

It was raining by the time Sean's conference call was over, and he drove carefully to Jess's place on the slick roads. The meeting had taken much longer than he'd thought and he hoped Jess wasn't going to be too annoyed by the lateness of the hour.

His fingers tapped against the steering wheel as he recalled the discussion with his agent and the studio executives. Getting one of his books made into a movie was going to be a thrilling achievement. It would be solid, irrefutable evidence of his success— something that even his family couldn't deny.

That was, of course, if it ever actually happened. So far, the whole experience had been one of the most frustrating and aggravating things he'd ever done in his life.

He sighed and backed off the accelerator a little. His annoyance wasn't worth a speeding ticket or— God forbid—an accident. Dezzie was too precious.

It's all going to be worth it.

Seeing Sebastian Douglas on the big screen was finally going to bring him a measure of peace. Topping the *New York Times* bestseller list hadn't been enough to impress his family. But a movie with one of Hollywood's most famous names starring? They couldn't dismiss his success then.

It's not quite there, Sean. Still a bit of work to be done. That was the weasely language the studio exec had used during the meeting about the screenplay. What the hell did that mean, exactly?

We want to get this off the ground soon. So you've got to give us your best, or we're going to take it out of your hands and call in the script doctors. The threat was clear. Sean was an author, not a screenwriter, but he'd wanted to maintain control over his creation. So he'd written the script himself in defiance of the studio's wishes. And that was potentially going to be the death of the whole project.

That and whether or not some precious director was available to do the job.

His agent had hung on the line after the exec had disconnected to reassure him. But the ego boost was unnecessary. What Sean needed was space. Room to concentrate. Time to get his head back into the draft he'd written more than a year ago and do whatever it was that would finally get *Sebastian Douglas, Demon Warrior* the green light.

Perhaps this house-sitting thing was meant to be. Six weeks in one place would ground him enough to focus on the script. And it might even help him meet the deadline on his new book that was approaching far too quickly for his liking, especially since he was having troubles with the werewolf characters he'd decided to incorporate.

Sean pulled up in front of Jess's building, but stayed a moment in his car to update his Twitter account. It had been a while since he'd given the crew a progress report.

Hi, crew! Staying put in Melb for a few weeks working on Sebastian stuff for you guys. It's supersecret, but it's gonna be good, I promise.

Within seconds there were multiple responses filling his phone's screen.

You tease! Can't wait. Sebastian is my dream.

Yippee! *Happy dancing*

Make Elvire give up on Roman and get with Sebastian, okay?

We love you, Sean!

He knew it was shallow, but the responses made him feel better, salving his bruised ego. In some ways, his readers—*the crew,* as he liked to call them—were a substitute family. A family that admired his success and appreciated his hard work.

Before he closed down the Twitter application, a direct message popped up.

Sean, if U R in Melb for a while can I organize a fan meet-up?

It was from Rachel, the self-appointed manager of his unofficial "fan club." She called herself Rach-Elvire on Twitter and her avatar online was a picture of herself in full Elvire costume hugging him at one of the comic conventions he'd attended last year. She seemed to turn up at every book signing, appear at every convention he attended and always seemed to know which hotel he was staying in.

But apart from a fondness for dressing like a vampire, she seemed pretty harmless, and her Sebastian Unauthorized Wiki website had been one of the first in an explosion of online fandom for Sebastian and his adventures. She'd even flown all the way to Sydney for the launch event of his latest book and had proudly presented him with a box full of cookies baked in the unique shape of Sebastian's favorite dagger. They'd been delicious.

He typed back to Rachel:

I'll let you know. I have a deadline, so it depends on how the work goes.

He enjoyed attending the occasional fan meet-up. But they were starting to get a little out of hand. The last one, in a café in Richmond, had the café's owner calling a halt to everything when regular customers couldn't get in the door for their coffees.

Here's my number—call me, Rachel replied with the eight digits of her phone number.

Cool. I'll let you know, he typed, although he didn't think it would happen.

He then sent a final message for all his followers.

Don't forget I'll see all you Melbourne peeps at the Comic Convention in a couple of weeks!

It would do as a reminder to Rachel that there was an official opportunity for a gathering happening soon anyway.

Feeling a little more buoyant than he had when he'd first pulled up in front of Jess's place, he checked himself in the rearview mirror, ruffled his hair to try to make it stand up and then got out of the car.

When Jess opened the door, Sean couldn't help but smile at the disgruntled look on her face. It was such a contrast to the adoring and supportive messages he'd just been reading.

"It's late," she said in greeting.

"Sorry." He pulled a face, deliberately giving her his best "please forgive me" look. "My meeting went longer than I thought and I couldn't do anything about it."

She hadn't invited him in, hadn't even opened the door all the way, holding it as if to physically bar him from her home—as if her expression wasn't unwelcoming enough. Despite the frown, she looked just as beautiful as she had in her wedding finery, although her appeal was different this time.

He'd quite enjoyed seeing her in the navy scrubs and ponytail she was wearing at the clinic. But she'd changed since getting home, and her dark wavy hair curled over her shoulders, and jeans and a soft knit sweater gently clung to her curves. The pale blue highlighted her gray eyes and the lack of makeup showed off a spatter of freckles across her nose and cheekbones.

A faint citrus scent wafted to him and reminded him of the way her skin tasted.

Not for the first time, he wished things had gone differently Saturday night. He might be stuck spending the next six weeks working on his screenplay, but that didn't mean he couldn't have a few distractions along the way—and Jess Alexander would be a particularly good one.

He realized now he shouldn't have slept with her. He should have left her waiting for more. It was what Sebastian did with Elvire—and Elvire practically salivated in Sebastian's presence now.

Elvire! Could that be what the screenplay was missing? A love interest? The movie had plenty of action, plenty of tension and more than a few frights. But there was no Elvire—because Elvire hadn't entered Sebastian's world until book two. Could there be a way to work her into the screenplay without disrupting the canon timelines he'd worked so hard to build?

"Earth to Sean? Must have been some meeting." Jess's voice cut into his thoughts. "Huh?"

Jess was waving a hand in front of his face and her frown had been replaced by a faintly bemused expression. "I said I'd go get Suzie for you. You were in another world."

Literally. Fiction versus reality. Sexy real-world woman in front of you—wake up, Sean. "Oh, yeah, sorry. The stuff from my meeting is still going round in my head. Thanks."

"I'll be back in a second."

Jess turned from the door and Sean thought for a moment she was going to close it in his face.

"Jess—I don't suppose you'd have a coffee on offer, would you?"

She halted and shot him a startled look over her shoulder. "You want to come in?"

He slouched against the door frame. "I've been talking for almost three hours straight. I could use a drink of some kind. Plus, you need to tell me again what I need to look out for with Suzie. Everything you told me at the clinic's gone from my head since the conference call."

"But..."

Jess's eyes flicked between him and the door as if she was deciding which image she liked better—his face, or the door closed with him behind it.

"I'm not a vampire," he joked.

That made her eyes go wide. "What?"

"I just mean that it's not dangerous to invite me into your home." Weak. And obviously not to Jess's taste.

"Oh, right," she said flatly. "Well...I guess I can find some coffee." Jess finally opened the door and gestured for him to come inside.

"Thanks. Milk with one sugar. Do you have real sugar? Hailey and Rob only have that fake calorie-free stuff and it's disgusting."

"There's plenty of sugar at the supermarket," Jess pointed out drily as he followed her through the hallway and into an open-plan living area.

Sean sighed. "Yeah. I guess I'll have to go there and get some." The thought practically gave him hives. He'd rather face a pack of rabid werewolves than aisles of grocery items. But if he wanted to change the assumptions Jess—and his family—made of him, he guessed he needed to get comfortable with things like supermarket shopping. He'd need to buy dog food before long, anyway.

"Take a seat, I'll be back in a minute."

Sean looked around to find himself in a pleasantly decorated room with a kitchen visible through an archway and glass doors that led out to a darkened deck. The room wasn't overly feminine, but it had a softness to the furnishings and the accessories that made it somehow obvious a woman lived here. A television flickered in the corner, the sound turned off. A book lay on the sofa, open, spine up. Sean couldn't help but investigate it—a historical, Booker Prize winner, literary tome. About as far away from the Sebastian Douglas series as it was possible to get.

Suzie lay on a well-chewed old dog bed near the window, snoring gently.

"Hey, pretty gal, how're you doing?" Sean crouched down beside the dog and scratched her ears. Suzie's

tail thumped and she stretched to make it easier for
Sean to pet her.

"She's going to be fine," Jess said behind him.

Sean watched as she bent over to place two steaming mugs on the coffee table.

"Phew, good." His relief was genuine. He really
didn't want to live down to Hailey's and Rob's worst
expectations. Having them return from their honeymoon to find their possessions and their pet in much
the same state as when they'd left was his goal. Who
knew? It could even start them thinking that he just
might be a capable adult. Besides, he was really very
fond of the smelly old dog.

Giving Suzie one last pat, Sean got to his feet and
walked over to Jess. "Thank you so much. Honestly,
I don't know what I would have done tonight without
your help. I really appreciate it."

Jess looked away, seemingly embarrassed by his
gratitude.

"It's fine," she said, waving him onto the sofa. She
sat, too—as close to the arm of the couch as she could
get without actually climbing it.

Sean took his coffee in both hands and sucked in
a deep breath of the steam rising from the cup. He
was going to need every bit of caffeine he could get
tonight—he wanted to make a start on the script revisions straightaway while the feedback from the producers was fresh in his mind.

"So what was the meeting about?" Jess asked.

Sean hesitated before answering. He hadn't told
anyone about the movie deal—in fact, he was strictly

forbidden from discussing it publicly. It would be nice to share the news with someone—but then what if it all fell through? Sean didn't want to have to admit failure to anyone and, for some reason, especially not Jess.

"Sorry, it's none of my business," she said quickly, jumping in when he remained silent.

"No, it's not that." Sean rushed to reassure her. "It's just… It's a long story and I'm kind of sick of it right now."

Jess nodded. "Fair enough."

Sean looked around the living room. Apart from Suzie, he couldn't see any other animals. "You don't have any pets?" he asked.

Jess shrugged and bit her lip before answering. "Not right now."

Her tone and the old dog bed Suzie lay in were more clues than Sherlock Holmes would have needed. "But you did until recently?"

"Yeah. Rocco. A black Lab. He died a couple of months ago. Old age."

"I'm sorry."

"Thanks. I still miss him."

A photo on the table next to the sofa caught his eye. "Where was this taken?" he asked, picking up the frame to take a closer look at the group it depicted. Rob and Hailey stood with their arms around each other, Hailey's eyes closed and mouth open in a fantastic hoot of laughter. Rob smiled at her with an expression of such love and wonder it actually made something in Sean's chest tighten. Beside them stood an older, grandmotherly looking woman, an older man by her side, both smiling dutifully yet warmly for the camera. And on the far side was Jess, an imposing-looking man beside her with his arm around her shoulders in a possessive gesture. Both of them wore smiles, but their eyes were cold. Jess had her arms folded in front of her and she leaned away from the guy, as if she didn't want him touching her.

If it had been a frame in a graphic novel it would have communicated a bucketload about the people in it and their relationships.

Jess shifted. "Oh. I, uh, forgot that was there. It's from a Christmas party we had for the practice three years ago. We all went out to the Yarra Valley and stayed overnight at a winery. It was…fun."

"Well, Hailey and Rob look like they're having fun, anyway." He didn't bother mentioning that Jess looked as if she'd rather have been water-boarded than pose for the picture—it was that obvious.

"Yeah, there was quite a bit of wine consumed that weekend."

"Who's…?" Sean trailed off as a thought occurred to him. Was Jess involved with someone? Married? Was that why she'd freaked out on Saturday night? He quickly sought out her left hand—no ring. He would have noticed on the night, surely.

"My ex-husband," Jess said, clearly guessing where his question was headed.

"Ah." He breathed an internal sigh of relief. Sean didn't do cheating. He knew his family didn't think much of his moral compass, but he *did* have one. His north just pointed in a different direction to theirs. "How long have you been divorced?"

"Just over six months."

"Not that long then."

Jess shrugged. "I guess not. But we were separated for a year before that." She shifted on the sofa again, curling back into herself—away from him.

A realization suddenly hit. "Oh, I get it."

"Get what?"

Sean hadn't realized he'd spoken aloud. Too late now. "Have you dated much since your divorce?"

Her blush confirmed his suspicions.

"So *that's* why you freaked out."

"I didn't freak out!"

"Yeah, you did."

"I did not."

"What would you call it, then?"

"I...changed my mind."

Sean frowned at that. "About what?"

"About...being there."

The idea that Jess regretted their time together made Sean uncomfortable. He'd been pretty sure she'd had a good time. "You wish it hadn't happened?"

"Yes... No. I don't know."

Confusion creased her forehead and she stared intently into her cup of coffee as if all the answers could be found within it.

"Hey, it's okay, you know." Sean moved closer and reached out to take her hand. She tensed and shot him a quick look, but she didn't move away. "It's okay to move on. You *should* move on."

"'Cause you're such an expert," Jess muttered, but her sarcasm was muted.

He squeezed her fingers. She was right. It was the mother of all ironies, him sitting here dispensing relationship advice. But he had learned one or two things during his years of experience with women. And he'd die before admitting it, but he'd had his heart broken once, too. That was actually when he'd decided that keeping things temporary worked best for him. Best for all concerned, really.

"Have I ever been divorced? No. But do I know about moving on after a relationship has ended? Yes. You have to get out and remind yourself that the world still exists—that there are more adventures to be had."

"Adventures?" Her eyebrows raised and she gave him a small smile.

"It's a good word for it."

She sucked in a deep breath and let it out in a long sigh. "I guess it is. It certainly takes courage, anyway."

"That it does."

They sat in silence for a while. Sean drew back, let her hand go and recovered his cup of coffee from the table. He drank a few sips with true gratitude—the first decent coffee he'd had in days. He really did need to go to the grocery store.

Jess ran a hand through her hair, seeming to gather herself. She gave a short, self-conscious laugh as she shifted, tucking one leg underneath her on the sofa. "Thanks—and sorry, I guess."

"What for?"

She shrugged. "I wish I'd handled Saturday night better. You were right—I freaked out. That's the bit I wish hadn't happened."

Color stained her cheeks and she looked straight ahead, clueing Sean in to how much the confession cost her.

"We can always have a do-over." The words were out before he'd really thought them through, but he realized he'd be quite happy to try a repeat of Saturday night—without the weird finale.

"What?"

He couldn't help but laugh at the way her whole body started, and the shocked look on her face as she jerked to face him.

"Oh, you're joking," she said.

Sean was sure he wasn't being vain in reading disappointment in her tone.

"Actually, no, I wasn't," he admitted. "In fact, given that I'm in town for a while, how about you show me around? It's been a long time since I've spent any time here—" a deliberate strategy to avoid his parents "—and I'd appreciate a local's insight. Not to mention the fact that I owe you one for tonight. Let me repay you with dinner."

"You want to go on a date?"

"Sure. Why not?" He gave her a gentle shove on the arm. "I get company and you get a chance to remember what it's like to be dating. Kind of a practice run. Courage, remember?"

"Oh, thanks, but…I couldn't…" she stumbled. Her fingers went to her mouth and she bit a fingernail before she realized what she was doing and clasped her hands firmly in her lap.

"Come on, what are you scared of?"

"I'm not scared."

Suddenly, Sean saw his chance. "Bo-oo-ok, bok, bok." He did his best chicken imitation, complete with flapping elbows.

Jess rolled her eyes in an expression he was now familiar with.

"I'm not scared," she repeated.

Sean did a few more "boks" for good measure.

She shook her head. "You're being stupid."

"I'm not the only one."

"Fine." She sighed.

"So, was that a yes?"

"Will it get you out of here so I can get some sleep? It's pretty late, if you hadn't noticed."

"I will absolutely leave you in peace."

"Then it's a yes."

"Thursday night? There's a new movie coming out that I want to see—if that's okay with you."

She nodded. "Thursday night."

"Excellent." Sean drained his coffee and then rose and headed for the door. Jess followed him slowly.

"I'll pick you up here at seven."

Jess shrugged. It wasn't the most enthusiastic of consents, but he'd take it. He liked Jess, and since he was stuck in Melbourne for six weeks, he needed to ensure he had an occasional distraction from writing—he knew from experience that spending too long inside his own head tended to send him a little loopy.

"See you then."

He leaned in, wondering if it would be pushing things to kiss her. The boundary seemed strange given the intimacy they'd already shared. But sure enough, Jess pulled back.

"Good night, Sean," she said primly.

He grinned. "Good night, Jess."

CHAPTER FIVE

How STUPID COULD one woman be?

Clearly the limits were pretty high. Jess took one final look in the mirror as she readied herself for her date.

Adventurous, not stupid, she mentally corrected herself.

How long since she'd last been on a date? She counted back as she adjusted her bra strap to make sure the scoop-necked top of her dress sat right.

Over a decade. She'd met Mark when she was twenty-five.

Sean would have been in high school. Only just, but still...

Ew.

The thought made her stomach twist.

"He's a grown man," she said aloud, scolding herself. Yes, he was younger than her, but he was years past being a boy. It wasn't as if she was breaking the law or doing anything unsavory. He didn't even look particularly young—he had one of those faces that could be anywhere between twenty-five and thirty-five depending on the light.

What she was doing, as he'd so rightly put it, was

moving on. It was about time. Everyone kept saying it. Even Hailey's usually gentle admonishments had become more insistent recently.

She *should* be over Mark. An appropriate amount of time had passed. She'd read the self-help books. Even gone to a couple of therapy appointments—but sitting around talking about feeling sad and powerless had only made her feel more sad and powerless, so she'd given up on that.

She and Mark didn't keep in touch. It was easier that way. Once all the property had been settled there was really no need. And Jess wasn't in any hurry to find out if Mark was still seeing Cathy—if she'd been more than the fling he'd insisted she was. A faint sense of nausea passed through her—as it always did when she thought back to those times.

And standing around thinking about her ex-husband was a brilliant way to prepare herself for a date. Not.

It certainly did nothing to alleviate the butterflies running riot in her stomach.

Thankfully Sean chose that moment to knock on her door.

The sense of relief she felt at banishing Mark from her mind was almost enough to overcome her anxiety about the night ahead. She slammed the wardrobe door closed and did a weird skip-run down the narrow stairs of her compact townhome, needing to expend some energy.

"Hi," she said as she opened the door, a little

breathless from the combination of nerves and her unnecessary dash.

"Very *Melbourne*," Sean said drily, looking her up and down.

"I guess." Her knee-high black boots, black tights and long-sleeved black dress had looked elegant but understated in the mirror, or so she'd thought. And perfect for a night out in the city known for its shunning of the majority of the color wheel. Now she wondered if she looked like some kind of widow or horror-story creature—hadn't Sean made a joke about vampires the other night?

"I like it." He smiled then, and it only made her nerves ratchet higher.

He wore dark jeans, boots and a casual white shirt of heavy linen with a faint gray swirl down the front. A casual canvas jacket in a pale khaki hung over his arm in preparation for the cool autumn weather. His hair was spiky again, like it had been at the wedding. The man was the epitome of casual style.

She wondered if his choice of clothing was a deliberate or accidental callback to his tux. A flash of heat went through her as she remembered the way he'd looked standing in front of her, white dress shirt undone, tie hanging around his neck, black trousers tented with his arousal.

She shook her head to clear the image.

"Shall we go?"

"Let's." He held his arm out. "The movie starts at nine—I hope you'll like it."

THE DATE, all things considered, was going pretty well, Jess figured. Dinner at a nice, but not too fancy, Italian restaurant had been delicious and conversation had flowed freely. They'd steered clear of personal topics, but discovered they both had a love of classic movies and had managed to laugh over their pretty much opposite tastes in music. At least in that one area he made her feel young—his love of classic rock had more in common with her father's record collection than her own iPod list filled with contemporary alternative folk-pop.

The movie—a Hollywood superhero blockbuster mostly designed for a teen audience—had been okay, but hadn't been the kind of film she'd thought Sean would choose after the discussion they'd had over their food about Hitchcock and Kurosawa and Almoldóvar.

But then, Sean was younger than her. Not that it really mattered, she told herself for the twentieth time. It didn't seem to be a problem for him, so she simply wasn't going to make it a problem for herself. They certainly didn't look out of place together—Jess was pretty sure no one was struggling to work out if she was his mother or his date.

As the lights came up in the cinema, Sean sat in his chair, a serious, contemplative expression on his face.

"What did you think?" he asked, frowning at the credits as they rolled up the screen.

Jess shrugged. "It was okay."

"Yeah. It wasn't as good as I thought it was going to be."

"I didn't have high expectations."

He cocked his head and gave her a searching look. "Why not?"

"Oh, you know. It was yet another one of those comic book movies. Those stories are all pretty silly, aren't they?" She said it just a moment before remembering Hailey's description of Sean's writing. She'd been vague about it, but Jess was sure she'd mentioned comic books. *Way to put your foot in it, Jess.* "Ugh. Sorry. That was dumb of me."

"It's okay." Sean waved her comment away but she was sure she'd seen a flash of something cross his face—just like at the wedding when Sean's uncle had made a similar dismissive comment.

"It's not okay," she insisted. "You write comic books, don't you? I'm afraid I don't know much about them and I tend to think of them as being for kids."

"I started with graphic novels—which are sort of like comic books—but I mostly write novels these days."

Jess breathed a sigh of relief that Sean didn't seem too insulted by her offhand comments. She searched her brain for something positive to say. What had Hailey said about Sean? Pretty much nothing good. But Rob had once mentioned that a friend of his had found one of Sean's books for sale in the United States—that was something. "Oh, cool. Um, Rob told me that you've even had one of your books sold overseas. It's great that you've had a taste of success."

"What did you think of the movie's ending?" Sean asked before she could go on.

"Well…" Jess struggled to think of something intelligent to say about it. "I didn't like what happened to the baddie. It was clear that there was more to his story than we got to see. I wanted to know more about what drove him to want to destroy the planet. Then it would have meant more when he failed."

Sean sat up straighter in his seat, nodding in agreement. "Absolutely. There's way more detail about all of that in the original story. We lost that complexity."

"But the style of the movie was fantastic. The lighting and camera angles and art direction were great." Jess surprised herself with her recall and critique, but she meant it. "I haven't seen too many of this kind of movie, but it definitely seemed very stylish. I'd recognize a scene as being from this movie if I caught a clip of it—just because of the visual aesthetic."

That seemed to please Sean very much for some reason, if his smile was any indication. "Yeah. You're right. The story was lacking, but the style was great. The director did as good a job with the script as he could."

"Who was the director?"

Sean named someone Jess had heard of—although didn't know very well. Then he stood, brushing his hands on the front of his pants. "What would you like to do now?" Sean asked. "We could grab a gelato, or find a restaurant for dessert."

Jess shook her head and put a hand on her stomach. "After pasta for dinner and chocolate during the movie, I couldn't eat another thing."

"Okay, well, how about a walk?"

"Sure."

Sean took her hand as they exited the cinema and began to stroll down the street in the cool night air. It felt strangely comfortable.

They passed a large bookstore and Jess halted. Maybe she could find a way to make up for her tactlessness earlier.

"Let's go in here," she said.

Sean shrugged. "Sure."

Once inside, though, Jess was at a loss. She'd had some vague idea of walking in and going straight up to the shelf to find Sean's book. Then she could buy it—maybe get him to sign it, too. But where on earth would she find it? She had no choice but to ask him. "Will your book be in here?"

Sean looked instantly uncomfortable. "Probably, I guess."

"Let's find it!"

"No, Jess, we don't have to—"

"Come on." Sean was standing still, and Jess tugged on his arm to make him follow her.

"Which section?" she asked over her shoulder as Sean reluctantly began to follow her.

He did a quick scan of the store. "Probably there—" he pointed to the rear of the store "—in horror and sci-fi."

"I've never even been to that section before. This is great." She was genuinely excited about finding Sean's name on the shelf. But then a dark thought occurred to her—what if the store didn't stock his book? Would it be embarrassing for Sean? She'd been trying to make things better, not worse.

It was too late now—she'd just have to deal with it if and when it happened.

Still dragging a strangely reluctant Sean behind her, Jess made her way over to the horror section. The multicolored spines of the general fiction shelves gave way to more somber hues of black and red and brown as the subject material of the books got darker.

"Okay, *P*, we have to find *P*," she murmured to herself. She scanned the bookshelves. Large sections for Dean Koontz and Stephen King—horror writers even she'd heard of—helped her navigate the alphabetical shelving. To the left she saw two books on the top shelf, face out, with the name Sean Paterson in large shiny silver block letters on the front. On the cover, a handsome man in a trench coat—the model wasn't a million miles away from Sean's own looks, just more polished, more movie-star-like—held a sword in one hand and a shotgun in the other, his expression a dark, intense frown that seemed to look right through to Jess's bones. His booted left foot was propped up on a gravestone.

"Sean, look! There you are!" Her relief was almost overwhelming. Thank God the store had his book on their shelves! "And they've got two copies in stock. That's great!"

"Uh, yeah." Sean was rubbing his jaw and looking both uncomfortable and embarrassed.

Jess thought it was simple modesty until her eyes scanned the next shelf.

At first, she wasn't sure what she was seeing.

Then her jaw dropped as she took it in.

A larger-than-life-size cardboard cutout of the trench-coat-clad model wearing a jaunty fedora and with a cigarette dangling between his lips stood on the floor near Sean, emphasizing the similarity in their looks. A banner hanging from the ceiling above it proclaimed Sebastian Douglas: The Demon Warrior's Newest Mission—Out Now!

Next to the scowling cutout, an entire section of shelves held copies of the book. Next to that were rows of other books, all with the name Sean Paterson emblazoned on their covers and spines. Each had the trench-coat-clad hunter on the front—sometimes alone, sometimes with others. On one he was accompanied by a phalanx of bloody ghosts, on another a supermodel in a corset and voluminous skirts with long blond hair and fangs leered at him with a lustful gaze.

An array of fantastical characters across the shelves. Dozens of them.

"But...I..." Jess floundered.

Sean shifted uncomfortably. "Jess, do you mind if we get out of here? I've found it can get a little awkward if people recognize me. Not that that's likely," he rushed to add, "but just in case."

"Uh, yeah. Okay. Sure."

Jess let Sean steer her away from the shelves, but not without taking one last good look as if to assure herself it was real.

Sean Paterson wasn't the author of a little comic

book or silly schlock horror story as Hailey had led
Jess to believe. He was a multipublished author, so
famous in his genre that his latest release commanded
elaborate in-store promotion like cardboard cutouts
and entire shelves dedicated to his new book.

Once they were back out in the street, Sean turned
to her.

"You look like you could use a drink. Or do you
just want me to take you home?"

Jess sucked in a deep breath and let it out slowly.
"Drink. I definitely need a drink."

She waited until they were settled into a booth in
a dimly lit corner of a nearby bar, each with a glass
of red wine in front of them, before she spoke again.
"Why didn't you tell me you were so successful?"

Her hand shook as she raised her glass and took
a long sip. A weird anxiety had her pasta dinner sitting like a painful lump in her gut. Sean hadn't lied
to her—not really. It just felt like it.

"What was I supposed to say? 'Oh, by the way,
Jess, I've sold a lot of books,'" he mocked.

"That would have been a start!" Jess was aware
she was overreacting, but she couldn't seem to help
it. A bubble of emotion rose inside her, so hot and
tight it made her feel close to tears.

Sean was young. He was handsome. He was
charming. And, now she knew, he was an incredibly successful author.

And he'd made her feel like a fool.

Why hadn't she thought to look him up on Google?

A quick two minutes on the internet and she wouldn't be sitting here looking like an idiot.

Come on, Jess, get it together. Stop being ridiculous.

She was thankful they were side-by-side so she could angle herself away from him while she regained her composure.

Sean was silent.

"So," Jess began when she'd taken enough deep breaths to calm herself, "why did Hailey tell me that you weren't very successful? The way she described it, you'd written one or two books that were, well, struggling. Even Rob never said much about it."

Sean shrugged. "Hailey has been spending a lot of time with my mother, from what I understand."

"And?"

"My father reads the newspaper. My mother only reads biographies and Nancy Mitford novels."

Jess shook her head, not sure what he was getting at. "So?"

"So they have no idea what I do, what I've achieved."

"Why haven't you told them?"

"I've tried."

"Really?" She still sounded stupidly shrill.

He shifted in his seat uncomfortably. "Yeah. But it's kind of hard to just come out and say, 'oh, guess what, I'm pretty successful.' They're not interested anyway."

Jess took a long sip of wine. He hadn't deliberately set out to mislead her. She was self-aware enough to know that she was overly sensitive to this kind of situation. She didn't like not picking up on things that should have been obvious—it made her look foolish. And she hated being made to look like a fool—a hangover from her marriage, during which Mark had made her the biggest fool in the world.

But Sean didn't deserve her anger. If his parents—and Rob and Hailey—really were that dismissive of his success, he deserved her sympathy, not her misplaced sense of betrayal.

She lowered her voice. "I'm sorry, Sean." Her own parents were incredibly proud of her accomplishments. They'd always boasted of her scholastic achievements, and nowadays loved to tell their friends about the fact that she owned and operated her own veterinary practice. Sure, she knew they'd been disappointed by her divorce, and she was positive they'd love to have some grandchildren to spoil instead of a business to boast about, but, in her parents' eyes, Jess felt appreciated and successful. She hated to think what it must be like if it was otherwise.

The memory of Sean's mother bearing down toward them like an aircraft carrier at the wedding came back to her. As did Sean's quick escape.

"So how did it happen? How did you get to be a famous author?" she asked.

Sean gave her a slightly suspicious look, as if he didn't trust the motives of her question.

"I'm genuinely interested," she insisted. And she was.

Sean looked down at his wine. For the first time since she'd met him, that invisible cloak of confidence he wore seemed to have slipped. He looked not just uncertain, but vulnerable. She wanted to hug him, but settled instead for resting a hand on his arm, her turmoil and anger forgotten.

"I started with graphic novels," he said quietly. "I wrote the stories and drew them at first, then I just concentrated on the story and had artists draw for me."

"What were they about?"

"I started with a series of books based on characters from Aboriginal mythology. My first stories were about the spirits that created the moon and the sun. And then I wrote about the spirits that lived in the shadows that the moon and the sun cast. I put the shadow spirits in the modern world, had them scaring and manipulating people to their own ends, but in ways true to the original myths."

"I've never heard of anything like that before." Jess was intrigued by his description—enough to want to read it. The story sounded fascinating—although she'd never read a graphic novel before and had no idea what it meant. "Sorry for being ignorant, but is a graphic novel the same as a comic book?"

"Sort of, but not really." Sean gave her a quick smile, and Jess got the sense that he was pleased by her question. "A comic book is generally a short story that's part of a long-running serial. A graphic novel tends to be one single story—although it can be part of a series—that has a more complex plot and detailed narrative."

"So they're not like the Richie Rich and Casper

comics I read as a kid? The ones with the ads for sea monkeys on the back page?" She hoped he'd realize she was joking.

He shot her a quick grin. "Nope."

"Right, got it. So you started with graphic novels, then what?"

"Then...my agent asked if I'd be interested in novel writing. I'd already been playing with the Sebastian stories, thinking they'd be graphic novels, but then I decided they'd work better as just stories. So I started writing the first novel. It did okay. Actually it became a bit of a hit."

"A bit of a hit?" Jess prompted, sure he was underplaying things.

"*New York Times* bestseller."

"Just a *bit* of a hit, then," Jess repeated sarcastically, rolling her eyes at his modesty. "And the latest book—is that doing well?"

"Pretty well. You saw the display."

Jess could only imagine that if "bit of a hit" meant "*New York Times* bestseller," then "doing pretty well" must be stratospheric.

"Wow. So, how come I haven't heard of you before? How come you don't get mobbed in the street?"

Sean managed a laugh at that. "It's not like I'm a movie star."

"But...you're famous."

"Yeah, to people who read horror novels."

"But, but..." Jess struggled to take it all in. Thankfully, her earlier anger had all but disappeared.

Sean ducked his head—a gesture Jess had come

to associate with him being modest. "I'm fortunate enough to be able to make a decent living doing something I love in a field that's ridiculously competitive. I know how lucky I am, and I know how quickly that luck could change. It's one of those impossible-to-predict scenarios—I just happened to come on the scene with a story involving vampires and demons and supernatural creatures at a time when the market was ready and waiting for new stories in that genre. I was in the right place at the right time—and I had the right stuff and was willing to work for it."

Jess liked that he wasn't completely dismissing his own role in his success. Sure there had to be an element of luck in getting published—Jess didn't know a whole lot about it, just what she'd seen in movies and on TV—but clearly Sean had been able to capitalize on his lucky break by working hard.

"How many books do you have out now?"

"It's hard to say—some of my graphic novels have gone out of print. There were around twenty of them. And the latest Sebastian Douglas book is number seven."

"How many are there going to be?"

"As many as I can write without getting stale or boring."

"What're the Sebastian Douglas books about?"

Sean rattled off a clearly practiced spiel about a loner who hunted evil creatures and kept the world safe with the reluctant assistance of his studious assistant, Rob. Sebastian's activities were a secret from the everyday world and as a result he never received any

recognition for his heroism. He—and Rob—simply
went on to the next job, the next baddie to be slain.
In his explanation, Sean referenced Sherlock Holmes,
and Batman, and a few other things she wasn't familiar with.

"Wow." Jess shook her head, still stunned by the
knowledge that the disreputable Sean Paterson, the
man with a woman in every port, was an incredibly
successful author. She really didn't understand why
his family was so dismissive of his achievements.
She knew, from Hailey, that Mrs. Paterson was very
concerned about appearances, being a woman who
preciously guarded her position in the upper class of
Melbourne society. But surely recognizing Sean's
fame could only enhance her cachet, not damage it?

Jess guessed that now was not the time to mine
Sean's clearly complicated relationship with his family.

"So now you know the whole Sean Paterson story,"
Sean said, giving her a gentle shove with his shoulder.

"I seriously doubt that."

Sean gave a little laugh. "Maybe you're right."

What Jess did know was that tomorrow morning,
as soon as she had a break, she was heading straight
for a bookstore to buy up as many Sean Paterson
books as she could get her hands on.

"And yet I still know hardly anything about the
Jess Alexander story. Turnabout's fair play." He raised
his eyebrows expectantly.

Jess managed to swallow the sip of wine she'd
taken, but then she had to clear her throat. This was

definitely one of the reasons she'd avoided going on any dates. Because eventually, at some point, she'd have to talk about herself. Knowing what to share and what not to seemed so simple—but in reality it was a minefield. One she didn't want to have to cross if at all possible.

Sean's attention—right from the very start—had been making her uncomfortably aware of a new element of her personality that she didn't want to admit to.

Cowardice.

Since when had the woman who'd backpacked alone through Europe, bungee jumped in New Zealand, treated feral cats and untrained pit bulls, not to mention started and runs her own business, been *afraid?* It was a description she didn't want to belong to her. She'd told herself that her lack of a social life since the divorce was just about being *cautious.* Careful. Circumspect.

But it was becoming more obvious that it didn't matter which thesaurus she consulted—what it all added up to was a serious case of *scaredy-cat.*

"I'm not that interesting." She tried to deflect. "I've never written any books. In fact, I didn't even do that well in English at school—I was more of a science geek."

"You're the cutest science geek I've ever seen."

Jess waved away his compliment, but the effects of that sexy grin of his weren't nearly as easy to dismiss. And that flash of heat was enough to remind her that she'd set out on this date without really thinking it through. *Without letting herself think it through.*

What was going to happen when it was time to go home? Was Sean expecting a free pass into her bed because of what they'd done on the night of the wedding? Did he think she was easy prey? Did he think she was *easy,* full stop?

At the same time, her body kept reminding her of just how skilled his lovemaking had been. Certainly better than anything she'd experienced during the final years of her marriage.

"You've gone all serious on me again." Sean's words broke through her tumbling thoughts. His finger reached out to touch her chin.

Jess dredged up a smile. "Sorry." She drained her glass of wine and sat straighter in her seat. "I guess it's getting late. Pumpkin time. My ball gown turns to rags and I lose all conversational prowess."

"As long as you leave your glass slipper behind, I don't mind."

His heated look made Jess's stomach do a slow flip in her belly. It wasn't exactly a pleasurable sensation.

Sean climbed out off the booth and offered his arm. "Shall we head back to the carriage, Cinders?"

"Sure."

They managed the drive back to Jess's house without incident, conversation flitting between inconsequential topics before settling on a revisiting of their critique of the movie. But despite her focus on discussing lighting and camera angles, by the time Sean pulled Dezzie up in front of Jess's place, her nerves were shredded. What would he expect? More important, what did *she* want? The fact that she couldn't answer that question was driving her crazy.

He killed the ignition and turned to her.

"Thanks, Jess."

"For what?" she asked, startled.

"For entertaining a vagabond like me. I don't spend a lot of time in Melbourne and I really don't know many people here—certainly not people I'd like to spend a pleasant evening out with. You've been a sanity saver. I tend to go a bit nuts if I spend all day with fictional characters and then don't interact with real, actual people."

Jess laughed. "I can't even imagine that." Spending a day writing stories was light-years from her own very practical, very grounded daily life. Just that morning she'd spent an hour drenched in puppy urine before she could get cleaned up. But that didn't mean his work was any less valuable. She fiddled with her purse before settling her eyes on him. "Sean, I'm really blown away by your success. I think it's fabulous. I'm sorry I didn't react well—it…it wasn't anything to do with you."

He shrugged. "I can understand why you felt that way. It came out of the blue."

"Yeah, but it's just…" Jess wasn't sure if she was saying this because she felt he deserved an explanation or she needed to explain herself. "I'm a bit over-sensitive. I don't like being lied to or feeling like a fool."

"Because of your ex?"

She twisted the handle of her purse in her hands. *Way to jump in the deep end, Jess.* "Yeah. It was… all a bit messy."

"I figured something like that."

The light in his eyes was kind and understanding, and something inside Jess uncoiled, her fingers relaxing their death grip on the bag's strap. "Thank you," she said. "Thank you for being patient with me."

"You're very welcome." He leaned over and pressed a kiss to her mouth, warm, firm, soft, delicious. Jess unconsciously swayed forward, eyes drifting closed, but then he pulled back and was gently shoving her arm.

"Now scoot," he said. "I'm sure you've got an early start tomorrow."

"Huh?" Her incoherent grunt wasn't exactly ladylike, but he'd scrambled her brain with that one simple kiss.

"Sleep well, princess," he said.

"But…" Jess trailed off. *Courage. Take a risk. Go on.* "Don't you want to come in? I have coffee—and sugar, if you still need some…"

He considered her for a moment, his expression unreadable. Jess's anxiety reached red-zone levels.

"Thank you." He cupped her face with his hand, his thumb lightly stroking her cheek. "But I'm here, in one place, for five more weeks. We've got plenty of time. Think about what you want to do on the weekend. I'll call you tomorrow to make a plan."

His arrogant presumption that she'd go out with

him again was Sean Paterson all over. But, like his confidence in life generally, it wasn't unjustified.

"Okay." Jess scrambled to get out of the car. Dezzie's powerful engines rumbled awake and, with a wave, Sean was gone.

Inside, Jess threw her bag on a chair and sank into her sofa with a sigh. Sean had urged her to sleep well, but she already knew she'd do nothing of the sort. She felt wired, as if she'd had too many cups of coffee, adrenaline running high.

No wonder she'd avoided dating.

Except…

At least she'd made a start now. She'd dipped her toe in the water. Surely no other dates could be as daunting as this; the first after a decade-long absence from the pool.

The night of Rob and Hailey's wedding hadn't gone as she'd expected, but there was no denying the sparks between them had been hot. Tonight had been—well, fun, mostly. Apart from the bit where she'd freaked out.

Just like on Saturday night.

Two "dates" and two freak-outs.

And Sean still wanted to see her again? *Did he consider her his community service?* Surely she couldn't be *that* fascinating to him. She was older than him, but it wasn't as if she offered him a wisdom or wealth of experience he didn't already have—he was the one who brought the dating prowess to the party. Wasn't that why younger men liked "cougars"? She shuddered at the label.

Jess wasn't sure she believed his "don't know anyone else in town" shtick, but even if that was true, a man like Sean only needed to head for the nearest nightclub to find himself companionship for the night.

But they talked so easily—Jess had honestly not met someone of either gender in a long time who she'd found so interesting and where the conversation had just flowed. Not to mention their chemistry. When he kissed her, her brain went into instant meltdown.

And he came with an expiry date.

When Hailey and Rob's honeymoon came to an end, Sean would be gone.

Strangely, that part of it was reassuring.

Maybe...

Should she consider Sean as practice? It smacked a little uncomfortably of "using" him, but then wasn't he using her, too—for company? And who could blame her? A twenty-eight-year-old stud was practically throwing himself at her.

Jess needed practice getting out and dating if she ever hoped to *not* spend the rest of her life simply watching television and adopting an ever-increasing number of dogs and cats. She'd already noted that she'd been spending more time than usual looking longingly at the animals up for adoption at the rescue center where she volunteered occasionally.

Even better, the stud seemed—for some unknown reason—to be cool with her strange behavior, her freak-outs, her reluctance to share herself.

Perhaps life was handing her this chance. One of the first nice things life had handed her since her marriage had headed down the toilet.

Jess looked over at the calendar hanging on the wall in the kitchen that she could just see from where she lounged on the sofa. A fling with a finite life-span; an *affair*.

It was perfect, really.

CHAPTER SIX

"The zoo?"

Sean laughed at Jess's uncertain tone as they found a spot in the parking lot adjacent to the Melbourne Zoological Gardens and got out of the car. She certainly didn't seem to like surprises. Which, in itself, wasn't a surprise.

If he were to distill her into one of the character profiles he liked to develop for his books, he'd say Jess was all about control and certainty. The amateur psychologist in him, the one that helped him write the believable characters his fans loved, was pretty sure she'd been that way all her life, and her divorce had only reinforced it. He hadn't missed the nervous expression on her face when he'd picked her up from her house that morning and refused to tell her where they were going.

Now that he was getting to know her, he was realizing that their night together had been quite out of character. It was lucky he knew for a fact she hadn't been drinking or he might have been harboring guilt about taking advantage of her.

But no, she'd been sober. Completely aware of what she was doing.

It meant there was an adventurous streak in there somewhere. Buried a little, perhaps, but there nonetheless.

He nudged her shoulder. "Come on, it'll be fun."

"Yeah. Yeah, okay."

She smiled then and he took her hand and led her to the gates. He'd already organized tickets—and a few other surprises—so they walked straight in and were immediately surrounded by lush gardens and air scented with the unmistakable smell of animals.

It was the perfect day for the zoo—coolish, but with warm, bright sunshine to keep things comfortable. Jess was wearing a flowery blue sundress with a white cardigan that was almost retro-style. Her hair was pulled back into a ponytail, which added to the look. Sunglasses covered her eyes, but her mouth curved, betraying a smile.

He wondered how long it had been since she'd just done something for fun—apart from last Saturday night.

They walked past the first few enclosures in comfortable silence, occasionally pointing out where a creature was hiding behind a tree or other structure. He noticed that Jess carefully read the signs that went with each animal, her forehead creased with concentration.

After they'd made their way around about a third of the displays, Sean decided to declare his hand.

"I have to confess, I had an ulterior motive for coming here today."

"You did?"

That worried expression was back. After the vague details Jess had shared when he'd dropped her home after the movie Thursday night, at least Sean better understood where her reticence came from. He didn't know what exactly had happened between Jess and her ex, but he was pretty sure he wanted to find a way to hunt down the bastard and give him a solid punch in the gut.

Strange. By dint of his relationship preferences, almost all the women he dated came with baggage. But he couldn't recall it bothering him before.

He smoothed his thumb across her forehead, smiling gently at her. "Don't worry—nothing nefarious is going on."

She started a little at his touch, but her mouth kicked up at one corner. "Nefarious? Good to know it's nothing *nefarious,*" she teased, making fun of his vocabulary.

He shrugged, smiling at her gentle taunting. "It's a very good word." He held up the leaflet that showed the map of the zoo. "I actually wanted to come here to look at wolves. And I wanted to mine your vet-brain with a few questions."

"Wolves?"

He took her hand and they started walking again. "I'm writing a new character into my next book. A werewolf. Or maybe a more generic kind of shape-shifter. I'm not sure. But I thought I'd come and look at the wolves, see how they move, find out more about them."

"A werewolf. Okay."

She sounded faintly amused, but not in a mocking way, Sean was relieved to note.

Jess stopped. "Let me look." She held out her hand for the map and then studied it for a moment. "I'm not sure you're going to have much luck," she said, shaking her head. "I don't think they have wolves here. At least not the kind from Europe or North America that would be traditionally werewolflike."

Sean peered over her shoulder at the map. He put his arm around her waist as he did, not that he needed to, it was just nice to feel her body against his again. She didn't resist. In fact, she kind of leaned into him, as if she'd been as hungry for the contact as he was.

"They have mane wolves, here," she said, pointing at a spot on the map. "They're from South America," she read, "but they look like they're more doglike."

"Well, that's a start. Shall we head that way?"

"Sure."

Jess looked up and her eyes widened, as if startled to find him so close.

Sean smiled and leaned in to kiss her. Those plump lips were just too tempting. He meant it to be a quick peck, appropriate to the setting, but once his lips touched hers, he didn't want to pull away. Ever.

Her mouth molded to his and Sean lost all sense of place and time. Children's shouting vanished. The acrid scent of a nearby animal disappeared. The warmth of the sunshine paled in comparison to the heat of her body. When her lips parted with a sigh, encouraging him to deepen the kiss, his one remaining shred of sanity pulled him back, reminded him of where he was.

"Whoa," he said.

Jess's eyes opened, looking up at him in blatant invitation, dark and seductive.

He stepped back, giving her a rueful smile that he hoped communicated his desire to continue, along with his reluctant recognition of their surroundings. It took just a moment longer for reality to click in for her and then color flooded her face.

A stupid, primal male pride swelled Sean's chest at her response. Jess Alexander, cautious, careful and restrained, had almost lost it in the middle of a public place because of one little kiss. From him.

"Come on," he urged, dropping his arm from around her waist and taking her hand instead. "Let's go check out these wolves."

AFTER TAKING A tour of the wolves and discussing their potential as were-creatures, Sean sprang his next surprise on Jess—the gourmet picnic he'd pre-arranged with the catering service at the zoo. Their food had been laid out for them on a classic red-and-white-checkered cloth in a shady area of a large, open lawn. Kids played and turned cartwheels nearby, other families were enjoying picnics, a few other couples had obviously also made the same arrangements.

"This is delicious," Jess said as she polished off a small tub of potato salad. "Thank you so much for organizing everything. I hate the fast-food stuff you typically get at places like this—hot dogs and chips and the like."

"You like to eat healthy?" Sean asked.

Jess nodded. She picked up a chicken-and-avocado sandwich triangle. "I do." She went on to talk about food and nutrition in a serious, science-y way that Sean loved. He leaned back on the picnic blanket and closed his eyes, his face turned up to the dappled sunlight, taking simple pleasure in having a full belly, a gorgeous day and an even more gorgeous woman beside him.

"Am I boring you?"

He chuckled. "Nope, not in the least. I love listening to you talk."

"What was I just saying then?"

"Something about processed foods being evil."

"Lucky guess," she grumbled.

"Are you a good cook?" he asked.

"I'm okay. Not a gourmet by any means, but I can make a great curry. And I'm pretty good at whipping up a cake every now and then when the occasion calls for it."

"I thought you just said sugar was the devil's work."

"It is. Except for cake. Cake gets a free pass."

He smiled at that then paused, wondering if he could take the conversation to the next level. Eventually, he asked, "What about when you were married? Did you do most of the cooking, or did you share it?"

JESS SAW SEAN crack an eye open and knew he was waiting to see how she responded to the question. Her hand froze halfway to her mouth as she considered what to say. Inwardly she gave a little shrug. If she'd decided last night that a few weeks of "practice dating" with Sean might be a good thing, then learning how to share herself again and open up was part of that. That meant she had to find ways to talk about her past in a casual way.

"We, uh, shared it, I guess," she said eventually, noting Sean's other eye opened to study her. "It depended on who got home first. We both had demanding jobs—which meant we were both home late a lot."

Sean rolled onto his side and propped himself up on his elbow, clearly preparing to make the most of Jess's confessional mood. "That's never a good sign," he said.

Jess avoided meeting his eyes. It had definitely been a sign. And if she'd been more vigilant, more confident, more willing to stand up for herself, she'd have called Mark on his lies well before he'd grown used to manipulating her. "I suppose it wasn't. Funny, I don't have nearly as many late nights at the surgery as I used to."

"It's easy to find stuff to do when you don't want to go home."

"Yeah." She shifted on the ground, tucking her legs underneath herself, leaning over to one side so she was facing him. It was a beautiful day and it was time to change the subject, but before she could say anything Sean was playing the role of inquisitor again.

"Why did it end?"

She shot him a look. He was really pushing her today.

This is practice, remember?

The nerves she felt at revealing this most vulnerable part of herself were important to overcome. If she was ever going to join the dating game and find herself a new companion she had to get used to talking about this stuff. She gave a silly laugh. "Do you want the official version or the real reason?"

"Whichever you want to tell me."

"Officially, we grew apart. Mark got more into his sailing, and I got more into my work and volunteering at the animal rescue." She looked down at her hand as she twisted one end of the tablecloth in her fingers. *Stop being a scaredy-cat.* "Unofficially— but in reality—Mark cheated on me. Multiple times, with multiple people."

Mark had made it clear that while she was adequate to cook his meals, do his laundry and listen to his "bad day at work" stories, when he wanted so-called *real* companionship, he looked elsewhere. Outside his marriage.

Sean was silent for a while. Jess dared to look at him, but his gaze was directed to a tree on the far side of the lawn area, his expression hard to read. *What did he think?*

Eventually his eyes shifted to her and he reached out a hand, curling his fingers around her ankle. His touch was warm and strangely comforting, even though his look conveyed neither pity nor sympathy—just the same interested curiosity as before.

"Why isn't the real story the official one?" he asked.

"Honestly, I don't really know anymore. Especially once I found out that most of our mutual friends knew what was going on, anyway. At the time, Mark convinced me it would be better for both our reputations if we went with the official story. And I guess I was gullible enough to believe him. It was...a weakness of mine."

Sean's eyes narrowed and the hand around her ankle tightened its grip. "How could it possibly be better for *your* reputation?"

The delicious food they'd eaten seemed to grow in Jess's stomach until she was uncomfortably full. But she knew the feeling was more about the conversation than her digestion.

Courage.

"I guess..." *Come on, Jess.* "I didn't want to tell people because...because I felt it was my fault. And I didn't want them thinking that, too."

Her reasoning was ridiculous, of course. All their friends—*supposed friends*—knew what was going on. Had known for years. Yet none of them had thought to tell Jess. They'd all made up their own minds about why Mark did what he did, well before Jess had thought to even wonder what they might be thinking.

Sean frowned. "Hang on, I don't get it. You didn't want them thinking *what?*"

"That I… That Mark had to…*go elsewhere,* because I…" *Wasn't enough.* She couldn't bring herself to say the words aloud.

Sean swore.

Clearly she didn't need to say it. The message was loud and clear anyway. As a wife, Jess had been second best: good enough for Mark, if he didn't have anything better on offer.

"Ouch." Jess reached for her ankle. "Sean, you're hurting me."

"What? Oh, God, sorry." He released his grip and stroked her reddened skin. He gave her a rueful look. "I'm so sorry, Jess. I think in my head I was pretending it was that asshole ex-husband of yours' neck."

That made Jess laugh in surprise. "I think I'd like to see that. It'd be interesting to see who came out on top—Mark isn't as tall as you, but he's fit. Although, of course, he's ten years older."

"I'd grind him to a powder," Sean said with surprising determination. The carefully blank expression he'd worn earlier had vanished. The gold flecks in his eyes still sparked but there wasn't a trace of his usual cheerful mischief to be seen.

"Well, thanks, I guess," Jess said. She wasn't sure what sort of reaction she'd expected, but Sean turning into her knight in shining armor and racing to her defense certainly wasn't it. From the people who knew the full story she was used to pitying looks and feeble reassurances about her attractiveness.

"Did he…" Sean paused and ripped a blade of grass from the ground, shredding it between his fingers. "Did he hurt you? Physically I mean?"

"Oh, no, never. He would never have done that." Mark had many faults, but he'd never threatened her in that way. He was, mostly, a gentleman. In fact, his manners and charm had been attractive to her right from the start. He was also funny and witty and always had something interesting to say about the world. There were reasons she'd married him.

"Right. He just satisfied himself with beating your self-confidence to a pulp."

Jess opened her mouth to protest, but closed it again. *That was pretty much it.*

And she'd definitely pushed her personal boundaries for disclosure far enough for one day.

"So, why werewolves?" she asked.

Sean gave her a measured look. She could practically see him working out whether or not he was going to quit the conversation there. But she was thankful when he did.

"I need to shake things up," he said. He rolled flat again, lifting one arm to shade his eyes. "Sebastian needs a new enemy. He's pretty handy with the vampires these days, so I need to give him a new challenge."

"But aren't werewolves… I mean, they're a bit of a cliché, aren't they?" The idea made Jess think of D-grade movies and that Warren Zevon song.

"Not the way I write them."

God bless that unsinkable confidence of his. Jess smiled.

One week later

FIVE DATES. FIVE!

And still nothing more than a kiss.

Jess stomped around her bedroom as she tried to decide between a coat and a wrap.

Their first date had been that superhero movie, then they'd gone to the zoo. On Monday, Sean had met her at the clinic after work and they'd found a quick dinner at a nearby Malaysian restaurant. Then they'd gone to another movie on Wednesday. Last night, Friday, they'd attended a wine tasting that Sean had found out about from a flier in Rob and Hailey's mailbox. They'd both got giggly drunk and shared a taxi home—another quick kiss at her front door and then Sean had been instructing the driver on how to get to Rob and Hailey's place.

And now it was Saturday night again. Two full weeks after Rob and Hailey's wedding. Jess had spent more time with Sean this past week than she had spent with her husband in the last month of their marriage.

So far, every single date had ended with a kiss at Jess's front door. Nothing more.

She threw the wrap over her shoulders and studied herself in the mirror.

No. Too drapey.

She pulled the wrap off and grabbed a strand of long black beads to try instead.

Nope. The beads didn't work, either. She took them off and threw them on her dresser.

She studied herself in the mirror again. The outfit looked fine: what she needed to do something about was her frown. Her fingers pressed against her forehead as if she could physically clear it. But that wasn't going to be enough: she was turning herself inside out trying to understand what was going on.

Sean had said he needed company while he was in Melbourne—perhaps that was literally all he meant?

Maybe the sex after the wedding hadn't been as good as she'd thought and he just wasn't interested in a repeat?

Or perhaps he just wasn't attracted to her? But he sure seemed like he was on the night of the wedding—he'd even said as much. And he still kissed her good-night at the end of each date. And when they were together, he was always holding her hand or putting his arm around her waist.

Maybe that was just his way of being friendly?

Perhaps he feared if they had sex she'd freak out again, and he wasn't prepared to deal with it.

Whatever the reason, it was slowly driving her insane.

All week her dreams had been filled with fever-pitched recollections of their night together and their romp on Rob and Hailey's couch.

And now, she felt sleep-deprived, grumpy and seriously on edge.

The doorbell rang.

Sean.

A stupid smile spread over her face. She shook her head at herself as she surveyed the image in the mirror one last time. Skinny black trousers. A pearl-gray top with a daringly deep neckline she'd bought that day. Strappy heels that she knew she was going to regret if Sean's surprise date involved anything more than walking to the car and back. And she'd decided to wear her hair loose and keep her makeup smoky.

She did a twirl.

Yes. Hot. Well, she thought so. Hopefully it wasn't too much mutton dressed up as lamb.

"Wow. You look…" Sean's words trailed off when she opened the door. He eyed her, hungrily—or so she liked to think.

"Aren't you a writer? I thought you were supposed to be good with words?" she teased, pleased nonetheless.

He took just a small step forward and leaned one shoulder against the doorjamb as his eyes raked her over once more. The jeans he was wearing should have been illegal. "Gorgeous. Scintillating. Dazzling. Extraordinary. Lovely. Exquisite," he reeled off.

Jess laughed and felt her cheeks heat. "Okay, okay. Thank you, dictionary-on-legs."

"For you."

She belatedly noticed he'd been holding one arm behind his back as he produced a single rose and presented it to her.

"Oh! It's lovely." She brought it to her face. It didn't

have any scent, but the color of the petals was stunning—a deep blush apricot at the base merging into a hot pink at the edges. Unusual and very beautiful. Very Sean. "Thank you." She couldn't remember the last time she'd been given flowers by a man. Mark hadn't ever been given to romantic gestures, not even in the early days when they'd been dating.

"You're welcome."

"Let me just put it in some water before we head out." Jess led the way to the kitchen. "How did your work go?" She'd taken up asking for an update on his writing each time they got together. At first she'd been surprised at exactly how many hours he *did* work. Hailey's descriptions were of a man who did a couple of hours work late at night and spent the rest of his time sleeping in or lounging around. In truth, Sean appeared to work the same hours as she herself did—if not more.

Jess had pretty much decided she couldn't trust anything Hailey had told her about Sean—all her information had come from his parents and they clearly didn't know their son at all.

"Pretty good. I finished chapter four of the werewolf/shape-shifter book and it's coming along. I'll need to ask you a couple of dog-biology questions later."

"And you didn't get too distracted on Twitter?" She put on her best mother tone.

He laughed. "No, not too much. I posted a photo of Suzie with her nose stuck in the peanut butter jar. That went down pretty well with the crew."

Sean affectionately referred to his online fans as "the crew." At first she'd been surprised to discover that Sean interacted with readers like that. But then she'd decided she liked it—she figured it made his readers feel a part of his world and it was nice that Sean had that kind of positive feedback on his work.

"I can imagine they loved it. Was it another late night?" She knew that when he was immersed in his story he often didn't stop writing until the wee hours of the morning.

"Not too bad." He smiled and gave her a wink. "I didn't want to be too tired for you tonight."

While his flirting still sent tingles through her, these days she managed not to flush with heat every time he made a suggestive comment. Still, his wink made her pulse speed up.

"Where are we going anyway?" she asked, trying to sound normal. She was used to Sean's surprise date destinations now. Still not entirely comfortable with it, but used to it.

"That's for me to know and you to find out."

She rolled her eyes, but knew there was no point pushing. Sean leaned against a counter and she was aware of his gaze on her as she found a vase and filled it with water, placing the rose carefully on the table. It would go in her bedroom later.

"So, ready to go?" she asked.

She turned to find him standing there, lounging against the counter, arms folded in a way that emphasized his biceps. He wore jeans, a simple, dark blue shirt and the khaki canvas jacket that was clearly his

favorite. She'd never before seen a more perfect speci-
men of manhood outside a movie screen.

"I'm ready—are you?" he asked with a sugges-
tively raised eyebrow.

At the sight of him, her heart did a weird lurch in
her chest—it thumped and thudded until her pulse
was pounding in her ears. The ache low in her belly
that had begun the night of Hailey's wedding surged
back to life.

But then all the questions that had been plaguing
her as she'd dressed returned. Why hadn't he sought
to rekindle their physical relationship so far? Why
had their every date ended in just a kiss? What did
it all mean?

Sean let out a breath and his smile slipped. "Uh-oh,
that's the serious-Jess face. What's the matter?"

*Don't think. You can't always be this cautious. Just
close your eyes and jump.*

Jess shut off her brain. Before she could analyze
the problem from all angles, before she could consider whether or not it was a smart thing to do, she
rushed at him.

He made a little "oomph" noise as she more or less
fell into his arms and shoved him harshly against the
counter, but when her lips found his, he was right
there, into the kiss.

His body was hard and warm and welcoming. His
lips firm but soft against her own. His hands settled
on her hips as if they belonged there.

She kissed him with abandon and he responded,

deepening the kiss, matching her desire with a hunger of his own.

His hands tangled in her hair, holding her head so he could take control, kissing her with a power and passion she knew he'd been holding back. He had to have been, because there was no way their kisses at the front door would have ended there if they'd been anything like this.

"Bedroom, upstairs," Jess whispered urgently as Sean's mouth trailed kisses across her jaw and down her neck.

He made a half grunt, half groan noise of assent into her neck as his tongue licked at her pulse. Then he lifted his head, shaking it slightly as if to clear it, and his darkened eyes found hers.

"Show me," he said, clasping her hand in his.

Jess was sure she'd never made the trip from the kitchen to her bedroom faster. Once they were standing beside her bed, Sean kicked off his shoes and socks and shrugged out of his jacket. Another quick move and his shirt was gone, too.

Barefoot, bare-chested—as astonishing as she remembered—this time in jeans instead of tuxedo pants. Still just as devastating. Jess was reminded all over again how handsome he was, how young and eligible and charming. And how old and broken she felt.

What the hell was he doing with her?

Was the answer to that question the thing that she was afraid of?

"I love that top, but I love what's underneath it more." He ran a finger lightly along the neckline, skating the tops of her breasts. Jess shivered. Grasping the hem, he lifted it over her head, and she raised her arms to assist.

A wicked smile spread over his face as he took in her ridiculously expensive black bra, and he raised one finger to trace the edge of the lace.

"Ooh, I like," he said. His eyes met hers, smoky and sparkly all at once, sensual yet mischievous.

But then his grin faltered and his hand fell away from her. He sighed. "Uh-oh."

"What?" Jess ran a hand through her hair. Her fingers were trembling but that was the least of her problems. Her breath came in short gasps and her heart felt as if it had taken up learning the drums. She fought the desire to grab her top and put it back on again.

He cupped her cheek with his palm. "I've been waiting all week for you to make the first move. I thought if you did, we'd avoid the freak-out. But looks like I was wrong."

"I'm not—" She broke off. She'd been about to deny it, but she knew it would be pointless.

Fear and excitement sometimes feel the same. Perhaps you've lost the ability to distinguish between them.

The thought came from nowhere, but she clung to it like a life preserver. "Okay, so I might be freaking out, just a little. But..."

Jess sucked up every ounce of courage she possessed and hooked a finger into one his belt loops, tugging him closer.

"But that doesn't mean I'm going anywhere. Not this time."

Sean raised an eyebrow. His hand slid around her waist to sit in the small of her back, the warmth of his skin against hers adding fuel to the flames that had temporarily banked.

Jess kissed his neck, the way he'd kissed hers a moment ago. She nibbled up to his ear, taking his earlobe into her mouth for a brief suck. His hastily indrawn breath in response made her smile.

"I'm nervous and kinda panicky and I can't stop shaking," she whispered into his ear. For some reason that made the confession easier. "It feels like I'm scared, only I don't think I am."

"I don't think you are, either," he whispered in reply. "At least, not of me."

She moved back so she could meet his eyes and shook her head. "I'm not scared of you." And she wasn't. There were so many things in the world to be scared of. Getting naked with Sean Paterson, knowing as she did the pleasure he could bring her, shouldn't be one of them. Anyway, he was leaving in a few weeks. Walking out of her life and not looking back. Even if it all went wrong, she'd likely never see him again.

There was no danger here.

"Good." He grabbed her hand and looked at it, smiling indulgently as her fingers trembled in his grasp. "You're beautiful," he said, and he brought her hand to his lips, kissing each fingertip gently.

It didn't take long for him to remove the rest of her

clothes—and his own—and they were skin to skin on her bed. He seemed to instinctively know just how she liked to be touched, and he continued murmuring to her in low tones, telling her how wonderful she was, how good she tasted, how hard she was making him.

By the time he left her briefly to get a condom, Jess was focused only on her need to feel him intimately inside her once more. Her rational mind had shut down, leaving her open only to the sensations of her body and the want that was building to an unbearable ache low in her belly.

"Sean?"

"I'm here."

And he was back, his warmth and strength resting over her, fitting himself between her thighs as if he'd always belonged there.

He groaned as he sank inside her, and Jess arched her back, trying to get closer. As close as they were, she felt a deep, primal need to connect along every inch of their bodies, to claim him as he was claiming her.

"Oh, Jess."

Her name was nothing more than a breath as Sean kissed her again, moving deeper inside her, joining them at their mouths, too. The ache continued to build, higher and higher as they moved together. It was overwhelming, almost too much, but before she could say *stop*, Sean called out and shuddered. Then she was there, too, a pulse of exquisite energy hit and flooded her body with ripples of pleasure from the center of her all the way out to her fingers and toes. It was nothing to fear. It was pure bliss.

CHAPTER SEVEN

JESS STRETCHED LANGUIDLY. Her muscles felt wonderfully sore. Beside her in the bed, Sean yawned extravagantly.

Last time they'd done this, it was at about this point that she'd freaked out. Perhaps because she'd had her little nervous moment earlier—or perhaps because she was somehow over it—whatever the reason, it wasn't happening now.

Jess felt sated, warm, comfortable. This time she was definitively sure she wanted Sean to do all that to her again and she wasn't letting him out of her sight until he did.

She still didn't know what any of this meant; where it was going. But for now, she would just put all that aside. She was simply going to live in the moment for once.

And at this particular moment, she was hungry.

"What's the time?" Jess asked. Sean was on her side of the bed, blocking her view of the little alarm clock she had there.

Before she could explain that fact, Sean had reached for his jeans and pulled his phone from a pocket. "It's almost nine."

"Hmm. Are you hungry? I think I'm hungry."

"I could eat." He sounded distracted and Jess realized he was still looking at his phone.

"What's up?" she asked.

"Oh. Text message from my agent." He didn't look happy about whatever it said.

"On a Saturday?"

"Apparently Hollywood never sleeps."

"Hollywood?"

Sean lay down, one arm behind his head. He continued to fiddle with the phone. "Um, yeah," he said, clearly not listening to her.

"Sean? What's happening in Hollywood?" She gave him a poke with her finger for good measure.

He looked up, a little sheepish. "It's not confirmed yet, but they're, uh, talking about making my first Sebastian book into a film."

Jess's jaw fell open. "Seriously?"

His look instantly hardened. "Why is that so hard to believe?"

Surprised by his bitter tone, Jess held up a hand. "Whoa, Sean. It's not hard to believe at all. I'm just shocked—that's amazing."

"Yeah, okay." He sighed, then ran a hand through his hair. He gestured to the phone. "My agent says they want the final version of the screenplay a week earlier than they'd originally said." He swore softly.

"I thought you were writing the book about Sebastian and werewolves?"

"That, too."

A movie. Wow. Since the bookstore visit, Jess better understood Sean's success. The day after that, she'd gone on the internet to see what she could learn about Sean Paterson the author, kicking herself for not thinking of doing it before. There were tens of thousands of hits—nothing to do with the fact that Sean Paterson wasn't exactly an unusual name. For at least the first several pages of search results, they were all the Sean Paterson she knew.

When she looked up Sebastian Douglas the hits multiplied exponentially—hundreds of thousands. Fan sites dedicated to discussing, appreciating, dissecting and generally enthusing about the world Sean had created. She'd even found a blog for people who liked to dress up as characters from the books and participate in role-playing games. Some of the costumes were amazing—a vampire called Elvire seemed to be a favorite with female fans and some of her outfits wouldn't have been out of place in a bondage dungeon. She couldn't help wondering how true to Sean's vision they were—she'd begun reading his books but she hadn't yet gotten to the point in book two where Elvire appears.

But a movie? That was *really* taking it to the next level.

"Tell me more," Jess urged.

Sean didn't glance away from his phone when he spoke. "You remember the two movies we saw last week? Both directors are interested in doing mine— it will come down to scheduling as to who makes it. My deadline for the finished screenplay was the week after Rob and Hailey get back. I guess now it's the same time."

"Can you do it?"

"Deadlines always motivate me. It'll happen."

"Wow, Sean." Jess sat up, pulling the sheet with her to cover her breasts. "This is amazing news. How did your family react? They must be thrilled."

He smiled at the phone and then shot her a grin. "Check this out." He put an arm around her to pull her close, sharing the phone screen.

At first the rows of messages made no sense. "What am I looking at?"

"Twitter. Some of the crew are holding a Sebastian-themed dinner party."

Jess squinted at the screen and read the messages there. They were mostly from someone who called herself *RachElvire*. The photo beside her name was too small to make out properly, but it was clearly a picture of Sean standing with his arm around the shoulders of a woman with long blond hair.

Hey @SeanPaterson—wish you were here. Main course: roast chicken. Sebastian weeps. #sebdoesdinner

Dessert momentarily interrupted by demon. Sebastian slays it. Dessert continues. #sebdoesdinner

Elvire has poisoned the wine with devil's blood! Oh noes! #sebdoesdinner

Rob has cure! Godiva truffles reverse the effects of devil's blood. #whoknew #sebdoesdinner

"That's…" Jess fought for the right description.

"Totally weird, right?" Sean said, grinning broadly.

"Yes, totally weird, but it sounds like they're having heaps of fun." Jess paused to think about it. "How does it feel for you? To know you've created something that so many people get so much enjoyment from?"

"It's… Yeah, it's pretty great."

Jess nudged him with her shoulder. "The erudite author. Once again lost for words."

He shot her a look before concentrating again on his phone. "I think I'll send them a quick note to say *bon appétit.*"

"They'll be thrilled." Jess thought about the messages she'd read. "Why does roast chicken make Sebastian weep? I know he's vegetarian—is it from when he lived with that foster family on the farm when he was a kid?"

Sean finished typing his message and tossed the phone to the end of the bed. He twisted to put a hand on either side of Jess's hips, bringing himself face-to-face with her. "Ms. Alexander? Are you reading my books?"

"Maybe," she said, deliberately coy.

"I think you are."

"I like Sebastian. But I think Rob is my favorite character."

"Why?" Sean asked. He lowered his head to trail little kisses along Jess's shoulder.

She arched her neck into Sean's caress. "Because he's so brave."

Sean paused his kissing to look up. "Brave? Rob's the research guy. Sebastian does more of the slaying and bravado stuff."

"I know. Sebastian's the hero. He doesn't think twice about plunging into the vampire nest with his sword drawn. Rob *does* think twice. He's scared. But when he has to, he does it anyway. That's why he's brave."

Sean seemed to think about that for a moment. "You're right. I hadn't thought about it that way before."

His eyes lost focus for a moment as she'd seen them do before. Every now and then Sean slipped into another world, one beyond reality, where Sebastian and Rob and Elvire lived and loved and fought.

"I haven't given Rob his payoff," Sean muttered.

"Huh?"

He rolled off her and rubbed his jaw thoughtfully. "Rob. He's the comic foil in the screenplay. But he needs a heroic moment. I haven't got one for him yet."

"Would you like a pen and paper?" Jess asked jokingly.

"Uh, well..."

She gave him a disbelieving look. He had to be kidding, right? They were in bed! She was under the impression they'd been about to make love again. "Seriously?"

"Sorry." He shook his head. "I'm sorry, Jess.

That message from my agent just put my head in the wrong space."

"If you want to go write, you can," she offered. So much for leaving the outside world behind and just living in the moment.

"No, no. Absolutely not. You can remind me tomorrow—Rob's hero moment. Okay?"

"I can do that."

That mischievous look was back. "Now, where was I?"

"Does this help?" Jess let the sheet fall, revealing her breasts.

"Yeah, that helps a lot." He grinned.

THEY MADE LOVE again and afterward ordered pizza, eating it while sitting on the floor in the living room, half-dressed, laughing about silly things.

"What are you doing next weekend?" Sean asked suddenly.

"Why?"

He shook his head. "Always so suspicious. Haven't my surprises always been good so far?"

"I guess so." In reality? Despite the sexual frustration, the past week had been the best week of Jess's life in a very long time.

"I have to go to a comic convention next week. It might be fun for you to see what goes on at these things. You probably won't want to hang around for the whole day, but maybe you could come with me for the morning and then I can meet up with you afterward."

"I've never been to anything like that before."

"Excellent. Now I just have to think up a few surprises between now and then."

He hadn't noticed that she hadn't exactly said yes.

Plans for next weekend. Plans for during the week. What was going on?

There was no need for the seduction routine anymore. Sean had to realize by now that if he wanted sex, Jess was going to give it to him. There was no need to keep up the pretense of dates and outings.

"Sean?"

He looked up from the pizza box where he'd just lifted another slice. "Hmm?" His smiled faded. "Oh, crap. You've got that serious look again."

"Sorry. It's just...I'm not good with no...*boundaries.*"

The pizza went back into the box. "What do you mean?"

"It's just... What *is* this?"

"Pizza with the lot?" he tried to joke. But she knew he knew what she was getting at.

Jess sighed. "I know, I know. I'm sorry. I'm a pain. This should be fun and I'm dissecting it already—thinking too much."

He grabbed her hand. "It's okay. It's very Jess."

"It's just I thought...once we...that you'd..." She cursed her tongue for deserting her. Why was it so hard to talk about this stuff?

His eyebrows rose. "You thought that once we'd slept together again, I'd be out of here? Very flattering, Jess."

"That's not quite what I meant. But you have to

admit, even on the night of the wedding, you were sure to make it clear that you weren't hanging around."

"I know. And that hasn't changed. It's just we have more time together, that's all."

His directness was both disconcerting and refreshing. At least with Sean she knew where she stood. "So that's what this is. An affair." She'd meant to sound coolly confident, but instead it came out like a question.

He wrinkled his nose. "An affair? Oh, I like the sound of that. It makes it seem all...*naughty.*"

Jess didn't return his smile. Her nerves were returning—those strange "freak-out" feelings that made her want to run away.

"Okay, okay." Clearly something in her expression gave away her distress, because Sean took both her hands in his and set his eyes on hers. "I get it—time to get serious here for a moment."

"Please."

"Right. Okay, let's be clear. I'm here until Hailey and Rob get back. You and I like each other. We seem to enjoy each other's company and we also have some rockin' chemistry. Agree so far?"

She nodded. "Agree."

"So that's what this is. We have four more weeks until the newlyweds return. We could spend those weeks by ourselves. Or we could have more fun like we've had this past week. That's pretty much the deal."

"A deal," Jess repeated.

"Does that work for you?"

Did it? It was perfect, wasn't it? She'd thought a one-night stand with Sean would be practice for getting back into the dating game. Then they'd actually gone on some dates—more practice. Now he was offering her a chance to have a go at a short-term relationship. An opportunity to work out how to share herself with someone else, without making herself vulnerable or putting her newly found, still-fragile self-confidence at risk.

"It...works for me," she said slowly.

Sean stuck his tongue out at her. "Are we done with the serious now?"

She rolled her eyes at his silliness. "We're done with the serious."

Monday

JESS SAILED THROUGH the workday with a spring in her step. Her patients had been the usual roster of parasite infections and household accidents—nothing serious and nothing but happy, on-the-mend pets by the end of the day. Just the kind of day she liked. Just the kind of day that was a perfect bookend to her wonderful weekend.

She found herself smiling for no reason at all. Andrea had given her a couple of funny looks at times, but she hadn't said anything. It was lucky that Hailey wasn't here. Hailey would have known instantly that something was going on, and she wouldn't have given up until she'd discovered exactly what was behind Jess's cheerful mood.

Better yet, Sean had called around lunchtime and he was coming by in half an hour or so to go for dinner—he'd shared at least that much of his plans with her. Jess had insisted it be somewhere casual so she wouldn't feel out of place in the jeans and sweater she'd brought with her to change into from her work uniform, but other than that she was growing pleasantly fond of his surprises. She'd begun to learn that it wasn't always about his desire to surprise her as his own impulsive nature—he wanted to do whatever he felt like at the time, and you couldn't preplan that.

Jess was just closing up and about to go get ready for her date when the surgery's phone rang. She thought for a moment about letting it go to the machine as it was already after-hours, but on second thought she grabbed it.

"Village Veterinary Clinic, Jess speaking."

"Hi, Jess."

He didn't need to introduce himself. Even though they hadn't spoken for more than six months, Mark's voice was as familiar to her as the three dark freckles that made a triangle pattern on the back of her hand.

"Mark," she said, stalling for time while she tried to work out what to say. In the end she settled for "What do you want?"

"I was just calling to see how you were," he said and there was no mistaking the hurt tone in his voice at her curt question.

Jess instantly felt chastised. There really was no

reason to be rude. "I'm fine," she said, making sure her tone was more conciliatory. And then, because she was too damn nice for her own good, she asked, "How are you?"

"I'm good, thanks. Busy at work as usual. And I'm vice president at the yacht club now, so that keeps me out of trouble."

"Congratulations." Jess sat down heavily in the office chair and rolled it across so that she could lean her elbow against the counter. She felt strangely weak, and she really didn't need to feel that way for a conversation with Mark. She had a feeling that there was going to be more to this call than polite chitchat. As far as she knew the divorce was final, all the settlements resolved. But there must be something that had gone wrong to have Mark call her out of the blue.

"How's the surgery?" he asked.

"Fine. It's doing fine. How's Cathy?" Jess hoped she sounded casually interested. And then, she discovered to her surprise, she *was* only casually interested. The thought of Mark and Cathy together didn't make acid churn in her stomach the way it always had. That was interesting. What had brought on that change? Was it just that she was finally moving on with her own life?

"Um…" Mark paused. "Cathy and I broke up. A few months ago, actually. I'm single."

No one had told Jess. Still, the friends they'd had in common tended to be from the yacht club, and by and large Mark had "won" them in the divorce. Jess wasn't too broken up about it—sailing had always been Mark's thing more than hers. Besides, they were also the "friends" who thought Mark's infidelity was none of their or *her* business.

"I'm sorry to hear that," she said. She wasn't sorry at all, but it was the right thing to say.

"These things happen," Mark said.

Jess barely kept back a bark of hysterical laughter at his seemingly carefree answer. "So why are you calling, Mark?" she asked, not bothering to keep up the polite pretense.

"I told you, to find out how things were going with you." There was a definite pout in his voice at that.

"Well, everything's fine. So is that it?"

There was a brief silence.

"I was talking to Bree and Nick yesterday."

Two friends from the yacht club. Jess hadn't been particularly close to them, but Mark and Nick were good friends. Bree and Jess had never really warmed to each other—for no special reason, they just hadn't clicked in the way Mark and Nick had.

"That's good," Jess said, wondering where the hell this was going.

"They were telling me they took the kids to the zoo last weekend."

"Good for them," Jess said. And then she realized what must have happened. She'd been spotted. With Sean. *That* was why Mark was calling.

For some strange reason her stomach dipped, like a burglar caught in the spotlight clutching a bag of stolen loot. She sucked in a breath and gave herself an internal talking-to. *It's none of Mark's business.*

"They said you were with someone. A guy." Mark sounded breezy, yet there was something more beneath it.

"Oh, really?" It was ridiculous to feel nervous. And yet she did. She picked up a pen and began twisting it in her fingers, unscrewing it at the middle and then screwing it back together again.

"You're doing the right thing," he said smoothly. So like Mark. Offering reassurance as if his okay was what was needed. Like a used-car salesman. She'd used to find that arrogance appealing—now it grated. "It's nice that you've found someone. It's what's right."

"It's not..." Jess began. And then she stopped herself. No way was she explaining the temporary nature of her relationship with Sean to him. In fact, she wasn't sure she could explain it in any way that wouldn't make it sound tawdry and base. Which it wasn't. What was happening with Sean was the most fun Jess had had in years. Not just the sex. The companionship, the going out, the simple pleasure of it all. He made her feel young again—not that she was ancient by any means. But until she'd met Sean, she'd been *feeling* old, worn-out by life. Sean reminded her that there was still so much to do, so much of life yet to live.

"It's not any of your business," she ended up saying, her tone calm but firm. She was ridiculously proud of herself for making a stand. She'd never fought with Mark. Never yelled at him for what he'd done. The divorce discussions had been extremely civilized—as long as she got Rocco, and Mark didn't touch anything to do with the surgery, she'd decided to go along with everything else without a fight.

Sometimes, though, she wished that they'd had that scene—her screaming at him for his betrayal, shattering vases against the wall. She figured it might have been cathartic. But it was too late now. At the time all she'd felt was so *hurt* and so *stupid* she could barely speak, let alone throw things.

"I know, I know. It's good for you, though. Nice that you're getting out."

His condescending tone rubbed against every nerve. She twisted the pen in her fingers more tightly.

"Well, thank you, I guess," she said. Hopefully the sarcasm was laid on thick enough that even Mark would get it.

"Now, Jess."

Now, Jess. Or *Come on, Jess.* It was something he used to say a lot. A slight warning in his voice. A school-teacherly tone. A *you're being a bit silly* condescension.

The pen snapped in Jess's hand, startling her. A blob of indigo ink spread on her fingers, only getting messier as she instinctively tried to rub it away.

"I've got to go," she said, reaching for the box of tissues on the desk and grabbing a handful to blot up the mess she'd made.

"I'd like us to be friends, Jess," Mark said.

Jess's attention was split between the call and the spreading splodges of ink all over her hand and desk. She swabbed at her palm with tissues, but that was only making things worse. And because she was distracted, it took a moment for Mark's comment to sink in.

"What?" she exclaimed as she realized what he'd said.

"Enough time has gone by for us to put the past behind us. I think we could be great friends again."

"I don't—"

He interrupted. "What are you doing tonight? I could come and pick you up. We could go down to the yacht club for dinner. That'd be nice. You could catch up with everyone."

I'd rather slide bamboo under my fingernails.

From outside, in the street, the sound of a loud rumbling engine approached. It pulled up in front of the surgery and idled for a while.

Dezzie.

Sean.

He was probably sitting in the car checking Twitter on his phone. Jess couldn't help but smile as she pictured it.

"Not tonight, Mark." In her head it was *Not ever, Mark.* But as much as she'd managed to distance herself from him, from their marriage, there was still a decade of habit that was hard to break. She couldn't bring herself to be so final.

"Okay. I can tell I've caught you at a bad time."

One thing that Mark and Sean had in common—seemingly bulletproof self-confidence. Clearly it was a trait that Jess found attractive in men. Maybe because it was something she wished she possessed herself?

"I'll call you again later," Mark continued.

"I don't—" Jess tried again.

Once again, he didn't pause to let her finish. "Have a great night. Bye, Jess."

Jess sat in a daze listening to the disconnected tone. For a moment the beep of the phone and the rumble of Dezzie's engine were in sync. The rhythm was strangely comforting, helping to blank her thoughts. She didn't want to think about any part of that call if she could help it.

Then the rumble stopped as Sean killed the ignition and she heard the creak of the car door as it opened and closed.

Shaking her head to wake up from her daze, Jess got up from the chair and headed over to the door. She unlocked it and opened it as Sean was a few steps away. He grinned at her and then his eyes dropped to her hand.

"Oh, God, are you okay?" He broke into a jog as he closed the distance.

"What? Oh." Jess looked down and realized she was clutching a wad of tissues around her fingers. She laughed, a little hysterically.

"What?"

She lifted the tissues and waggled her ink-stained hand in his face. "Nasty ballpoint accident. It might be life threatening."

Sean looked genuinely relieved. "You just looked kind of pale and when I saw the tissues…" He trailed off. "I'm glad you're okay."

He leaned in to plant a quick kiss on her lips.

"Nearly ready to go? I have reserved us a table at a particularly grotty pub that apparently serves the best chicken parmigiana in Melbourne."

Jess widened her eyes theatrically. "That's a big call."

"I know. I think we'll report them to the parma police if they're found to be lacking. Shall we investigate their claim?"

"Sure." Jess widened the door to let Sean in and headed back to the consulting rooms. "Let me get some alcohol wipes to see if I can make my hand look less ugly, and then we can go."

Sean followed. "You're lucky you weren't sucking on it. You might have ended up with a dribble of ink down your chin."

"That might have been funny if it had been a red pen." She turned and grinned at him. "You would have been able to tweet about having dinner with a real vampire."

"Ooh, now wouldn't that be fun." Sean took a couple of steps, herding Jess against the wall, bracketing her legs with his own. He gave her a hungry look that had nothing to do with chicken parmigiana. "I missed you," he said, his lips just inches from hers.

"You only saw me yesterday."

"I know."

Then he was kissing her and Jess wondered what time he'd made their reservation for at the pub. Because if she had her way, they might be very, very delayed.

She pushed Mark's phone call to the back of her

mind, shoving it in a box and tossing the box into a dark, dark corner. There were probably things about it she should think about. Things she should work out and deal with.

But she didn't want to.

And Sean's kisses were so very nice.

CHAPTER EIGHT

A few days later

SEAN SAT BACK in his chair and let out a long breath. He checked the word count of the current document—*Sebastian versus the Werewolf* was his silly working title—and he was pleased with his progress.

Things were beginning to look up. Two days ago he'd sent off new pages of the screenplay and they'd been well received by his agent and the producers in L.A. Maybe he actually had half a chance of meeting his deadline and finally getting this thing off the ground.

Sean was spending more time than he should with Jess, but after a night with her he always returned to his writing renewed somehow, so it was worth it. Definitely.

Suzie snuffled and rolled over in her sleep. She'd taken to sleeping on the floor at his feet when he wrote. Maybe she found the clacking of keys soothing. Strangely, he found the dog's presence kind of comforting. He'd always loved animals but never thought of himself as a pet person—he'd never lived anywhere long enough to be able to have one. But

Suzie's clumsy affection had gotten under his skin. He'd genuinely miss her when he left.

Sean had set himself up at the dining room table, looking out the front window into the garden and the street beyond. Rob and Hailey had a spare bedroom furnished as an office, but it was cluttered and cramped, with hardly any natural light. When he was writing, he often spent time staring out into the distance as his brain organized his thoughts. It was nicer to look out at a view than at a wall or an overflowing filing cabinet.

Too often, these days, his daydreams slipped to recalling his dates with Jess. She really was an amazing woman. By turns funny and serious, carefree and cautious. He couldn't remember the last time he'd honestly had such enjoyable company. And not just in bed.

Their "arrangement" wasn't the first of its kind in his life. In most cases, he found short-term relationships more satisfying than one-night stands. It was just...*nicer* to get to know someone a little. And, as a side benefit, the sex generally got better when he did.

It certainly had with Jess—and their first night had been pretty hot to start with. In a way it was probably good that their time together had a limit— if the sex kept improving exponentially, eventually he might explode.

He chuckled to himself at the idea.

These past couple of weeks, his comfort at being

settled in one place had given him hope for himself, for the future.

One day, he would be capable of what Rob had achieved. A house. A dog. A...*gulp*...wife.

He'd had that one disastrous try at playing house. Ten months was all he'd managed and both of them had been left with scars, he had no doubt. But he was beginning to realize that it was something he would want to try again. One day.

He just had a few things to prove first.

He'd thought book seven topping the bestseller charts around the world might be enough. But it wasn't. And because his parents never read genre fiction, it hadn't even registered with them.

But a movie. They couldn't ignore a movie. A big-name star, a big-name director. Perhaps, even, a red-carpet opening night right here in Melbourne. He'd have to talk to his agent about that. His parents would be sitting in the darkened cinema, watching as "Written by Sean Paterson" rolled across the screen. He could almost taste the satisfaction.

And then, as sometimes happened when his brain seemed otherwise occupied, a scene came to him. He bent over the keyboard, fingers flying.

It was dark outside when he looked up again.

Time had a way of disappearing on him once he got involved in his writing—he lost track of the outside world.

He had a sudden thought—had he missed a date with Jess? His stomach dropped, but then he realized no, it was Friday. They were going to the convention together tomorrow. Tonight she was catching up with a friend—as she was perfectly *allowed* to do. Even if he'd been a bit put out that she hadn't invited him along.

Still, that was just how Jess operated. She wasn't going to introduce a guy to her friends unless there was something serious going on. Certainly not a… *what had she called it?* Oh, yeah, an *affair*. Such a cool word.

He decided to send her a text message—something hot and suggestive, just to make her blush while she was out with her serious friend—and grabbed his phone. When he saw the screen, he realized that while he'd been in his writing zone he'd missed a text message from Rob.

How r things at home? How's Suzie? Rome is a fizzer. Crappy weather & shit hotel. Basically not having much fun. U?

He frowned. His brother was on his *honeymoon*. Wasn't it supposed to be a daze of fun and frivolity? Even if it was raining?

What's up? Sean typed and sent. There had to be more to the story.

A minute later, his phone rang.

"Rob? Is everything okay?" Sean was instantly alarmed.

"Yeah, mate. All good. How's it going?"

His brother sounded tired and flat. Not at all like the dizzy newlywed he should have been.

"What time is it over there?"

"Getting close to midday."

There was a pause. Sean didn't know what to say and Rob clearly wasn't about to volunteer anything. He'd said everything was good, but clearly something was up.

"So, crappy weather, huh?" Sean ended up asking.

"Yeah. It's meant to be spring here but they've had a cold snap. The wind is freezing and the rain just won't stop."

"Guess that makes the tourist routine a bit ordinary."

"Yeah."

More silence. "So, where are you right now?" Sean asked.

"I just ate some breakfast at a restaurant near the hotel. The coffee's pretty good—I'm gonna sit here for a while, grab another one."

"Where's Hailey?"

"She's on her way. Been a bit of a slow start. She…" Rob trailed off.

"She what?" Sean prompted.

"She's walking toward me right now," he said quickly. "How's Suzie?" His tone noticeably brightened, but Sean could hear the hollow note. *What was going on?*

"Suzie's fine," Sean said. There was no need to mention the emergency visit to Jess—especially when his brother already sounded so stressed. Sean was beginning to get worried. "What's going on, mate? Is something wrong? You don't sound right."

"Fine, fine, that's great," Rob replied, clearly distracted. Then there was a rustle and Sean heard him speak to someone else—Hailey, he assumed. "Yeah, I've finished. I got you a water. There's more in a jug over there. They can do some fruit if you want."

Hailey's reply was muffled.

"Rob?"

Rob came back to the call. "Sorry, bro. I'll call you later. Everything's good."

"You sure?"

"Yep. Fine. Glad to hear all's well with the house. Give Suzie a hug for us. Gotta go."

Sean was halfway through saying goodbye when the call disconnected.

He sat for a while, staring at the phone.

Maybe it was just postwedding blues—if such a thing existed. Rob and Hailey had been together for so long there couldn't possibly be anything wrong with their relationship. It wasn't as though Rob was getting married to someone he hardly knew. There couldn't have been any surprises after the wedding night. Could there?

Puzzled, Sean decided to let it go—for now. He'd text again tomorrow and, depending on the answer he got, maybe he'd call back.

He looked around the room—the only light was coming from the street outside. And Suzie was sitting up, tail wagging and head cocked in a hopeful way that indicated she was expecting some food to come her way in the very near future. Time to step away from the computer for a bit.

Saturday

WHEN SEAN HAD invited Jess to attend the comic book convention he was speaking at, she hadn't been sure whether or not to tag along. She had no real knowledge of comic books or graphic novels—and, thanks to Sean, had only recently learned there was a difference between the two.

But she figured it might be fun to explore something she didn't know much about. And, more important, she was keen to see Sean in his element, so to speak, talking with his like-minded fans.

"I'm imagining it's going to be like a book club meeting, only bigger," she said as Sean drove them to the Melbourne Showgrounds, where the event was being held.

"Ummm, no. It's not quite like that."

"What then?"

He shrugged. "It's hard to describe. It's great, though. It's a whole bunch of people who have similar interests getting together and sharing what they love."

Jess grimaced. "You're making it sound like some kind of orgy."

Sean just laughed.

"Are you nervous?" Jess asked. She couldn't even imagine doing any kind of public speaking—the very idea sent ice water through her veins.

"Nope." Sean gave her one of those sexy winks. "The only difficult questions they're going to ask me are about my books—and who knows them better than me?"

"I guess you are the expert."

They pulled up to a security guard at the entrance and were directed into a VIP car park. It was still early and the doors hadn't opened yet, but there were already groups of people milling around outside the exhibition halls. She figured they must also be special guests, or people working at the convention, because some of them were in costumes—she recognized characters from *Star Wars* and *Harry Potter,* but there were other colorfully exotic outfits that she couldn't place at all.

A tall, gangly teenager wearing a bright T-shirt that declared him as Event Crew came rushing over as they approached the registration desk.

"Sean Paterson?" he asked, a little breathlessly.

Sean smiled and smoothly shook his hand. "Yeah. Hi."

"I'm great…I mean, it's so great to meet you. I've read all your books, like, lots of times each, and book three is my favorite even though I love them all equally, really," he gushed. "I play Rob when my mates and I do RPG. I've even written a little fan fiction… Oh, I can tell you about that later. I'm Josh. I'll be working with you today. Come through to the green room and I'll organize your pass for you."

Sean grabbed Jess's hand. "This is Jess Alexander, my assistant for today. Can you arrange a pass for her, too?"

Josh barely gave her a glance. "Yeah, sure. This way."

"Assistant?" Jess asked with raised eyebrows. They followed Josh through a door plastered with a large Strictly No Admittance sign, a security guard standing beside it.

Sean nudged her with his shoulder. "Just play along, Miss Moneypenny," he joked.

"Help yourself to coffee—I'll be back in a minute." Josh gestured to a table against the wall that had a typical catering setup for tea and coffee, along with platters of fruit, muffins and pastries. Josh turned on his heel, but then spun back again, his face a picture of uncertainty. "Oh. Unless... I mean, I'd be happy to make your coffee for you. Yeah. You take a seat and I'll—"

Sean held up his hand to interrupt the kid's babbling. "Josh, it's cool. You grab the passes, I'll handle the coffee."

Josh gave a lopsided grin that revealed his relief. "Oh, great. Great. Well, you just make yourselves at home and I'll be back in a sec."

"Talk about starstruck," Jess said once Josh was out of hearing distance. "He's got to be your biggest fan. It's a wonder he managed to speak at all."

She wondered if there were going to be more fans like Josh today. People so thrilled to meet Sean they lost the power of speech. She hadn't given that side of things any thought at all. What was it going to be like if there were *lots* of fans like Josh? Fans like those Twitter people who held a Sebastian Douglas–themed dinner party? They all knew Sean's world so well. They could talk about vampires and supernatural beings in a way that a boring suburban vet couldn't hope to compete with. Suddenly, Jess wondered if it had been a good idea to come at all.

Sean waved off Josh's fawning, but from his smile she could tell he was pleased. "He's just a kid. He's fine. You want a coffee?"

"Sure."

They headed over to the table and busied themselves with making drinks. Sean grabbed a plate of food, too, while Jess surveyed the room. Sean had said there might be stars from a few TV shows attending, but Jess didn't recognize anyone. Then again, she didn't watch many science fiction shows or read many books in Sean's genre. There were about half a dozen event crew staff scattered throughout the room, each clearly attached to a guest or two they were looking after—like Josh was taking care of Sean. A security guard stood by the door and there was another burly guy hovering near the food table in that uncomfortable-looking way that screamed bodyguard. Clearly at least one person here was famous enough to warrant protection.

"Are you Sean Paterson?" Jess heard someone with an American accent ask.

"That's me. Hi. It's nice to meet you."

Jess turned back to where Sean was chatting and all the breath left her body in a rush.

"This is my friend Jess," Sean introduced her. "Jess, this is—"

"I know," she managed to whisper, not entirely sure what words were leaving her mouth. The connection with her brain had somehow been severed. "Oh, my God," she said, after no other words occurred to her.

Sean squeezed her arm. "Jess, breathe," he muttered to her under his breath. He gave a "what are you going to do" shrug to their famous companion.

Ethan Falcon just smiled easily, as if it was an everyday occurrence to be confronted by a speechless, gibbering female. Probably, a small still-functioning part of Jess's brain thought, because it was.

A heated flush began to prickle her neck and rise up her face. She *loved* his show. But it was about a crime-solving writer, not anything fantastical or comic book related. She had no idea what he'd be doing here. Her mouth opened—surely she could say something simple, like "I love your show"—but nothing came out.

"It's a pleasure to meet you," Ethan said. When Jess still didn't say anything, he turned back to Sean. "So I hear a whisper that Sebastian Douglas might be coming to the big screen?"

Sean raised his eyebrows. "Whispers, huh?"

"No such thing as a secret in L.A.," Ethan said with a laugh.

Sean nodded and held up crossed fingers. "With any luck. Still a few hurdles to jump, but it's almost there."

"Well, that's great news. Don't forget to let my agent know when you get around to casting, okay?"

"You'd make a great Sebastian," Sean said warmly.

"He's a great character. I've only read book one, but I'm gonna have to grab the others. Book two'll be on sale somewhere here, right? Maybe you can sign it for me later."

"Love to."

The two men shook hands. Ethan turned back to Jess with another smile. "Lovely to meet you."

"Uh, you, too," she managed to croak. Her cheeks were on fire.

Sean steered her gently over to a couple of chairs in front of a low table as if she was frail, or in shock. Both not far from the truth.

"Here, sit. I'll bring the coffee over."

Jess watched in stunned silence as an event crew person walked over to Ethan and began ushering him toward the door. They were talking about microphones and other logistical things—clearly he was the first speaker of the day.

"Recovered yet?" Sean asked, returning and putting a cup into her hands. His tone told her he was highly amused.

"It's not funny," she protested, pressing the cool backs of her fingers to her still-flaming face.

"*Au contraire*. It's hilarious. Jess Alexander has one of her famous freak-outs when faced with Ethan Falcon. I wish I'd filmed it to play back for you. The look on your face!" He chuckled.

"Okay, okay," Jess conceded. She took a sip of her

coffee as her pulse began to return to normal. Her nerves didn't really settle, though. The heat of embarrassment was still too close to the surface, and having Sean call her reaction a "freak-out" wasn't helping.

"Mr. Paterson?" Josh, their event attendant for the day, returned, holding two laminated passes on lanyards.

"Please, call me Sean."

"Okay, Sean. These are your passes. It's important that you wear them all day. Unfortunately, not all of our security personnel will recognize you." He gave an exasperated tsk at what he clearly considered to be serious incompetence before continuing, "And it's vitally important that your assistant wears hers or she won't be allowed backstage with you."

Jess felt like saying *I'm right here,* but she'd already gathered her level of relative importance to Josh and figured there was no point.

"Here's a copy of your schedule," Josh continued.

Jess tuned out as Josh and Sean went through the activities for the day. She felt totally discombobulated. This outing wasn't turning out to be anything like she had expected, and it had barely started.

Running into one of her favorite TV stars and behaving like an idiot was going to haunt her for the rest of her life. And that was all without realizing that there were going to be a lot of people around competing for Sean's attention. She had a feeling Josh's dismissiveness was only a taste of what she had to look forward to being at Sean's side today.

"Do you want to go listen to Ethan's session?"

Sean asked her, breaking her out of her reverie. "We could watch from backstage, because I'm on after him. Would that be okay, Josh?"

Jess was sure anything Sean wanted would be fine by Josh, and sure enough Josh nodded and bounced on his toes like a puppy. "Absolutely."

Jess nodded reluctantly. It had to be better than sitting here, thinking about her embarrassment. "As long as I don't have to meet Ethan again." Once was bad enough.

Sean smirked. "I'm sure we can avoid him."

Josh led them through a winding corridor and out through a side entrance. The crowd had swelled immeasurably during the time they'd been inside, and now there were literally hundreds of people lined up to enter the pavilion Josh was leading them toward. A significant portion of them were in fancy dress. So maybe the people she'd seen earlier weren't working at the show. But why, then, had they made all that effort?

"Why are all the people dressed up?" she asked Sean in a low voice.

"It's called cosplay. It's part of the fun—people dress up as characters from their favorite comics or books or TV shows. There's a competition at the end of the day for best costume."

"Sean!" Someone called out from the crowd and most of the people surrounding them turned to look.

"Sean, hang on a second!"

A woman separated herself from the crowd and began to run toward them.

Josh stepped forward. "We need to keep moving—"

"It's okay," Sean said. He smiled at the advancing woman. "Hi, Rachel."

Jess was nothing less than struck speechless by the woman's appearance. She was—for want of a better word—stunning. Long, long blond hair—probably a wig—framed her pale face. Lots of makeup outlined her eyes in black and her lips were bloodred. An ornate black satin corset showed off a tiny waist and full, creamy breasts, and the outfit was completed by a Victorian-style ruffled skirt with a bustle and short train. A black lace choker wrapped around her neck, along with a long strand of black beads. At her waist, a plaited whip hung in silent threat.

She could have walked off the set of a historical movie—although Jess wasn't sure exactly what sort of role she would have played. An extremely high-class "lady of the night" perhaps.

"It's great to see you, Sean." Rachel leaned in to hug Sean, one arm wrapping around his back, the other clutching her period-appropriate reticule. Sean hugged her warmly before his eyes caught Jess's. They flashed with something Jess couldn't identify, but then he pulled back from the embrace.

"It's great to see you, too, Rachel. Is this a new outfit?" he asked, stepping back to give an assessing look.

Rachel preened and did a pirouette, showing off her swishing skirts.

"I knew you'd love it. It's Elvire before she was turned," she said. "But only just!" At those words she pushed the lace choker down to reveal two puncture wounds that looked so real it took Jess a moment to realize they were fake. A fake vampire bite.

Sean laughed. "It's great."

"You weren't too specific about what color she was wearing when Alain bit her, but I decided to go with black."

"Good choice."

Rachel gave Jess a quick, dismissive glance. "Can you take our photo?"

Jess found a compact digital camera shoved in front of her and she took it out of reflex. Rachel's attention was again fixated on Sean.

"I mean, if that's okay with you, Sean. It took me weeks to make this costume. I'd love to be able to have a photo of us together for the website."

Josh stepped in. "Photos aren't allowed until the signing session this afternoon."

Sean shrugged. "Oh, one can't hurt. Come on then."

Rachel snuggled in next to Sean, under his arm, while Sean put his hand on her waist.

Jess held up the camera and snapped a shot of Sean's cheeky grin and Rachel's smug smile.

Suddenly the outfit Jess had decided on that morning—jeans, shirt and ballet flats—felt boring and matronly. Not that she wanted to dress as a Victorian-era prostitute, either, but she felt…invisible.

"One more," Rachel insisted, turning in Sean's arms to press her breasts against his chest and look up at him adoringly. Sean played the part and smiled that sexy smile of his at the camera.

Jess clicked the shutter and then held out the camera, hopefully signaling that her time as photographer was at an end.

"That's it, no more," Josh declared, taking the camera from Jess and handing it back to Rachel. The young man rose immeasurably in Jess's estimation just for that.

"Thanks, Sean," Rachel gushed.

"It's Sean Paterson," someone from the queue outside the building said loudly. "He's taking photos."

A few people began to detach from the orderly line and make their way over to where they stood. Many of them were in costume—some she recognized from the covers of Sean's books: trench-coated Sebastians, bow-tied Robs, a couple more exotically attired Elvires.

"No more photos," Josh announced.

A general noise of disappointment came from the people who were advancing.

"That's not fair," someone said.

"Sorry, guys," Sean said, giving them a wave. "My fault. I'll catch you all inside or later at the autographs, okay? Bye for now."

Rachel grabbed Sean's arm and forcibly pulled him back to press a kiss to his cheek. She whispered something in his ear. Sean nodded, his smile a little forced. "Okay," he said. "Later."

"This way." Josh hustled them to another door manned by a security guard. The guard stepped forward, creating a barrier between them and the disappointed fans.

With one last wave from Sean they headed into the dark corridor inside.

As she blinked to adjust to the dim lighting, Jess had the strangest feeling that she could identify with Alice's thoughts when she fell down the rabbit hole on her way to Wonderland. Suddenly nothing made sense anymore. A man from TV had talked to her. The characters from Sean's books were walking around in the light of day. And she…she'd clearly taken a potion that made her very small indeed.

CHAPTER NINE

JOSH LED THEM to the back of a temporary stage set up inside one of the Showgrounds pavilions. It was dark, and Jess stumbled over a cable as they headed toward a couple of seats lined up backstage.

"Careful," Sean warned, taking her elbow and steering her until she was safely seated.

The hall behind the black curtaining was filled with the noises of talking and chairs shuffling. Echoes from the metal walls and concrete floor made it impossible to tell how many people were out there.

Sean took the seat beside her, his knees bouncing up and down.

Jess was relieved to find that Ethan Falcon was on the other side of the stage from where they were seated, being fitted with a microphone. At least they wouldn't come face-to-face again anytime soon and she could avoid further embarrassment.

She clasped her hands together tightly in her lap and focused on the sensation of her fingers digging into each other. Even in the dim light she could see the tips of her fingernails turning white. She couldn't go home until after Sean's speech—unless she wanted to appear incredibly rude. But once he was done she could claim a headache, grab a taxi and leave Sean to this world where he fit in and she didn't.

Her fingers relaxed a little. Now that she had a plan, she felt better.

"You okay after your run-in with stardom?" Sean whispered.

Jess fought to find some polite small talk. "I'm fine. So, is Ethan going to be in your movie? He'd be a brilliant Sebastian."

Sean gave her an indulgent smile. "Nah, probably not. He's in that TV show. TV stars are impossible to schedule. Besides, he's too old to be Sebastian."

"Too old?" Jess protested. How old was he? Only a few years older than she was, surely.

And that probably made him a decade—or more—older than Sean, she realized with a sinking feeling in her gut.

She kept forgetting about the age difference between them.

In so many ways, it felt like Sean was older than her. He was always introducing her to new experiences, making her think about things differently, encouraging her to see life in a fresh light. Just look at what he was introducing her to today! These were things you'd expect an older mentor should do, surely, not a…a *boy toy*. Ugh. She shuddered just thinking the word.

"Are you cold?" Sean asked. He slipped an arm around her shoulders and pulled her in closer.

Then there was nothing but the roar of the crowd as Ethan took the stage and spoke with the emcee for a while, before taking questions from the audience. All too quickly—from the noise of disappointment in the audience—it was over, and a voice was announcing a short break before Sean's appearance. Sean's name was greeted with a few shouts and an enthusiastic round of applause.

"Can I go out and sit in the audience?" Jess asked. She suddenly wanted to watch Sean from the perspective everyone else had.

Sean looked surprised. "Sure, if you want."

Josh looked a little flustered at the request. "I can't guarantee you a seat out there. You might be up at the back."

"That's okay."

"The book signing's after this, isn't it, Josh?" Sean asked.

Josh nodded.

Sean gave her a quick kiss. "Okay, well, why don't you just meet me there?"

"Just show your pass to security and they'll let you through the queue," Josh advised.

Jess nodded. She'd find Sean at the book signing and then tell him she was heading home early. With the way she was feeling, she felt confident she wouldn't have to entirely fake the headache.

Josh guided her to a spot where she could slip out from behind the black curtains that divided the stage space. A security guard seemed startled to see her as she appeared, but he and Josh exchanged a few words and then the guard gestured to a single empty seat just three rows from the front.

A fizz of nerves tingled in Jess's belly as she sat down. Despite her own unsettled feelings, there was something contagious about the spirit in the room: the enthusiasm and anticipation of the people around her.

And part of her nerves were entirely on Sean's behalf. He'd said he wasn't nervous, but she was nervous *for* him. There were hundreds of people in the crowd. Hundreds of people watching the stage, waiting for Sean.

The host came out and called for silence before making a long introduction, listing Sean's many amazing achievements.

Jess experienced a strange moment as he took to the stage, one arm raised in greeting to the roaring crowd. For just a second, everything around her receded—the almost-deafening noise, the dusty smell of the concrete floor, the discomfort of the molded plastic seat, the weird snaky feeling in her belly. There was only Sean. Wearing jeans and a simple checked shirt, he looked totally at-home in the spotlight.

Pride surged through her. He was amazing. But the pride was quickly followed by doubt. Uncertainty. How on earth did she fit in here?

Sean smiled and waved, then greeted the host with a warm handshake.

They took their seats on the stage and the emcee began with a few questions. Sean concentrated all his attention on the host, looking at him in that way that he had—as if there was nothing in the world more important than the person in front of him. It was almost overwhelming to be on the receiving end of that gaze, Jess knew firsthand.

There were a few questions about his working style and Sean answered them breezily, giving no indication of exactly how hard he really worked. She knew the kind of hours he put in, she knew the time he spent not just writing, but interacting with his fans and dealing with the business side of publishing. He might be the black sheep of the Paterson clan, but the accounting genes were still in there somewhere—she'd seen the spreadsheets on his computer screen that gave a clue to the fact that he wasn't just a writer—he was a clever businessman, too, who had maximized his success with smart investments.

The host turned the questions over to the audience. Belatedly, Jess noticed two long queues had formed in the aisles—people lined up behind microphones in the hope of asking Sean a question.

The first girl who spoke was only a short distance from Jess—close enough that Jess could see her hand shake as she steadied herself against the mic stand.

"Um, hi, Sean," she started, voice wavering with nerves.

"Hi," Sean replied. He leaned forward in his chair and gave her a reassuring smile. At least, Jess figured that was how he meant it. If the girl was anything like Jess, the smile would only make her nerves hike up a little further and her heart melt a little more.

"What's your name?" he asked kindly when it seemed her nerves had struck her dumb.

The girl blushed furiously, and Jess was reminded

of her encounter with Ethan Falcon. A bolt of empathy went through her.

"I'm, uh, Danielle. I've got a question about Rob." She then went on to describe in minute detail a scene clearly from one of the books Jess had yet to read, finishing by asking, "So, I just wondered if you intended for Sebastian to discover that, or if Rob is still hiding it from his brother."

Sean paused for a moment. "Danielle, you clearly have a better understanding of my books than I do." He shot a grin out to the audience.

A ripple of laughter went through the room.

"But let me see if I can explain my thinking."

As Sean continued to answer questions, Jess wished she'd read more of his books before coming today. She was only halfway through book three, and she'd been reading in every spare moment that wasn't taken up with work or Sean. The questions people were asking were incredibly specific and were giving away some of the story lines Jess had yet to discover.

Finally, after at least half an hour had passed, the host called for the final question. A disappointed sigh went through the crowd.

The final questioner—another woman dressed as a vampire—took to the microphone. She was nervous, too, but her nerves showed in her overloud voice and the fact that she bounced on her toes as she spoke.

"First off, I just want to say, thanks for being awesome," she said, gushing.

Sean ducked his head in a humble manner that was

nothing less than totally adorable. "Uh, well, you're welcome, I guess."

The crowd laughed.

"I just wanted to tell you that my favorite character is Elvire," the woman continued, her loud voice echoing. "She's smart, she's hot and she's not *completely* evil. I want to know if she and Sebastian are ever going to get together."

A man sitting in front of Jess furiously whispered to his female companion, "Why is it that getting Elvire and Sebastian together is all that chicks seem to care about? There's so much more to Sean's books."

"Because Sebastian's hot," his companion whispered back. "We want a sex scene."

Jess put a hand to her mouth to stop the bubble of laughter in her throat from escaping. She couldn't wait to tell Sean what she'd overheard.

Meanwhile Sean was providing a long-winded and circuitous response that managed to sound intelligent but didn't really answer the woman's question, leaving the whole Elvire/Sebastian romantic possibilities topic completely mysterious.

"Okay, okay." The woman put up her hand. Clearly she was smart enough to see through the ploy. "I get it. You're not going to tell us."

Sean gave another of those mischievous grins. "Nope."

"But because you didn't give me a real answer I get one last question," she protested.

The host began to interrupt, but Sean held up a hand. "Okay, one last question."

The woman took an audible breath before asking, "Is Elvire based on anyone you know? Like, your girlfriend or whatever?" She giggled and looked over at someone else in the audience who gave her the thumbs-up signal in encouragement. "Do you have a girlfriend? And, if not, do you want one?"

The room broke into uncomfortable laughter and a few people behind her hissed in indignant whispers. Jess wasn't sure how she knew, but she had a feeling the woman had broken an unwritten rule by asking such a personal question.

"Thanks for the offer," Sean said with a grin, appearing not fazed in the slightest. "I'll take it under advisement. As for Elvire, all my characters have elements of people I know in them, but no one character is based on one person." Then he gave a nod to the host.

"And that's all we have time for, folks," the host said, standing up. "Let's have one more round of applause for Sean Paterson. You can find him in the main exhibitor hall, where he'll be available for photos and autographs for the rest of the morning, before he joins the 'supernatural superheroes' panel this afternoon."

Sean and the host disappeared from the stage.

Jess sat for a moment, listening to the talk around her. Without exception, everyone's comments were positive—how charming Sean was, how down-to-earth, how much they loved his books. More than a few were commenting on his appearance and how handsome and charming he was.

"I imagine Sebastian looks like Sean," the woman in the row in front of Jess said to her friend. "Totally hot." Jess had been about to get up and leave, but she stayed to eavesdrop a little longer—imagining the fun she'd have relating the conversation to Sean later.

"I can see why!" her companion exclaimed. "I've seen photos, but I had no idea he'd be that gorgeous IRL."

"He's taken, though," the first girl said. "He does have a girlfriend, even if he didn't say so on stage."

Jess's ears pricked up. This wasn't exactly the conversation she'd expected to hear.

"Really? Who?"

"She runs his fan club for him. They keep their relationship pretty quiet, but she looks after all his social media and stuff, so he can focus on writing."

The girl looked very disappointed at that. "Yeah? Aw, I always thought it was really Sean at the end of his tweets."

"Sometimes it is. But sometimes it's her. You see her at pretty much all Sean's things. Actually..." The girl lowered her voice, and Jess almost missed what she said. Almost, but not quite. "That's her, there."

Jess sat up straight and risked turning around, wanting to find out who the girls were pointing to. Stupidly, a tiny part of her wanted them to be pointing to her, even though she knew they wouldn't be.

As Jess turned, Rachel swept past, her full skirts impossible to miss.

Of course.

The girls continued to whisper to one another as Rachel flounced off to the exit.

"That's an awesome Elvire."

"Did you see the bracelet she's wearing? Apparently that's what Alain gave Elvire before he turned her into a vampire."

"Hang on, that's not in the book."

"Exactly. Apparently Sean gave it to her, with a love scene between Alain and Elvire that's never been published, for their anniversary."

The girl groaned. "Oh, God, what I'd give to read that. Or to have Sean write special scenes just for me."

"I know, right?"

Jess stood and grabbed her purse. As she left the row of seats she risked taking a good look at the two girls who'd been whispering. They couldn't have been more than sixteen, and they were dressed as Sebastian and Rob, one in a trench coat and fedora, the other in Rob's trademark suspenders and bow tie.

Was anything they said accurate? Or just the whisperings of jealous teens?

Surely stories like that didn't come out of nowhere.

Maybe Rachel was an ex-girlfriend?

Maybe Rachel was just a fangirl who'd let a few rumors grow legs?

There were a hundred logical possibilities—many of them far more believable than Sean having a relationship with an avid fan.

But then again, maybe Jess was an idiot. It had happened before.

ALTHOUGH SHE'D PLANNED to go find Sean and make her excuses, Jess couldn't bring herself to face him. Not until she had things clearer in her mind. She thought about finding a taxi and heading straight home, but instead found herself wandering, taking in the sights and sounds around her. The noise and chatter and activity were strangely helpful—there was so much going on, that her own thoughts couldn't dominate. And she knew if she went home she'd just sit and stew.

Much to her surprise, she found herself still at the convention a few hours later when Sean's last speaking session of the day was about to begin.

She sat through the session—which was interesting, although the panel spent a lot of time talking about graphic novels and she really didn't understand the detail—and at the conclusion showed her pass to security in order to be allowed backstage.

She'd decided to put the overheard conversation behind her. Even if Sean was having—or had had—a relationship with Rachel, it was none of her business. They'd made no guarantees about fidelity during their "affair." And what he'd done before, or after their time together was over, was none of her business.

But the thought of other people talking about her, about her relationship—even misguided teenage girls—left a stale, bitter, all-too-familiar taste in her mouth.

Sean's face lit up when he saw her but for once his sexy smile didn't melt her tummy.

"Jess! When I didn't see you at the signing I figured you'd left. I thought you'd gone home hours ago."

"I'm still here."

Sean's arm wound around her waist. "I hope you haven't been too bored."

"No, no, I haven't been bored at all."

Her tone was clearly off, because Sean frowned at her. "You okay?"

Jess sucked in a breath and forced some enthusiasm into her voice. She'd made her decision about how to handle things and she was going to stick to it.

"I'm fine!" Maybe that was a little too bright. "I went to a really fascinating session this afternoon about female role models in science fiction. I even made a list of TV shows I want to watch."

Sean smiled, clearly pleased. "Excellent! We can head straight to the DVD store after this if you want."

"Sure, that'd be great." Really she just wanted to go home and sink into a hot bath and not think about the world for a while. "I just heard your last panel, too. That was interesting."

"Did you like it? Here, let me introduce you..."

Sean introduced her to the other panelists—all writers Jess had never heard of. At least that meant that unlike her encounter with Ethan Falcon she was able to avoid being starstruck and could hold up her end of the conversation.

After a few minutes of polite chitchat, Jess was surprised to note that Sean's usual exuberance was beginning to fade. She could hardly blame him. She felt exhausted just from the few hours she'd spent wandering around—she couldn't imagine how he must be feeling after a full day of being the object of all that attention.

He confirmed her suspicions a moment later when he leaned in to whisper to her, "Are you ready to get out of here?"

Farewells took some time, as Sean had to go find Josh and sign out—as well as sign a T-shirt and book for his young fan. Then, as they made their way to the car park, even in the dimming light of approaching dusk, Jess could see a trio of female fans camped out beside Dezzie. The ruffle of black skirts instantly gave away that one of them was Rachel.

Jess couldn't help it; her sigh of irritation was audible. She was tired, crabby, and having yet another gushing group of fans ignore her was the last thing she felt like dealing with.

"Hey, guys!" Sean had clearly found some extra energy, because he sounded as sparkly as he had first thing this morning. "What's up?" He began to walk toward them, leaving Jess standing behind him. "Just give me a minute," he said to her over his shoulder.

"It's okay," Jess said, even though Sean didn't hang around to hear her response. If he had, she was sure it would have been obvious that she didn't mean it.

One of the girls clasped her hands to her face, her eyes bright. "See! I knew it was his! This is Desdemona, right, Sean?"

"I told you it was," Rachel said imperiously.

Jess watched as Sean dug out a grin from his last reserves of energy. "Hi, guys," he greeted them warmly.

She hung back, knowing that she wasn't important—wasn't going to be the focus or even a part of this interaction. The twisted feeling in her gut returned with a vengeance.

"We missed getting a photo this morning 'cause Jen was sick. I didn't want to come without her so we didn't get here till after the photos were done, and they wouldn't let us get one at the panel, but Rachel said if we waited here we might catch you and you might take a photo with us now because we really worked hard on our costumes," one of the girls said in a rush.

All three were dressed as Elvire—the two younger girls in very homemade, clumsy attempts in comparison to Rachel, but recognizable as the character nonetheless. One of them wore an extremely ugly blond wig.

"You look great," Sean said.

"Not as great as Rachel, of course, but we still tried."

Sean shook his head. "You *all* make great Elvires."

Jess was ridiculously pleased when Rachel's expression showed that she wasn't at all happy with being lumped in with the other two.

"Can we have a hug? And a photo?"

Sean held up his hands, in an exaggerated "keep away" pose. "Jen's not contagious, is she?" he said jokingly.

"Nah." The girl who was clearly Jen, the one wearing the cheap wig, spoke up for the first time. "I just had to do chemo this week and it meant I felt a bit crappy this morning."

Sean didn't skip a beat. "Well, then, I'd say you deserve a hug. C'mere."

Jess had to give him credit for his seamless response. She was left swallowing a lump in her throat as she watched the two girls hug Sean in turn and then pose for photos—Rachel acting as official photographer this time.

Sean spent some time talking to the two girls, finding out they were best friends, that Jen had a rare form of leukemia, and that she read and reread the Sebastian Douglas novels to help distract her from her illness and its treatment.

The whole conversation was so matter-of-fact and so terribly affecting that Jess was close to tears by the time Jen and her best friend walked off, giggling and grinning, Sean having made their day—if not their year.

"Thanks for that, Sean," Rachel said, lounging familiarly against Dezzie. "Sorry to spring that on you. I did send a DM to warn you, but I figure you haven't had time to check."

"No, I haven't been on Twitter today," Sean confirmed. "But thanks. I'm glad you made this meet happen for them."

"I saw their tweets and how disappointed they were. I knew you'd want me to."

"You were right."

"No problem."

There was a pause and Jess couldn't decide if it was awkward or loaded. Perhaps both.

Rachel gave the slightest, most fleetingly dismissive glance in her direction, and then lazily pushed herself away from the car.

"Cool. I'll let you head off, then," she said, her eyes solely back on Sean.

"Great. Thanks again, Rachel."

"And Sean—" she stepped forward to kiss Sean's cheek and give him a quick embrace "—don't forget about that catch-up."

Sean nodded as he stepped back, shooting her his trademark smile. "Sure. I'll call you."

THE RIDE HOME was silent; Sean was too tired to speak. He loved attending conventions—loved the opportunity to get face-to-face with his fans—but they were utterly draining. He considered himself a people person, he needed interaction with others to stay sane, but his work was a solitary endeavor and he was used to being alone a lot of the time. Being surrounded by people for hours on end took every ounce of energy he had—especially the kind of interactions he'd just had with the sick girl.

Jess stared out the window—she looked as tired as he felt. He wondered what she'd thought of the whole thing. He wanted to ask, wanted to hear her tell him how he'd done on stage, what she'd thought of his popularity, his success. But something in him stopped the words from coming out—he just knew it would sound ridiculously needy.

Surely, after the day he'd had, the applause, cheers, autographs and photos, he didn't need further affirmation from someone.

Yes, you do, a little voice inside him whispered. *It's never going to be enough.*

He shook himself to get rid of the unwelcome thought. It was childish, immature. Just the kind of description his parents took enormous pleasure in leveling at him.

Sure, he enjoyed a pretty carefree lifestyle. He didn't often have to deal with the kind of things Rob dealt with: malfunctioning household appliances, marriage, a dog that needed constant care, building a career at Paterson Associates with the intention of one day being its leader. Just because Sean preferred discussing the merits of hotel rooms to discussing trends in kitchen cabinetry didn't mean he wasn't a grown-up.

Look at him now: dating a thirty-five-year-old divorcée. Jess was already beginning to relax the tight hold she seemed to have on life thanks—at least in part, he liked to think—to his influence. She was also beginning to regain a little of the confidence that bastard ex-husband of hers had robbed her of. Their time together was going to be good for her, and once he'd moved on she'd be ready to go and find herself a new partner, maybe even a new husband. She was too wonderful to go unclaimed.

Yep, she definitely wouldn't be on the market for long.

Sometime soon, Sean would be in Sydney—or

maybe L.A.—and he'd be talking to Rob and Hailey on Skype and one of them would randomly mention that Jess and her new man had been over for a barbecue.

His hands tightened on the steering wheel.

Someone swerved into his lane without indicating, cutting him off. He swore loudly and hit the horn with a heavy hand. Jess shot him a glance with raised eyebrows, but didn't say anything. He wasn't usually given over to demonstrations of road rage.

Exhuastion was making him irritable.

He realized he and Jess hadn't made any plans for the evening, but he was driving to Rob and Hailey's place on automatic pilot, assuming they would spend the night together. It almost felt like a habit, a comfortable routine. But of course it wasn't—they were still temporary lovers, nothing more.

"I can't wait to grab a beer and crash on the couch," he said as he turned into Rob and Hailey's street. The idea of lazing around, watching TV, with Jess snuggled next to him was pretty much close to heaven.

The idea stopped him short.

Usually, after a convention, he was exhausted but also wired. After a couple of hours' recovery, he often went out afterward—to a pub or a club or the gym, working off the energy he'd collected throughout the day. He didn't feel that way now. Tonight he wanted to sit back and relax, hear more about Jess's experiences at the convention. She had such a different perspective on the world than he did, and he enjoyed seeing her view of things.

Was he just getting old?

Or was it something to do with Jess herself?

He felt strangely unsettled by the realization.

Jess murmured a vague agreement in response to his suggestion.

"You look wrecked, too." He realized too late she might misunderstand. "I mean gorgeously wrecked, of course," he said with a smile. "You're always beautiful, but you look tired." He pulled the car up to a stop in front of the house.

"I am." She sat straighter in her seat and shook her head, as if coming out of a daze. "Actually, sorry, I haven't been paying attention. I wanted to ask you to take me home. I think I want to sleep in my own bed. I know you have writing to do, so maybe we could just talk tomorrow."

It was probably a good idea. Maybe that was all this attachment to her was—habit. After all, they'd spent nearly every night together this week—a first for him in any kind of relationship, even when he'd been living with someone. Strange—it had been so comfortable. If someone had asked him to predict how he'd feel, he'd have said "stifled," when in actuality the time he'd been spending with Jess had been anything but. He'd had fun. Felt weirdly contented. And been more productive as a result.

But it couldn't last. It was probably a good thing that they got some space.

Besides, his deadline was still looming and the producers in L.A. still weren't happy about some of the final details around the screenplay and the movie as a whole. He owed it to himself—to his fans—not to get too distracted right now.

"Yeah, okay," he said. "I'll take you home and call you tomorrow. Or Monday."

Jess swallowed hard, but when she spoke, her tone was light. "Yeah. Monday's fine."

An annoying jolt of disappointment went through him but he quickly quashed it. Of course Monday was fine. It would have to be. If it was fine with Jess, then it was more than fine with him.

But, weirdly, he was already feeling strange about spending the next forty-eight hours without her.

Sean forced himself to make a lighthearted comment. "Monday's ten-dollar steak night at the chicken parma place. We'll have to give it a run for its money."

Jess didn't respond to the invitation. "The traffic shouldn't be too bad now, so if—"

Her words faded as Sean looked past her to the house.

Something was wrong.

The words were out of his mouth before he even realized what he was saying. "I'm pretty sure I didn't leave any lights on."

In the early evening gloom, Rob and Hailey's house was lit up like a Christmas tree. His already tight stomach rolled with foreboding. "Shit."

CHAPTER TEN

"STAY HERE," Sean said as he stepped out of the car.

Jess wasn't sure whether to stay in the car or go with Sean to help, but she knew she'd be of no use against an intruder. At least if she was out here, she could call the police if Sean encountered anyone.

Although, why would a burglar turn the lights *on*?

Still, she dug her phone out of her bag and dialed the emergency number in preparation.

But then the front door opened, as Sean was still only halfway up the path, and out walked...

Rob?

A million miles away from his bookish, gangly namesake character in Sean's books, Rob was just as handsome as Sean, but in a more classic, clean-cut-executive kind of way—taller, blonder, more polished. Right now, though, he looked a mess. Even from the car she could tell he was upset, from the way he ran his hands through his hair, to the way he embraced his brother with a stiff hug—hanging on for much longer than was socially acceptable.

Before she knew it, Jess was out of the car and running up the path.

"Rob? Are you okay? Is Hailey okay?"

"Jess?" Rob looked up, startled.

"Let's all go inside and get some coffee going, yeah?" Sean suggested.

Rob disappeared without explanation once they were inside the house and then came the sound of water running—Rob was showering.

"What's going on?" she hissed in a whisper to Sean, who was making coffee.

Sean shrugged. "I don't know. Last I heard they were in Rome, but not having much fun because of the weather."

"Where's Hailey?"

"I don't know."

"Is she okay?"

Sean banged a cup down on the counter. "Jess, I know as much as you do. Let's wait for Rob to tell us what's going on."

Jess perched on the edge of a chair, her entire body tense. All her anxiety from the convention, about what was going on between Sean and Rachel, vanished in her worry about Hailey. She and Hailey were not just coworkers, they were good friends. If something had happened to her...

She and Sean sat in silence, hands around their mugs of coffee, and listened as the shower turned off and doors in the house opened and closed.

Rob finally appeared in clean clothes and with wet hair. He grabbed the coffee Sean had left out and slowly walked over to the table where they sat, pulling out a chair and slumping down into it.

As if knowing her master needed comfort, Suzie

materialized, nuzzling her head into Rob's lap. Rob began patting her automatically.

"So," Sean began after the three of them had sat in silence for long enough. "What happened?"

"We're getting a divorce," Rob pronounced with doom, his eyes unfocused.

Jess felt a bubble of hysterical laughter rise in her throat. *Was that it?* She'd been imagining a car accident, kidnapping, a terrorist attack. Working out how to arrange for a body to be returned to Australia from Italy. She coughed to clear her inappropriate reaction and reached for Rob's hand.

"Where's Hailey, Rob?" she asked, as gently as she could. Was Hailey still in Europe? Alone?

"She's here, in Melbourne. But she's staying with Vanessa," he said, naming one of Hailey's best friends—the woman who'd been maid of honor at the wedding.

"Don't be crazy! I… You… The wedding!" Sean sputtered. "You guys were, *are* so perfect!"

Rob just shrugged.

"You'll work it out," Sean said, slapping Rob on the arm. "You guys have fought before, and made up before. You always do."

Rob shook his head. "Not this time. It's not just a fight about who took the garbage out or whether we go out or stay home on the weekend."

"Then what is it?" Jess asked.

"She's pregnant."

Jess's jaw dropped open. That was pretty much the last thing she expected Rob to say.

"You do mean *Hailey*, right, man?" Sean asked in a teasing tone.

Rob's look told them he was a very long way from being able to joke about this.

Rob ran a hand through his hair again. "Rome was a disaster. Hailey was so sick all the time. We thought it was food poisoning, at first, but then she took a test...."

Sean frowned. "I don't understand the problem. You guys have always said you wanted kids. I know it's a little earlier than you'd planned, but…"

Rob sat up straighter in his chair. "Exactly!" He put his coffee cup down on the table with a thump. "That's what I said!"

"Hailey doesn't see it that way," Jess guessed. She'd spent eight hours a day, five days a week with Hailey for over two years. She knew how important it was to her to finish her university degree. To achieve her goal of becoming a vet herself. A baby right now would punch a massive hole in those plans.

"Right. But, I mean, it's not like we have to worry about money—Mom and Dad can help if we need it. And she can always go back to uni later."

"Is she going to get…?" Sean trailed off, clearly unwilling to say what they were all thinking.

A pained look crossed Rob's face. "I don't know. She said she doesn't know what she wants to do. But from what she was saying back in Rome, I think she might."

"It's all going to be okay," Jess said soothingly. "You've come home to give yourselves time to work things out. You're right—this is serious, but perhaps you both just need some time." Jess felt like crossing her fingers behind her back as she spoke. *I hope it's true.*

"That's what Hailey said—she needed time. But I don't understand why. It's pretty obvious there's only one option here. I just don't get why she doesn't see that. No matter what I said to her, it didn't seem to get through that thick skull of hers."

There was more than a tinge of anger to Rob's words. Jess could just imagine what kind of "discussions" they'd had in Rome.

"Don't go jumping to conclusions just yet, okay?" she said.

"Yeah, I guess." Rob slumped in his chair, his anger fading. "I just don't understand why she's not happy. I'm happy about it. I'm really happy." His eyes filled with tears, and he looked about the most miserable man on the face of the earth.

Jess felt herself tearing up, too, in sympathy. She felt torn. She could see Rob's pain written across his face, but she could easily imagine how distressed and anguished Hailey would be about her situation right now, too. There really wasn't a compromise here. Someone would get what they wanted, the other person wouldn't. Simple—and complex—as that.

"It'll work out somehow," Sean mumbled. "Counseling. Something." He looked distinctly uncomfortable at the display of emotion from his brother.

His discomfort clearly communicated itself to Rob, because he cleared his throat noisily and scrubbed at his face with both hands, blinking away his tears. "You're probably right," he said. He picked up his cup and took a long drink of coffee, and when he put it down, he'd managed to regain his composure. Then he frowned at Jess. "Jess? Not to be rude or anything, but what are you doing here? Is Suzie okay?" He gave the dog still sitting loyally at his feet a protective squeeze.

Oh, crap.

In her worry for Hailey, Jess hadn't thought about explaining her presence here with Sean. Her stomach twisted. This was not how it was supposed to work. Her fling with Sean was a secret. Not a very closely guarded one, sure, but certainly not something she had expected to share with people she was as close to as Rob and Hailey. She and Sean hadn't yet talked about what would happen when Rob and Hailey returned from their honeymoon—thinking they still had a few weeks to work it out. But Jess hadn't planned on letting them know about their arrangement.

"I, uh…" she began, and looked at Sean with wide eyes, pleading for help with an explanation.

Sean jumped in. "Jess was kind enough to help me out at the convention today. I sucked her in with the promise of meeting Ethan Falcon and a free copy of my book."

"You met Ethan Falcon?" Rob asked.

"Yes, and made a fool of myself."

"It wasn't that bad," Sean said.

"It was pretty bad."

"Well, yeah, it *was* pretty bad." His mouth twitched and he winked at her—the mischievous, sexy Sean that she'd fallen for at the wedding.

She knew he was changing the subject—using her embarrassment to lighten the moment and give Rob a break. But he'd just covered up their relationship—lied to his brother. Why wasn't she relieved about that? It had been what she'd been hoping he'd do, hadn't it? The idea that Sean wanted to hide their affair, too, made something deep inside her twist painfully.

Now wasn't the time to pursue it.

"You should have seen me." Jess shook her head, smiling when she recalled the moment, despite everything. "I must have looked like a goldfish."

Sean put a finger to his chin. "Now that you mention it..."

Jess reached over the table to punch his arm playfully. "Hey, there's no need to rub it in."

"Oh, I'm going to be living off that story for weeks."

"You are not!"

"I am, too. I can see so many opportunities for blackmail."

"You wouldn't."

Sean raised an eyebrow. "You think?"

"There's no one who'd really care anyway."

"Just imagine me, camped out in your waiting room," he began with a storyteller air. "And each time a patient walks in and sits down with their cat, I lean over and go, 'Have you heard what happened when Jess met—'"

Jess laughed at the image he painted. "Oh, you're an idiot."

He held up his hands. "I'm not the one that flipped out."

"You did not just say that!"

Rob sniffed loudly and drained his cup of coffee. His eyes were trained on the table in front of him, unfocused. He was in his own world, but Jess was seized with horror at the inappropriateness of her flirting with Sean as Rob sat there with his life falling apart.

Sean obviously had the same realization, because he fell silent as he was about to offer his next rejoinder.

"Look, mate," he said to Rob instead, "why don't you go get some sleep and we'll talk about all this in the morning. It's bound to seem insurmountable while you're tired and jet-lagged. Tomorrow you can call Hailey and get this whole thing sorted."

Rob nodded. "Yeah, I guess."

"Good idea," Jess added. "Get a good night's sleep. You'll feel clearer in the morning."

"Absolutely," Sean chimed in.

"Jess, I probably shouldn't have told you about…" Rob said, waving a hand in the air to fill in the missing words. "With you being Hailey's boss and all." He winced. "She'll probably kill me if she finds out."

Jess frowned. He was right. Hailey would have wanted to break the news on her own terms. But Jess could handle it—it was Rob and Hailey's business right now and no one else's. "It's okay." She tried to sound as reassuring as possible. "I promise I'll keep it to myself. Hailey's still officially on leave, anyway. I probably won't see her for another couple of weeks—and you guys will have this worked out by then."

Rob slumped back in his chair again and his bottom lip pouted dangerously. "I hope so."

Sean's chair scraped noisily as he stood. "Jess, let me get that book I promised you, and then I'll take you home, okay?"

"That'd be great," she said, going along with the cover story, but relieved to be leaving—the sooner the better.

Sean disappeared into the house.

Jess reached for Rob's hand and squeezed it. "Rob? Try not to worry. I know this is tough, but you and Hailey are meant to be together. You'll find a way to work through this, I just know it."

Jess knew no such thing. In fact she knew firsthand that relationships were anything but permanent, anything but certain. *Meant to be together* meant nothing, really, in the face of cold, hard reality.

"Jess, you ready to go?" Sean called from the door. He walked into the kitchen and made a big show of handing her a copy of one of his books—the one in the series that she was up to reading, she noted.

"Mate, I'll grab some beers for us while I'm out," he said to Rob. "In case you need something to help you sleep."

"Sounds good," Rob said.

Jess gave Rob's arm a squeeze as she went past, wishing there was some way she could help, some medication she could prescribe to relieve his pain.

She was struck by the memory she had of Rob and Hailey at their wedding—gazing into each other's eyes with such dedication as they promised to love, honor and cherish.

Jess had made those same vows to Mark—and look how that had turned out.

Maybe relationships just didn't work. Maybe it wasn't how human beings were supposed to live.

So few animals mated for life—it just wasn't practical on many levels. Perhaps back when the average human lifespan had been thirty or forty years, when you needed to band together for safety, security and prosperity, long-term commitments had made sense. But now?

"You've got the serious-Jess face on again," Sean said as they made their way through light traffic toward her house.

"I'm just thinking about Hailey."

"Yeah."

They fell silent again, both, Jess thought, wondering how the two young lovers were going to make this work.

Sean pulled Dezzie up to Jess's front door and killed the engine, as was his habit.

"I'd like nothing better than to come in with you and snuggle up in bed and sleep for about ten hours, but I'd better get back to Rob."

Belatedly Jess remembered how exhausted Sean was and then her own tiredness washed over her— if anything, strengthened by her forgetfulness. The discomfort of the whole day came back in a rush—

the nerves, the uncertainty, the awful *invisibility* of being with Sean. Mark had made her feel like second best in a wily, secretive way. Being second best with Sean was a fact of life—there were hundreds of people lined up for a piece of him.

"I wish…" she began. But then she stopped. There was no point getting into it. What she and Sean had was a temporary thing. Fighting with him was pointless.

"You wish what?" he asked.

"Nothing." She rubbed a hand over her eyes—fatigue was making them sore. "We absolutely should not be doing this now. I should not be saying this now. I'm so tired and today was insane. I don't even feel like I can make words come out the right way."

"Jess? C'mon. Tell me what's going on." He twisted in the seat to face her.

Well, if he really wanted to know… "I wish you'd prepared me better for today."

"In what way?"

"I had no idea…" Her voice had already begun to get shrill and she forced herself to take a breath and lower her tone before continuing. "I had no idea what I was walking into. I thought it was going to be a few people talking about your books. Not dressed-up fans, and autographs, and celebrities."

"But—"

"I was totally lost. Totally out of place."

"No, you weren't. You—"

"I felt like a fool." *And that was the crux of it, wasn't it?* Mark had made her feel stupid because everyone had known what was going on in her marriage except her. And today, she'd gone to the convention having no idea that she'd be relegated to the role of "assistant" and then ignored for the rest of the day as Sean dealt with his fame. It was just like their first "date," when she'd walked into the bookshop and discovered Sean Paterson was more than just a dinky comic book writer.

"Jess, I thought you'd find it fun."

"Well, I didn't." That wasn't quite true. It actually had been an eye-opening and fascinating experience for the most part. But that wasn't the point. The point was that once again she'd been woefully underinformed about what her supposed partner was doing.

Sean look wounded. "I'm sorry, I guess."

"You guess?"

"I'm sorry. I'm sorry that you felt out of place. That wasn't my intention."

"Next time, a little warning would be nice." Even as the words left her mouth Jess was wondering why she'd said it. *Next time?* There wasn't going to be a next time.

"Fine." Sean looked straight ahead, both hands gripping the steering wheel tight. "I just… I wanted to share my world with you." His voice was small.

Jess didn't know what to say. She heard the vulnerability in his voice, but her own messed-up emotions didn't allow for her to reach out to him right now.

She reached for the door handle instead. "Sure. That's fine. You'd better get back to Rob—he needs you right now."

Sean stilled her with a hand on her arm. "Is everything okay? With us, I mean?"

She nodded, but didn't meet his eyes. "Yes, fine. It's just...been a big day."

"You can say that again."

"Uh, Sean?" There was one more thing she couldn't let rest. Not when she knew it would chew her up until she did. *In for a penny, in for a pound— isn't that what they said?*

"Yeah?"

"Are you...have you been...you know, *involved* with Rachel?"

"Rachel who?" His confusion was genuine and went some way to reassuring her.

"Rachel, *Elvire*-Rachel. I overheard at the convention—"

Sean snorted a laugh. "No, no. Rachel's like the head of my fan club. She's a nice girl. A little intense, but she means well."

Jess had the strong feeling that wasn't how Rachel saw things. "Okay then." There was no point trying to analyze it any further.

"You sure you're okay?"

"Yep, positive. I'll let you get back to Rob. Good night."

"Night, Jess. I'll call you, okay?"

Jess sat unmoving for a moment as a realization struck. Their deal had been to have an affair until Rob and Hailey returned from their honeymoon. That was supposed to be another three weeks away—but now they were back.

Rob was home, which meant Sean no longer needed to house-sit. He'd made it clear he wasn't the type to stick around anywhere for long. And she'd just behaved like a jealous and controlling harpy—just what a guy like Sean loved. Not.

Did this mean their time together was at an end? Was this going to be her last moment alone with him like this?

Without pausing to think, Jess twisted in her seat and grabbed Sean's face, pulling his lips to hers. He made a muttered sound of surprise, but quickly responded, returning her kiss with all the heat and passion she had grown used to.

His lips were soft and warm and he tasted faintly of coffee. His hand cupped her face, his thumb stroking her cheek as he parted her lips and deepened the kiss. By the time Jess pulled away she was panting, her whole body humming with need.

"Wow," Sean murmured, rubbing his thumb across his bottom lip.

"Yeah," Jess said. She didn't trust herself to say anything further, scared she might say something stupid—or worse, begin to cry.

Sean didn't say a word as she opened the car door and made her way to her house as fast as she could. Her fingers were trembling and it took forever to find her keys in her bag, and another age before she managed to get the right one in the lock. But then, finally, she was inside.

She took a deep breath and let it out shakily, leaning back against the door for support.

It was another moment or so before she heard the rumble of Dezzie's engine come to life and the echo of the car as it pulled out onto the street and drove away.

ALL DAY SUNDAY, Jess told herself she wasn't waiting for Sean to call. But she was. Despite her resignation from the night before that their affair was likely over, she needed to hear from him—get confirmation of her assumptions.

She jumped every time her phone so much as looked like it might ring. And it felt ridiculous: as if she'd somehow regressed to being a fourteen-year-old girl waiting for the hot boy at school to pick up the phone and dial her number, obsessively checking her mobile phone every couple of hours.

Of course, she *could* call him.

But he was dealing with Rob and that whole situation, as well as still trying to meet his deadline. It wouldn't be fair to interrupt him.

And *she'd* been the one to get all jealous and insecure—which was absolutely not what their temporary thing was all about. Calling him would just be further evidence of that.

When—*if*—he had time, he'd call her.

Assuming he hadn't already moved on.

It was entirely possible he'd already headed off to Sydney as had been his original plan before he'd been roped into house-sitting. Jess tortured herself wondering whether he would really leave without saying goodbye. The Sean she knew wouldn't, but the Sean of Hailey's description wouldn't hesitate.

Worse, he could have moved on in *another* way. Despite what he'd said about his relationship with Rachel—and Jess wanted to believe him, but history had taught her to remain cautious—she wasn't under any illusions. It wouldn't take Sean long to find someone new. Whether it was Rachel or someone else.

Not that it was any of her business.

Sunday passed in a blur and then she was at work. Thankfully there were enough distractions to keep her mind occupied and she managed not to spend every moment wondering about Sean and whether the thing between them was over.

Not *every* moment, anyway.

She'd actually had this grand plan of how they would bring a close to their relationship. The night before Rob and Hailey arrived home she and Sean would go out for a special dinner and then spend one last night in bed together, knowing it was their last hurrah. It would be sad, but also a kind of celebration—they'd review how much fun they'd had, and personally Jess could think about how far she'd come, how ready she was now to hit the dating scene again.

But at the moment, she didn't feel at all ready to set herself up on one of the online dating sites, or register for those singles dinners. She wasn't *finished* yet. She'd been cheated of her special "one last night," and it seemed she hadn't even begun to work through some of the issues she'd been left with as a result of her marriage.

If only they'd had more time. Time for Jess to find out if she could ever trust someone again.

Not that she blamed Rob and Hailey, but still.

Poor Rob and Hailey.

When she wasn't obsessing over her own predicament she was worrying about them.

Sean could at least call to give her an update on their situation.

AT THE END of a Monday that had passed in a blur, Jess said good-night to Andrea and then finished with the cleanup. Thank goodness Margie was back next week and she wouldn't have to deal with the admin anymore.

Distracted by the computer that seemed to be refusing to print out the report she needed, Jess didn't realize that she hadn't locked the door until the bell rang loudly, announcing a visitor.

"Sorry, we're closed," she said automatically, before looking up.

Her mouth went dry as her visitor smiled and closed the door behind him.

"No pets, just me," he said.

No, Mark had never been much of an animal person. Rocco had always been *her* dog, not *their* dog. It should have been a red flag right from the start.

"What are you doing here, Mark?" Irritation and anxiety warred inside her.

He shook his head and gave her a bemused look. "What's happened to your manners, Jess? No 'hello' and 'nice to see you'?"

His tone was joking, but all Jess could hear was his criticism. And that was something she was glad for.

He'd made criticizing her into such an art form during their marriage that it had gotten to the point that she'd no longer recognized it for what it was. Like a slap with a silk glove. Without stopping to think whether the critique was fair, she'd find herself apologizing for whatever mistake she'd unintentionally made: wearing the wrong shoes with an outfit, putting too much peanut butter on her toast, talking for too long about her workday.

Not anymore.

"My manners are just fine," she said, straightening up and clasping her hands together tightly, glad for the barrier of the reception desk between them. It had been more than six months since she'd seen him last—since they'd had their last face-to-face meeting with the accountant to finalize the divorce settlement. She'd often dreaded accidentally running into him—for a while had even made sure she never left the house without full makeup and styled hair, just in case. But that vigilance had relaxed as their paths hadn't crossed—making it obvious just how far apart they'd grown.

But she still saw the details only someone intimately familiar with him would notice. He wore the same musky Hugo Boss aftershave—and she still liked it. His shoes were perfectly shiny—he had a thing about scuffs. And that sinewy body in an Italian wool suit was still strong and capable.

Mark was fit and powerful. There had been a time

when being held in his arms had felt like one of the safest places to be. He'd promised to protect her from the world. Which had been wonderful, until the protection had become smothering. He kept her in a gilded cage, while he felt free to run wild....

He took a step forward. "I know you were busy the other night when I called, so I figured I'd pop in and see you this evening. Let's go grab a glass of wine and a couple of laksas at Chinta Ria and catch up."

A glass of chardonnay and a bowl of Malaysian noodle soup at the nearby restaurant had been one of their favorite weeknight indulgences—during the better times.

"Sorry, I can't."

He put his head on one side. "There's no reason we can't be friends, Jess."

A little voice inside her piped up. *Are you overreacting? What exactly* are *the reasons you can't have a civilized relationship with your ex-husband?* "I don't think..." she began, not sure what to say.

"Really? Come on now, Jess. You're being a little silly about all this. It's just dinner—an hour, maybe two at the most."

He was right. Shouldn't she be able to spend an hour with him? An unmistakable longing went through her—despite everything, a part deep inside of her missed him. It was tough to spend ten years with someone and then suddenly not have them in your life. So much shared experience that felt as if it wasn't worth anything anymore. Stories and times that really couldn't be shared with anyone else.

She sucked in a deep breath. Perhaps this was the mature approach—people were friends with their exes all the time, weren't they?

Before she could speak, he stepped closer to the desk, frowning.

"Or are you seeing that new guy of yours tonight? Do you need to rush home to do *his* bidding?"

His bidding? Jess caught the careful emphasis. Instead of Mark's bidding? Swapping one yoke for another?

No. No way. Never again.

"Don't you have someone to get home to, Mark?" she asked, her voice chilly.

He didn't seem bothered. "I told you, I'm single right now."

He was single and so, right now, she was important. But as soon as someone else came along she'd be shelved again—put back on the second-best rack. Ignored. Begging for scraps of attention. Pretending that everything was fine, because she didn't have the courage to admit what was really going on.

And just like that, something inside her snapped. She reached blindly and grabbed the nearest thing to hand: a sample bag of cat kibble from the display on the counter.

Her aim was perfect, but Mark's reflexes were practiced from hours spent dodging the boom on the yacht.

"What the...?" he exclaimed, ducking as the bag of kibble exploded against the wall behind him, scattering tiny brown stars across the floor and onto his suit.

The look on his face...

Jess surprised them both by bursting out laughing.

"Jess, really?" He shook his head like a disapproving father at a toddler's tantrum, brushing a few stray pieces of cat food from his suit, shaking the kibble dust from his shoes.

Oh, goodness, this was fun. Jess reached for another bag while Mark's attention was on his dusty clothing and deliberately aimed for the wall above his head, hoping for another kibble explosion to rain down over him. Unfortunately her throw didn't have the same power, and this time the bag simply crumpled and fell to the floor with a thud.

Oh, well.

It was the throwing that was the real fun.

"What's gotten into you?" Mark said, staring at the second bag of kibble before looking at her with wide eyes.

"Life," she said. "I'm having one."

"Has this guy got you hooked on drugs or something?"

Jess laughed again. Her laughter had a hysterical quality, she was aware of that, but at the same time she was truly finding Mark's outrage at her behavior genuinely amusing.

"*This guy* hasn't got me hooked on anything." But even as she said it, she wondered if it was true. Maybe he had her hooked on *him*.

Mark frowned. "Jess, I'm worried about you. You've always been easily led, and if the wrong person is influencing you—"

"Mark, I'm not your toy anymore." Jess was hyper-aware of all the things going on around her—inside her. The usual tang of disinfectant in the office was overlaid with the slightly fishy, dusty smell of dried cat food. Her blood was pounding, but her breathing was even, if a little fast. She sounded calm, although she clenched her fists by her side. Realization of why Mark had chosen *now* to reappear in her life crystallized. "I know you're annoyed because someone else has picked me up out of the sandbox and your sense of ownership has been rekindled. But there's nothing you can do about it."

"It's not like that at all," Mark blustered.

Jess shrugged, her laughter gone. "Maybe. Maybe not. You'll never see it, even if it is." She stepped forward, coming out from behind the desk to face him front-on. "But what I want you to know is, no, we can't be friends, Mark. I don't think we have been for a long time. Friends trust each other. Friends are loyal. We have neither loyalty nor trust between us. I don't think that can make for much of a friendship."

Mark stared at her, wordless.

Jess managed a small smile and felt the prick of tears behind her eyes. Goodbyes were always sad, even if they were necessary—perhaps even more so then.

"Goodbye, Mark."

He visibly gathered himself together, reaching one hand out to grab her arm. "Jess, let's—"

"Don't." She slid sideways to avoid his touch.

"I think you're being silly."

She nodded. "Perhaps I am. And perhaps it's time I was. Right now, that's the way I want it. And, for once, you are going to listen to me, and do what *I* say." She swallowed hard. "Please leave. And don't come back, don't call me. There's nothing left to say."

They shared a long look and Jess could see it in his eyes when he accepted her terms. But Mark was Mark and he couldn't leave it there.

"Are you sure? Because you know I always loved you. And I know you loved me."

"This time I don't need you to tell me how to feel, Mark." A little spurt of anger revived in her belly. "I know that as soon as you find your next conquest, I won't matter to you anymore—even as a friend. I'm not willing to be second best again."

He sucked in a deep breath and let it out slowly. And then, in a weird, disturbingly intimate gesture, he leaned forward and pressed his lips to her forehead. "Good for you," he whispered.

With a sad but boyish smile that reminded Jess of why she'd fallen in love with him in the first place, he turned and disappeared.

The ring of the bell on the door echoed around the empty room for long seconds after he'd left.

Jess drew in a shaky breath and sagged against the counter.

Laugh or cry? Dance for joy or curl into a ball in the corner? Could she do all those simultaneously?

Instead, she settled for finding the broom and sweeping up the kibble mess. Slow, measured strokes of the broom that somehow felt as though she was sweeping up the broken emotional mess in her brain at the same time.

By the time the floor was clean and the ruined bags of kibble put in the trash, her equilibrium was somewhat closer to normal. And, strangely, she felt lighter than she had in years.

CHAPTER ELEVEN

WEDNESDAY.

Jess lurched from upset to curious to downright relieved depending on who popped into her thoughts.

Still no word from Sean—four days since they'd spoken last.

Still no word about what was happening between Rob and Hailey.

Also, no contact from Mark since his Monday-evening visit, which was pleasantly surprising.

Jess mopped the floor with special vigor, relishing the twinge in her legs. After Mark's visit on Monday she'd gone home and changed into running gear and done a full lap of Albert Park Lake. It had been at least a year since she'd last done the circuit and the workout had left her sore and out of breath, but also given her a sense of satisfaction. She'd gone again last night.

Running had been one of her coping mechanisms during the early stages of the divorce—she relished the blank of her mind as she focused on getting oxygen into her lungs and pumping her arms and legs that little bit faster—but she'd let it drop to the wayside as she became more settled with her life.

Right now blanking her mind was a welcome respite. She didn't want to think about how much she missed Sean. It was indecent to be so attached to someone after such a short time. And it definitely reinforced the importance of their relationship being temporary—for her own self-preservation, if nothing else.

But that didn't stop her from finding a goofy grin on her face when she recalled the way her tummy tightened when he winked at her. Or from her breath becoming short when she remembered what it was like when his beard stubble rasped against her neck.

Mark's crack about her doing Sean's bidding had been way off—Sean had never tried to control her or manipulate her—not like Mark had. But his reminder that she was "easily led"? Well, it wasn't something she wanted to admit about herself. But clearly she did let herself get in over her head too quickly.

Over the past few days she'd grown to realize that she was still too damaged, too broken, to jump into a new relationship. She still didn't know how to draw boundaries around herself as an individual when she was part of a couple.

The affair with Sean *had* been a good idea, all told. She'd learned a lot about herself. Including the fact that she wasn't ready for a commitment.

Which was just as well, because clearly Sean wasn't, either.

All in all, she should be relieved about that.

Why, then, was she still counting the hours since she'd seen him last?

For the second time that week, the bell over the door announced an after-hours unexpected visitor. But this time the visitor was welcome.

"Hailey!" Jess exclaimed. She leaned the mop against the wall and went over to hug her sad-looking friend.

"Surprise," Hailey said after they'd pulled back from their embrace, her voice flat, her face pale.

"What are you doing here?" Jess wasn't sure how well she managed to fake her surprise or how much to pretend she didn't know.

"I thought I'd pop in and say hi," Hailey said. She looked around the empty waiting room. "You done for the day? It'd be good to chat."

"Yep, we're done. Just have to finish cleaning up and cash out the register."

"How about I give you a hand and we can go get a coffee?"

Jess wondered what Hailey wanted to talk about— was she going to tell her about her situation?

"You finish up back there—" Hailey gestured to the consulting rooms "—and I'll do the register."

"You're sure?"

Hailey managed a small smile. "I think I remember how to do it. It hasn't been *that* long."

"Okay."

With Hailey's help it didn't take long to finish tidying up, and then Jess and Hailey wandered along the street to their favorite coffee shop. It felt like old times; there had often been evenings when they'd have a drink together before heading home. Sometimes after bad days—like the day they'd put down three beloved family pets in one afternoon—and sometimes just to chat.

This wasn't quite the same as those times—Jess felt as if a dark cloud were following them along the street.

"I'll get it," Jess offered. "What would you like?"

"Chamomile tea," Hailey said. "I'll get us a table."

Chamomile tea. A bit different to the café latte that would be her usual order. Did that mean anything? Was she still pregnant?

A few minutes later Jess joined Hailey with their drinks. A silence fell as Hailey fiddled with her tea, jiggling the tea bag, squeezing it out. Jess didn't know where to begin. She didn't want to betray Rob by giving away too much, but at the same time, Hailey was her friend, and she looked awful.

"I thought Margie would be back by now," Hailey eventually said.

"Next week," Jess said. "And I can't wait. We got a postcard from the Cook Islands—they've been having a great time. Although Margie got a cold just after they left and had to see the doctor, but she's fine now."

"Great," Hailey said, her eyes a little glazed. Jess knew she hadn't really been listening. Then she fixed Jess with a look. "So, I know that you know."

"Ah."

"It's okay. I'm not mad at Rob. Not for *that*."

"I'm glad. It wasn't really his fault. He was telling Sean, and I…I just happened to be there."

Hailey nodded, thankfully too wrapped up in her own thoughts to question exactly *why* Jess had been there.

She looked down at her tea, stirring it unnecessarily with a teaspoon. "So, what do you think?"

Jess was startled by the question. "I'm not sure what you mean."

Hailey still didn't look up. "What do you think I should do?"

"Oh, Hailey." Jess sighed and leaned forward on her elbows. "I can't tell you what to do. Not about this."

Hailey looked up then, her eyes brimming with tears. "I wish someone could."

A lump formed in Jess's throat and she reached across the table to squeeze her friend's hand. "I know, hon, I know."

Hailey shook Jess's hand away, but only so she could reach for her purse and find a tissue. She dabbed at her eyes and blew her nose noisily.

"Sorry," she said when she was a little more composed. "I keep crying. Not sure if it's a symptom or just because of how crappy this whole situation is."

"You're fine. Don't worry about it."

"I'm staying with Vanessa."

"Yeah, Rob mentioned that."

"I feel so bad intruding on her because she's got stuff going on, too. She broke up with Matt because he wouldn't get engaged. I think with *my* wedding going on, she wanted to start planning her own wedding, so she gave him an ultimatum. He left, and she's really angry."

"Poor girl. But let me guess, her advice hasn't been especially objective?"

"She's on a hate-all-men rampage. She thinks Rob is being an asshole and that I should do whatever I want. She thinks I should get the marriage annulled." Hailey frowned. "Is that even possible? I thought 'annulled' was if you didn't sleep together or something, but Vanessa reckons it's just if you change your mind within thirty days."

"I think she might be thinking of the cooling-off period when you buy a house," Jess said, trying her best to keep a straight face.

"Yeah, that's what I thought. I don't think Rob and I can get an annulment. Not after the wedding night we had, anyway." She managed a smile. "You should have a seen the room, Jess. It was filled with yellow roses."

Jess knew yellow roses were Hailey's favorite.

"And there was Lindt chocolate, and French champagne—and even Rob's favorite beer. And rose petals on the bed, and candles in the bathroom, and that really expensive rose-scented bubble bath from Jurlique that I love. It was just…perfect." Hailey sniffed loudly and reached again for her tissue.

Jess had a flashback to the wedding, to climbing into Sean's car and stealing away from the reception early. He'd convinced her that Rob and Hailey didn't need the car because they were staying at the hotel—and he knew this because he'd "decorated" their room. At the time, Jess had figured he'd filled it with condoms and sex toys and tacky lingerie.

She'd known Sean had a strong romantic streak, but the idea of him collecting the candles, rose petals and bath oil and putting it all together? It made her ache to share a night like that with him.

She looked down at her coffee and the hurt of missing him became a physical thing in her gut. Not good.

Best get back to the matter at hand.

"Have you spoken to Rob?" she asked.

Hailey shook her head. "Only to Sean. He called me and asked if I'd come over and he told me you knew what had happened. I said I wasn't ready to talk to Rob yet."

Jess hated herself for the instant reaction that flashed through her: jealousy. Sean had called Hailey, but not her. Almost four whole days since she'd seen him or spoken to him and she was strung out like an addict needing a fix.

Stop being ridiculous. Hailey needs your help and attention right now.

Jess took a sip of coffee and then focused on Hailey. "So, Vanessa thinks Rob's being unreasonable. Do you agree with her?"

Hailey swallowed hard before answering. "I don't think she sees how complicated it is. This isn't just my decision. Rob is a part of it."

Jess nodded. She hoped Hailey wouldn't be too unduly influenced by Vanessa's extreme advice. "I think you're right."

"I just wish there was an easy answer. Or that

someone would just tell me what to do so I didn't have to be...*responsible* for it."

"I know." Jess couldn't count the number of times she'd had exactly that thought when her marriage began to collapse around her. In her darker times she'd wished that Mark would just come home and announce he was leaving her for Cathy or whoever he was screwing at the time—take the decision out of her hands. But he'd been too much of a coward to do that, and besides, why would he disrupt his life when he got to have the stability of a wife and the excitement of a mistress all at once?

"It's not that I don't want to have...it." Hailey stirred her otherwise untouched tea again. "It's just that I had this plan. And now I haven't even got to see Europe the way I was supposed to. And if we go through with it, when will I get the chance? It'll be years." She was tearing up again.

"Have you tried doing a pros and cons list?"

"Hmm?" Hailey sniffed.

"I know it sounds a bit simplistic, but I've found that sometimes just writing a list of pros and cons can really help. But don't just go by the number of items in each list. Give each one a weight. Because sometimes you can have just a few things in one column and lots in the other, but those few things outweigh everything else."

It was what she'd done before she'd finally gathered her courage and confronted Mark to ask for a divorce. The cons column was huge—loss of friends, financial ramifications, losing their house, being alone.

The pros column had just one item: not being second best. But that one item had weighed a lot.

"I could give that a try I suppose." Hailey didn't sound very sure.

"Well, it doesn't work for everyone. But definitely give it a try. You'll find a way to work this through, I'm sure of it."

"I'm glad you're sure. I don't feel sure about anything at the moment."

"Hailey, you're smart. You are one of the most compassionate people I know. And you know what you want from life as well as what you have to offer it. You're going to get through this—I'm certain."

"Thanks, Jess." She managed a tearful smile. "I knew you were who I wanted to talk to about this. I know you're my boss, but we're friends, too, although not BFFs, you know? But you're so sensible."

Jess thought she understood Hailey's clumsy praise. Jess was close enough to understand what Hailey was going through, but not so close she couldn't be objective.

"And you've been there, done that, with your divorce and all," Hailey continued. "So you know what it's like. I mean, not that I want that to happen…I can't even imagine how awful that would be. I'd hate to end up like…" Hailey shuddered and her breath caught in a sob.

Jess told herself not to be insulted. She could see how from the perspective of a twentysomething newlywed, becoming a thirtysomething divorcée was a horrible fate. Sometimes the realization that that was what had happened to her life took her own breath away. Except, since Monday, she was absolutely sure that being divorced and alone was a hell of a lot better than being still married to Mark. That bag of cat food had been a turning point. Maybe she'd get herself a cat and a dog when she was ready to replace Rocco. Then she could buy lots of that brand of kibble as a daily reminder of her victory.

But divorce was a long way from where Hailey and Rob were right now.

"Don't get ahead of yourself," Jess warned. "You have time to think things through. You've still got two and a half weeks of holiday and then you can—"

"Actually," Hailey interrupted, "that's another thing I wanted to talk to you about. I was wondering if I could come back to work. I'm not nearly as sick as I was in Rome—being home makes me feel better, I think. And I'd just like to return to a somewhat normal routine. It'd be nice to have something to think about other than…*this.*"

Jess bit her lip. "I've got Andrea…" Her business brain went into gear. Hailey had taken leave without pay for her extended trip. Jess's clinic was profitable, but by no means a gold mine. She couldn't support the full-time pay of two assistants when she only needed one, even just for three weeks. And she didn't feel right breaking the contract with Andrea. Although not as good as Hailey, the young woman had proved herself to be a capable and pleasant workmate, who had confessed she'd taken the temp job to save up for a trip to visit her boyfriend's family in the U.K.

"I wouldn't expect it to be like *normal*," Hailey protested. "Andrea can do my job. I could do Margie's job until she's back next week. And then I can just do whatever you need me to do—clean up, write notes, that kind of stuff. *Please*, Jess."

"Hailey, I'd love to, but I can't really afford—"

Hailey's eyes went wide. "Oh, you don't have to pay me! No, absolutely, I understand that. I'll just be like, a volunteer, until my real job starts again. That's totally fine."

It wasn't as simple as that. "Hailey, I'd *have* to pay you. It's illegal to have someone working without paying them. If anything happened—if you got hurt, or if for some reason things between us went wrong, not that I think they would, but... I could get in a lot of trouble."

"*Please*, Jess? I promise I won't tell anyone, not a word. And I absolutely won't get injured. I won't do anything that could result in that. I won't go near any animals. I'll just sit at the desk and answer the phone if that's all I can do."

Jess let out a long breath. It was a big risk—there could be nasty penalties from the tax office or the work safety authority if they were caught. But Hailey was a friend, and she trusted her to keep her word. Plus, Hailey's tearstained, pleading face was one even Scrooge would have to give in to.

"Okay. But if you feel even vaguely sick at any

time, you have to go home straightaway. And I'll have to find a way to explain it to Andrea—I'll just say something about you having to come back early from your honeymoon because you got sick. Does that sound okay with you?"

Hailey did a little jig in her chair. "Oh, thank you, Jess. You're a lifesaver. I'm so relieved."

"When are you going to talk to Rob?" Jess asked gently.

"I'm still so mad at him," she said, slumping back in her chair. "In Rome, he was so mean. He was all excited, bouncing around the place, and then I told him I wasn't sure. And he got angry! We couldn't talk without me crying or him yelling. It was a disaster." She managed a small smile. "I threw a cone of gelato at him."

Jess couldn't help but laugh at the image that conjured and the reminder of her own throwing-stuff-at-men episode. Mark should be thankful. Gelato was way messier than cat kibble. "Oh, Hailey."

Hailey laughed, too. "I know. Very mature."

Jess shrugged. "Sometimes you've just gotta find a way to get through to them."

Hailey let out a big sigh. "Yeah." She slumped back in her chair again. "You know what, though? I'm pretty sure I do know what I want. I knew right away. And it's what he wants, too. All I wanted him to do was hear my side, but he wouldn't listen."

"Maybe he's ready to listen now."

"Maybe. But I'm not done being mad at him."

Jess raised her eyebrows. "That's probably not very helpful."

"I know," Hailey said sulkily. "I will talk to him. Promise."

"You'll talk to him soon? Before you make any final decisions?"

"Yes." Hailey played with her untouched tea, dipping her finger into the cup and watching the ripples. "I still love him. Even if he is being an asshole."

"That's kinda the definition of love." Jess thought back over her own life. That was the problem—when you loved someone, you needed to compromise. It was just so hard to tell when that line crossed over from compromise to doormat.

"Yeah, I guess."

There was a beat of silence. And then Jess couldn't help herself.

"What do you think he's been up to? Do you know if he and Sean are still at the house together?"

Yeah, that was pretty smooth. Hopefully Hailey wouldn't pick up on the real reason she was asking the question.

"Probably. I dunno. They might just be hanging out and drinking beers. Or Sean might have left already."

"Oh, right. Yeah, of course," she mumbled.

She'd already wondered if that might be the case. If she might have missed out on her one last night. Was she being an idiot for not calling him? But she figured the fact that he hadn't called her meant one of two things: he was still busy with helping Rob, or he'd moved on and/or no longer wanted anything to do with her. Either way, she couldn't call him, especially not if it was the latter that proved to be the case.

Better she work out now how to get on with her life without Sean Paterson in it.

SEAN WAS PRETTY SURE he was wearing a fuzzy felt hat. On the inside of his skull. It was squeezing his brain, making his eyesight blurred and soaking up every bit of moisture from his mouth and throat.

He smacked his lips loudly, trying to wake himself up.

Exactly how many beers had he and Rob consumed last night? Let alone over the past few days? It didn't bear thinking about—and right now the urgent call of his bladder pressed him to crawl out of the bed in Rob and Hailey's spare room and get to the bathroom.

That taken care of, he wandered through the house. Rob was passed out on his bed, facedown, fully clothed. Sean would have checked on him, but the snoring was loud reassurance that his brother was still breathing, at least.

Sean made his way to the kitchen and filled the kettle with water, wincing at the stupidly loud noise the water made as it splashed against the metal.

The kitchen—the whole house—was a pigsty. It was as if a tornado made up of drunken teenagers had whirled through the place. Beer bottles were scattered everywhere. Empty pizza boxes and plastic take-out containers littered the floor and table. The trash was almost overflowing with pizza crusts and rib bones. Discarded socks seemed to be tossed all over the place, but strangely Sean didn't remember either he or Rob showering or changing clothes in recent memory.

A stack of DVDs teetered dangerously on the TV cabinet. Pillows and a quilt were scattered over the couch—the couch he and Jess had made such excellent use of, he recalled, smiling indulgently at the memory. Sean was pretty sure the quilt was covering up one helluva a red wine stain.

He and Rob had been on an extended, self-indulgent bender.

Jess would be appalled. He couldn't help imaging her expression—she'd screw up her nose and look all cute. Then she'd roll her eyes at him as he made a joke about it, but then she'd smile that little smile....

How long had it been since he'd seen her?

This whole thing with Rob had started with a few beers on Sunday morning in an attempt to cheer up his brother after Hailey had once again refused to take his call.

Then Sean had called Hailey that afternoon and although they'd spoken, she'd still refused to talk to Rob.

After that they'd switched to bourbon, and pretty much everything since then was a blur.

He knew they'd watched all six of the Star Wars movies, loudly critiquing them as they went, and adopted the sleeping habits of vampires—rarely bothering to get out of bed until the afternoon sun was beginning to fade.

And he knew that at least once a day, he'd urged his brother to call Hailey to talk, without any success.

But, if nothing else, Sean felt closer to his brother than he had in years. They hadn't talked about much, hadn't discussed his marital situation or family stuff, but then they never really spent time talking about stuff like that. Just hanging out together was enough. And when Hailey was being so unreasonable, there really wasn't anything else to do. All Sean could do was try to help Rob forget his troubles. For a little while.

Sean's phone buzzed. It took him a few seconds to locate it, but when he did he swore—quietly—at what it showed. Five missed calls from his agent. Several dozen unread emails. God knew how many tweets.

And it was Thursday afternoon. Thursday!

Had he really lost five days to watching movies and drinking beer and generally enabling his brother to wallow in misery?

He had a deadline, for God's sake!

Sean wasn't used to family dramas sucking up his time. He left dealing with all that to Rob. Last year, when his father had had a heart scare, Sean had been in San Diego. Rob had kept him in the loop, but Sean hadn't felt the need to come home. And when his mother had her purse stolen at a café in Richmond, along with a dozen other similar little dramas, Rob had dealt with all that, too.

But now Rob was the one who needed help. He'd insisted their parents not be informed about the situation between him and Hailey, but it was only a matter of time before Stephen and Victoria Paterson became aware that their son and new daughter-in-law were back in town early from their honeymoon. And when that happened Sean didn't know what he'd do. Hand over the situation to them to manage and then quietly disappear? It would definitely be the easiest option, but strangely it didn't sit comfortably with him.

Stephen and Tori Paterson had never been particularly good with subtlety—the kind of subtlety this situation required. Things were always black or white with them—no shades of gray. He hated to think what they might consider a helpful course of action for Rob and Hailey in their current situation. It'd likely involve sitting the two of them down and giving them a stern lecture about the responsibilities that come with marriage. With no understanding of Rob or Hailey's wishes.

They wouldn't stop to ask what Rob and Hailey wanted.

They never had with him.

And he'd showed them.

In fact—maybe it was a good idea to get the indomitable Patersons here. If Rob and Hailey were anything like him, they'd immediately run off to do exactly the opposite of whatever Stephen and Tori advised.

But Rob and Hailey *weren't* like him.

The kettle boiled and Sean tipped the hot water into a mug he'd filled with a couple of heaped spoonfuls of instant coffee. The smell alone was enough to cut through some of the fog in his brain.

He pushed the scattered pillows from the couch to the floor and sank down into the sofa.

Maybe he *should* call his parents. Because clearly Sean's own approach wasn't helping. Continuing to drink themselves under the table each night wasn't going to solve anything. So far it hadn't done much beyond create massive hangovers for them to try to drown each day with several dogs' worth of hair.

He just didn't know what else to do to help his brother. Words were his profession, his life, but he didn't have the right ones here.

He stretched his legs out on the sofa, recalling a much pleasanter moment he'd spent in a similar position. He realized he was smiling at his coffee and shook his head at himself, taking a scalding mouthful of it instead.

Jess.

Jess would know what to do. He'd had that thought pretty much every day, but then something had happened and he'd never gotten around to calling her. Besides, it felt kind of disloyal to heartbroken Rob to sneak off and call a girl. Even if it was for advice. He knew as soon as he heard her voice he'd want more than that. He'd want to go see her, touch her.… But he couldn't desert Rob. Not yet.

Phone sex.

They hadn't done that. That could be *very* fun to explore.

Although, after five days his body wanted more than his own hand for pleasure, even if Jess's voice was on the other end of the line.

Go and see her anyway.

The keen anticipation that shot through him at the very idea was absurd. His belly went fluttery—and it wasn't hangover-related. He missed her. And he couldn't remember the last time he'd ever missed a woman—not even his mother when she'd decided she didn't want to speak to him after he dropped out of university.

Jess had gotten under his skin. Somehow.

What would that mean for when he eventually left town?

Before he could think on it further, there was a sudden, very loud crash from the kitchen—the unmistakable sound of breaking glass.

"Shit!" Sean sat up suddenly, sloshing hot coffee down the front of his T-shirt.

Scrambling from the sofa at the same time he was trying to hold the hot, wet shirt away from his skin, he made his way into the kitchen.

There, standing in the middle of a spreading mess of food scraps from the upturned, open bag of kitchen trash, stood Suzie, a butter-wouldn't-melt expression on her face and half a pizza crust sticking out of her mouth. Her large tail had swept over a stack of beer bottles, and another couple went crashing down as she wagged it in joy at seeing Sean. He could have sworn she smiled at him as she munched up the pizza and licked her lips.

"What the hell was that?"

Rob stumbled into the kitchen, rubbing his face, bringing with him the unmistakable scent of stinky unwashed guy and stale alcohol. Sean figured he probably smelled much the same—only now with spilled coffee added to the mix. And ouch, his stomach hurt—he'd burned himself with the hot drink.

"Suzie," Sean said, gesturing to the mess.

"Oh, Suzie!" Rob scolded. "What have you done?"

"It's kind of funny," Sean said, beginning to laugh. "You can't even really tell how much of the mess she caused, and how much was already there."

"It's not funny," Rob said, but he was shaking his head wryly. "She used to do this when she was a puppy, but she grew out of it." He took a step forward and bent over to talk to Suzie, waggling his finger at her. "Why did you make a mess, huh? Why did you need to get into the trash? What, do we not feed you?"

Suzie wagged her tail harder, looking as if she was being praised rather than scolded. Yet again her tail knocked over a few more beer bottles, sending them crashing into each other like pins at a bowling alley and making Sean wince at the noise.

Rob froze and then his head slowly turned back to Sean. "Uh, *did* we feed her?"

CHAPTER TWELVE

SEAN OPENED HIS mouth to say yes, but then he realized his memory was too fuzzy to be sure of anything. "I…I don't remember. I know I fed her on Tuesday."

"What? You didn't feed her yesterday?" Rob spun around, no mistaking the anger on his face.

Sean put up his hands. "Hell, she's your dog, man."

"You're supposed to be house-sitting. That means taking care of the dog."

Seriously? "What do you mean, friggin' house-sitting? You're home! Your dog, you feed her."

Rob blew out a breath. "I don't believe you. You can't even handle the simplest responsibility."

"Oh, mate, you did not just say that." Sean shook his head in disbelief. Rob, too?

Rob nodded. "Yes, I just did."

"After all I've done for you these past few days."

"Ha! What, pour liquor down my throat and make me watch dumb sci-fi movies? Thanks very much for that."

Suzie started barking, as if she were a participant in the argument.

"I was *distracting* you!"

"You were doing what you always do—when something difficult comes up, you pretend it doesn't exist."

Sean was struck dumb for a moment, unsure how an argument over feeding Suzie had escalated so fast and so savagely. But Rob's criticism made his pulse race and his already-aching head pound. He clenched his fists by his side—he knew his brother was having a rough time, but he couldn't let that stand. "You have no idea what I do. No idea what I manage."

"Yeah, a few comic books and a novel or two. When are you going to grow up and stop living in fantasyland?"

The words came straight from Stephen Paterson, but strangely they were coming out of Rob's mouth. Sean found himself unsteady on his feet, as if Rob had physically wounded him. Usually, he'd spout off a quip, or a self-deprecating joke. But not today. Not now.

"When is the Paterson family going to realize that I *have* grown up? Last year I earned more than you and Dad combined."

Rob waved that away. "It's not about money. It's about responsibility."

"Yeah, and just look at *you* being all responsible. You haven't even tried calling Hailey since Sunday."

"I'm giving her *space!*" Rob yelled, stepping closer to Sean, clenching his hands into fists, too.

"You're an idiot! She doesn't want space, she wants to talk. She's a girl! Girls *always* want to talk. You just don't want to listen. Like everyone else in this family—none of you want to listen!"

"*Such* an expert. Exactly how many relationships have you had that have lasted more than a week? You've got no idea."

All the charitable, fraternal thoughts Sean had been thinking as he'd made coffee vanished in a haze of pent-up anger. Suzie's barking got louder.

"*I've* got no idea? You're hiding out from your wife. You're the one who doesn't want to face what's going on."

Rob scoffed. "This, from the king of not facing stuff. Whenever anyone gets close to you, you run away. Your closest relationship is with Twitter!"

"Yeah, that's right, keep criticizing me. It'll stop you from realizing that your whole life is a fraud."

Rob took another, threatening step closer. "*I'm* a fraud?"

Sean refused to step back, to give up ground. He yelled back into Rob's face, "Of course you are. The good boy. The good Paterson son. Doing everything right. With your fancy suburban house and your cute but ditzy wife. You've even knocked her up and got yourself a head start on producing an heir! Mom and Dad'll be thrilled about that."

Sean didn't see Rob's fist coming. All he felt was the impact of bone on bone as Rob's knuckles connected with his cheekbone. His head reeled. He staggered back from the punch.

At first, he was too stunned to feel anything. *Rob had hit him?*

Then the pain blossomed, so sharp his vision blackened for a moment.

"Oh, shit."

Rob's muttered curse penetrated the fog of pain.

Sean blinked and managed to see his brother run his hands through his hair.

"Shit," Rob said again.

Dizzy, Sean put out a hand to steady himself against the wall.

Suzie growled, but Sean wasn't sure if it was directed at him or at Rob.

"I can't believe…" Rob began. He shook his head and took a couple of steps back to lean on the kitchen counter. As he did, there was the unmistakable noise of broken glass crunching.

"Uh-oh."

Sean's thoughts were fuzzy, and it took him a moment to make the connection. "Did you just stand on broken glass?" he asked, blinking rapidly to clear his vision.

"Uh, yeah. I think so." Rob winced as he lifted his right leg. "Crap, I've sliced my foot."

Suzie stopped growling and trotted over to her master.

"Suzie, no—" Sean called, but it was too late. The golden retriever let out a yelp, and then only made things worse by retreating back over the glass she'd just walked on with an awful half whine, half bark that clearly signaled a dog in pain.

"Suzie!" Rob called, but the dog had apparently decided to get the hell out of Dodge and was limping gingerly to her doggy door. Leaving smeared bloody paw prints on the tiles as she went.

Both men watched Suzie's retreat and then turned to stare at each other, both in shock. Rob's eyes widened. "I hit you," he said, as if he wasn't sure.

"Yeah, you did," Sean said mildly. His anger had completely drained, leaving pain and exhaustion in its place. "Asshole," he added for good measure.

Rob grunted, as if he still didn't quite believe it.

Sean gestured to the bloody paw prints and Rob's foot. "For now we've got bigger problems. Let me go put some shoes on."

He stumbled to the bedroom and located a pair of runners and then headed to the bathroom for the first-aid kit.

In the kitchen, Rob had hoisted himself up on the kitchen counter and was peering closely at his cut foot, which was bleeding profusely.

The floor crunched underfoot as Sean made his way over.

"Suzie knocked the bottles over trying to get to the trash," Sean explained for no reason other than to have something to say about a topic other than their fight.

"I figured. You need to go find her."

Sean shook his head, but then realized that had been a bad idea. Movement exacerbated the pain in his face, which was developing into a bastard of a headache. "Let's get you bandaged up and then we'll get Suzie. I'll probably need your help with her."

"Okay, but make it fast. I'm worried about her." He paused to peer at his foot. "I don't think my cut's that bad."

"Yeah," Sean agreed, although they were both lying. He could tell immediately that Rob's foot would need stitches.

"I already picked out all the glass I could see," Rob said.

"Okay then."

Sean grabbed a gauze bandage from the kit and after putting a cotton pad directly over the cut, wound the bandage tightly to stem the bleeding and keep the pad in place. "That'll do for now," he said, tucking in the end.

"We've got to get Suzie," Rob said, his tone urgent.

Belatedly Sean realized that Rob was going to be of no help. He was barely going to be able to walk, let alone put shoes on and head outside to check on the injured dog.

Sean turned away from Rob and gestured to his back. "Come on, hop on."

"What the hell?"

"You've got to get out of this kitchen and you're not going to be able to put shoes on over that bandage. So hop on."

"You're gonna give me a piggyback ride?"

"Only if you shut up in the next five seconds. Otherwise I'm leaving you here to crawl out over broken glass on your hands and knees."

Rob snorted a laugh, but reached out and wrapped his arms around Sean's neck.

"Ready, one, two, three."

Sean groaned as Rob's full weight landed on him, and he staggered his way over to the carpeted

hallway. Jeez, his brother had really stacked on the
pounds since the last time he'd done this. Twenty
years ago.

Rob was laughing as Sean put him down, but as
soon as his injured foot hit the floor he gasped and
leaned against the wall for support.

"You reckon you can find my car keys and get
yourself out to the car while I get Suzie?" Sean asked,
wondering how he was going to manage a crippled
brother, an injured dog and his own aching face. The
pain was beginning to radiate down his neck, and he
could already feel his eye swelling.

"Yep. Are you gonna be all right to drive?"

Sean nodded, once again instantly regretting moving his head. "Yeah. I should be fine. I stuck mostly
to beer last night while you were on the bourbon,
and I quit a lot earlier than you. I've got a bitch of a
hangover, but I feel sober."

"Okay. You get Suzie."

"Will do. I'll meet you at the car."

"Take it easy with her. She'll probably be in her
kennel. That's where she goes when she gets hurt."

*The bloody dog hurt herself enough to have a reg-
ular retreat.* "Next time you ask me to house-sit,
remind me that Suzie is the Evel Knievel of dogs,
yeah?"

"Sure."

Sean made his way out to the backyard and sure
enough, Suzie was lying in her kennel, licking at her
bloody paws. Sean couldn't see how bad the cut—or
cuts—were, but just given the amount of blood on

the kitchen floor, he knew she definitely needed professional attention.

"Oh, Suzie." Sean crouched down in front of her. "I'm so sorry. I'm so, so sorry you got hurt. It was because we were being irresponsible slobs—and you got hurt."

Suzie gave him a classic puppy-dog-eyed look, which only served to dig the sword of guilt into his chest.

"Come on, sweetheart. Will you let me help you? Shall we go see Jess and get your paws fixed up?"

Sean didn't want Suzie walking—getting dirt and grime in her wounds, and possibly driving deeper any glass that might be stuck in there. But he also wasn't sure if she would let him carry her.

"Come on, girl, let's see how we can do this."

With difficulty, Sean managed to coax Suzie out of the kennel and hoist her into his arms. Thankfully she seemed none too bothered by being carried and she bore his stumbling gait with patience.

It seemed like forever, but just a minute or two later, he was sitting in Dezzie's driver's seat, Rob in the back holding Suzie. He was out of breath and his head pounded. Carrying a sixty-pound dog while battling a black eye and a killer headache wasn't the healthiest of exercise options.

"So, hospital to drop you off and then I'll take Suzie to Jess's?" Sean asked, looking at his brother in the rearview mirror. Rob's focus was on Suzie, stroking her head and murmuring to her.

Rob shook his head. "Nope. Suzie first."

"But—"

"Suzie first," Rob repeated firmly.

Sean was going to argue, but he didn't have the energy. And it wasn't as though Rob was going to bleed to death in the meantime. They could drop Suzie off first.

As he drove toward Jess's clinic, Sean gave himself a quick once-over in the mirror. His hair was a nightmare, his beard untamed. A red welt on the side of his face was rapidly swelling, threatening to close over his eye. He wore jeans and a T-shirt that stank of BO, beer and stale coffee.

Yeah, he was a real peach.

Jess probably couldn't wait for him to walk through her door. He gave another glance to Rob—he didn't look any better.

After they'd been silent for a long while—broken only by Rob's murmured comforts to Suzie—Sean decided to speak up.

"You know, we really should clean up the house," he said. It was Paterson-brother-speak for *truce*.

"Yep. And, after that's done, we could watch that movie *Serenity* again. I liked that." Paterson-brother-speak for *I'm sorry*.

And you need to talk to Hailey, Sean wanted to add. But he couldn't. Rob had been right—Sean either ignored relationship problems or he walked away from them entirely. He had in fact structured his life in order to make that possible. Who was he to give his brother advice on his marriage—or his potential child?

There was no one less qualified in the world.

Jess. Jess would know what to do.

JESS WAS LEANING over Hailey's shoulder to double-check the computer before closing for the day. Andrea appeared and leaned heavily against the wall, giving Jess and Hailey a weak smile as she watched them finish up.

They'd had to put down a beloved cat that afternoon and Andrea was taking it hard. Missy had been fifteen years old with advanced feline senile dementia. Her owner, Mrs. Goldsmith, was a widow in her sixties, and while accepting of Missy's fate, she'd been absolutely distraught. The three of them were feeling the impact of comforting the grieving woman.

"Let's all go get a drink," Jess suggested. She knew if she went home, she'd just crawl into a ball and cry. The cat had been the final straw to a tough few days.

Five days since Sean had called.

She was pretty sure he'd left town, although Hailey was so studiously avoiding talking to Rob, she didn't know for sure.

While Jess felt totally pathetic about the whole thing. What had happened to the idea that this fling thing was going to be empowering? Confidence building? Make her feel like facing the dating world?

All she felt like facing was a large block of chocolate and a bottle of chardonnay.

But she wouldn't let herself wallow. Every day she

put on her professional mask and got on with life. She'd done it before. She would do it again.

Andrea shook her head. "Thanks, but I think I just want to go home and have a cry and hug my boyfriend."

Jess couldn't blame her. If it was an option open to her, she'd definitely choose it. "Sounds like a good idea."

"I'm up for a drink," Hailey said, looking up from the computer. Then her face fell as she clearly remembered alcohol was off-limits. "Oh, but..."

"It's okay," Jess said quickly. "Maybe we all just need an early night. Andrea, why don't you head home? I'll finish up here and Hailey's nearly done anyway."

Andrea made a weak protest, but minutes later she'd collected her purse and was gone.

"Poor girl," Hailey said sympathetically.

Jess nodded in agreement. "She took that one hard."

"I still remember that King Charles spaniel in my first week working here, the puppy that had been hit by a car." Hailey's eyes teared up at the memory.

"They're all sad." And they were. But after ten years as a vet, Jess had developed a way of distancing herself. If she hadn't, she would have been locked up in a mental hospital long ago. Unfortunately, even in her little practice, putting down beloved pets happened more often than she would like.

Hailey spun around in the chair as she turned off the computer. "Okay, I'm done."

"It's been taking me an hour to get that right each night," Jess grumbled.

Hailey grinned. "Aren't you glad to have me back, boss?"

Jess rolled her eyes but she was smiling. "Yeah, it's good to have you back."

Crash!

Both Jess and Hailey jumped as the front door opened and hit the wall with a bang, the bell clattering violently and then crunching to silence as it was crushed.

A bearded wild man, carrying a bloody golden retriever, leaned heavily against the door, panting with exertion.

Jess took an instinctive step back, prepared to reach for the phone and call the police when recognition hit.

"Sean?"

Beside her, Hailey sucked in a shocked breath. "Suzie?"

Another wildly ungroomed man appeared in the doorway, hopping on one foot. He froze as he looked over at the women.

"Hailey?" he said.

"Rob?" Hailey echoed.

There was a beat of silence as all four people took in the situation.

"Now that we all know each other, can I put the dog down somewhere?" Sean huffed. He shifted her in his arms and Suzie whimpered. "She's not exactly a lightweight."

Jess was the first to unfreeze, the sound of an animal in pain registered immediately and her professional instincts kicked in. "Through here," she said, leading the way back into the clinical area.

Sean followed, breathing heavily, but when he reached the stainless steel bench, he took his time in setting Suzie down with gentle care.

"There you are, girl. Jess will make you all better now." He bent down to press his cheek against Suzie's.

"What happened?" Jess asked, reaching for cotton swabs to clean away some of the blood and find out exactly what kind of injury she was dealing with.

Hailey and Rob appeared in the room, Rob still hopping on one foot, while Hailey rushed to Suzie's side, pushing Sean roughly out of the way.

"She stepped on some glass," Sean said, staggering back.

"It was an accident," Rob added.

"My poor Suzie," Hailey said, shooting evil looks at both Sean and Rob. Thankfully she then went into professional mode, helping Jess with keeping Suzie calm and cleaning away the blood. Jess carefully examined Suzie's paws, checking them for cuts. There were two, but thankfully the amount of blood had been deceptive—neither were terribly deep.

"We need to examine them to make sure there isn't any glass still in there," Jess said softly.

Hailey nodded.

By the time they had checked out the wounds, put in a couple of staples and administered an anti-inflammatory injection for the pain, Suzie was licking Hailey's face.

"I know, baby, I missed you, too," Hailey crooned.

Jess turned to the untamed savages who'd brought Suzie in. The two men stood side by side against the wall like naughty children outside the school principal's office. Both of them were a mess and Jess could smell them even from a distance. They looked like they'd been sleeping in the wilderness for days after somehow bathing themselves in beer.

Sean's beard was impressive given he'd only had five days to grow it. His hair was flat and greasy. A large stain spread across the front of his T-shirt, and his left eye was beginning to swell shut.

Drop-dead gorgeous Sean was nowhere to be seen. People would actively cross the street to avoid looking at this deadbeat version of him.

And yet a stupid little spark inside her bounced around just at the simple joy of seeing him.

He hadn't left town and forgotten her.

But he definitely had some explaining to do.

"What on earth have you been doing?" she asked.

"I cut my foot," Rob said, when Sean stayed irritatingly silent.

"Are you okay?" Hailey asked, leaving Suzie's side to go to her husband. "Did you hurt it rescuing Suzie?"

Rob scratched his beard. "Ah, well—"

"Yep," Sean broke in. "It's my fault. I left out beer bottles that got smashed and Suzie walked in. Rob cut his foot getting her out of the glass."

Rob shot his brother a quick look that Jess caught. She didn't know what had really happened, but that clearly wasn't it.

"What happened to your face?" Hailey asked Sean.

"Rob hit me for letting Suzie get hurt." Sean shrugged. "I deserved it."

Hailey's frown softened when she looked at Rob.

"You really did that?"

Rob shrugged and ducked his head, looking embarrassed.

"A bit extreme, don't you think?" she chastised him, but her tone was soft and indulgent.

"Yeah," Rob agreed.

Jess stepped forward. "What about your foot? Do we need to look at it?"

"I'm okay," Rob mumbled.

"It needs stitches," Sean said.

"Sit down over here," Hailey ordered.

Rob meekly obeyed and Hailey knelt in front of him, lifting his foot into her arms and unwrapping the clumsy bandage from around it.

"Jess, what do you think?" Hailey asked as she examined the sole of Rob's foot.

Jess didn't even need to get close—the blood dripping on the floor was enough for her to know he needed medical attention. "Sean's right. He needs to go to the hospital."

Rob made a few muttered protests, but Hailey put a finger to his lips.

"Just shut up and let me look after you, okay?" she said.

Rob looked up at her and his eyes were shiny with tears—nothing to do with the pain of his injury, Jess was sure.

He blinked hard. "Okay."

Hailey retied the bandage and helped Rob stand. "Jess, can you take care of Suzie while I take Rob to the emergency room?"

"Sure. I'll take her home with me. She can stay overnight if that's easiest."

"Thank you."

Hailey and Rob both bent over Suzie, who was patiently lying on the exam table. She looked not only relaxed now, but a little bored with all the drama. Her expression brightened as her two owners leaned over to hug and pet her.

"Oh, Suzie, you silly thing," Hailey said.

"Suzie," Rob said gruffly, ruffling her fur with long strokes.

"I love you so much," Hailey said. There was a pause and Hailey looked across the table at Rob—this time her eyes were bright with tears. "I really do."

"I love you, too," Rob said, and although he continued to pat the dog, his eyes were on his wife, looking at her with such longing and passion it was almost a palpable force in the room.

Hailey gave a quick nod and sniffed loudly. "It's all going to be okay, you know."

"Yeah?"

"Yeah. I was just mad at you because you wouldn't listen."

"I'll listen now."

"Good. Because we'll probably have a long wait at the emergency room."

"Lots of listening time, then."

"Yes."

Jess felt a lump in her throat and she swallowed hard. The two young newlyweds still had a lot of things to talk about, but she was immensely relieved that they'd begun the process of working things through.

"Okay, let's go get you stitched up," Hailey said, going around the table to Rob. "Can you walk?"

"I might need to lean on you.…"

Rob put his arm around Hailey's shoulder.

Hailey winced. "Ew, you stink!"

"Sorry," Rob muttered.

They took a couple of hobbling steps together.

Sean stepped away from where he was leaning against the wall—looking for all the world as if he needed it to stand upright. In fact, as he straightened, he stumbled over his own feet, righting himself just in time.

"I can help," he offered. "I'll help you get out to the—"

Hailey held up a hand to cut him off. "I think you've done more than enough. Please don't be at my home when we get there after Rob's stitched up."

Sean shut his mouth with an audible click and slumped back against the wall, nodding obediently.

Rob stilled and gaped at Hailey. "You're…you're coming home?"

Hailey gave an impatient snort. "Well, someone's got to keep you out of trouble."

As Rob and Hailey walked past, Rob reached out an arm to squeeze Sean's shoulder. Sean gave him a half grin, half grimace and a wink, then winced as he clearly was reminded of his injured face.

Once the newlyweds had hop-walked out of the surgery, Jess jumped into action. She had no idea what to do with the turmoil inside her—*Hug Sean? Slap him? Interrogate him?*—so instead she slipped on her comfortable, professional mask. It had protected her all week.

"Now it's your turn," she said. She found a cold pack and cracked it to activate it. "Here, put this on your face."

Sean accepted the pack and held it to his cheekbone gingerly. "Thanks."

She shook her head at him. "I have no idea what's been going on, but..." She gestured to him from top to toe, words failing her.

"It's probably better that you don't," Sean mumbled.

"Did you get cut?"

Sean shook his head, then stilled it immediately with a gasp of pain. "Ow! I have to remember not to keep doing that."

"Let me look."

Sean lowered the ice pack and Jess gently felt along the line of his cheekbone and eye socket.

"I'm not a people doctor, but I'm pretty sure nothing's broken."

"Nothing's broken," Sean confirmed. "It wasn't hard enough for that. It's just gonna be a helluva bruise."

She stared at him for a moment. "Should I ask?"

"Probably not. Not now, anyway. I need to ask a favor."

Jess raised an eyebrow. *A favor?* Was he really in the position to ask for that? She wasn't sure whether to be annoyed, amused, disgusted or disapproving. This wasn't anything like the way she'd imagined things would be if and when she saw Sean again. Of all the emotions roiling inside her one was beginning to edge out the others: *anger.* She was angry with him for ignoring her for five days—especially given it looked like he'd spent that time regressing to his university days.

And yet...to her dismay, she still wanted him. The desire he aroused in her was still there—even though he looked and smelled like a derelict.

You're a hopeless case, Jess.

Sean's puppy-dog smile—the one he called on when he needed people to do things for him—was lopsided behind the ice pack. Jess stifled the hysterical urge to laugh.

"Can we go to Rob and Hailey's and do a quick cleanup before they get back from the hospital?"

"What?"

"It just...it would go better for Rob if we cleaned up a little before they get there. It's kind of a mess. And, to be honest, that's an understatement."

"That's your biggest concern right now?"

"Um, yeah. Why?"

Did he really need her to tell him?

There were so many things they had to clear up. For a start, why hadn't she heard from him in five days? And why had Rob hit him? Plus, she wanted to tell him what had happened with Mark—which was a weird thing to want to share with her temporary lover, she realized, but she did.

"What's up?" Sean asked, looking genuinely confused.

Doubt seized her. Was it her expectations that were the problem here?

Sean didn't want to deal with her anger as a neglected girlfriend.

She was a fling, a fun-time gal, as far as he was concerned. And here she was doing the Jess thing and getting all serious about it. At this moment all he needed was a friend who could help him out of a mess he'd made. Literally.

So the past five days had been pretty hellish. But the preceding weeks had been, well, glorious. Maybe she owed him this one last favor. She could help him clean up, and then they could say a proper goodbye. At least the whole thing would be finalized, wrapped up neatly. That would be better than the uncertainty she'd been living with.

She nodded. "Okay, let's get going."

Jess didn't bother doing a full cleanup of the surgery, figuring she could do the rest in the morning, and so, a few moments later, they were ready to leave.

"Dezzie's out the front," Sean said.

"And that's where she'll stay," Jess said firmly. "We're taking my car."

"But—"

It only took a look to silence him.

The drive to Rob and Hailey's was quiet. Suzie shifted around in the backseat more than Jess would have liked, but hopefully her wounds had begun to seal. She'd check them again when they got to her place.

When she stepped inside the house, her nose wrinkled. "What on earth have you guys been doing?"

"You're so cute when you do that," he said as he briefly touched his forefinger to her nose.

She arched an eyebrow. His flirting had definitely lost a lot of its charm coming from his bruised and disheveled state. Not to mention the influence of her own conflicted feelings. "Seriously?"

Sean had the grace to look a little sheepish. "Sorry. If we just get rid of the garbage, that'll make a big difference."

He headed for the kitchen and Jess heard the sound of glass crunching underfoot. She automatically restrained Suzie—the last thing they needed was for the gorgeous but not-all-that-bright dog to injure herself again.

"In here," she commanded Suzie, showing her into Rob and Hailey's bedroom. "Stay." She closed the door.

She found Sean in the kitchen, pulling out a roll of garbage bags.

"If you tackle the living room, I'll—"

Jess took the roll of plastic from him. "You'll go have a shower."

"No, I—"

She held up a hand. "Not an option, Sean. You stink. It's gross. Go shower. Then come help me."

Sean didn't bother arguing, just shuffled out of the kitchen like a dog with its tail between its legs.

Jess looked around at the devastation of the usually pristine home. Sean was wrong—clearing out the garbage was merely the first step in the huge cleaning effort that would be required to get this place even close to seemly, let alone back to Hailey's usual exacting standards.

But they had to start somewhere. And Sean was right about one thing—when Hailey and Rob got back from the hospital they needed to talk about their future, not fight over housekeeping.

First she opened all the windows to let out the stale male funk that had seeped into every crevice. And then she started on the garbage.

By the time she was carefully vacuuming the kitchen floor, Sean reappeared in clean clothes, with wet hair and smelling fresh. He still looked a sight, his face beginning to bloom colors, but it didn't look as if his eye was going to swell completely shut—although it was very puffy. He hadn't shaved, either, but she liked the beard on him.

"Wow," he said, looking around at the order she'd already managed to restore.

"You can take those out to the trash," Jess said,

pointing to the garbage bags she'd tied up by the back door.

"Aye-aye."

Reasonably sure she'd gotten all the broken glass from the floor, Jess put away the vacuum and headed to Rob and Hailey's bedroom to check on Suzie. The dog had curled up on the bed, and lifted her head and wagged her tail when Jess appeared.

"How're you doing, girl?" Jess asked softly. "Have you licked those bandages off yet? Are we going to have to get you one of those plastic collars that you love so much?" She checked Suzie's paws, pleased to find the bandages still in place. "Good girl. All those accidents have got you used to these things, haven't they?"

The room was stuffy and smelled of stale beer. She looked at the messy sheets.

If Hailey and Rob came home and had managed to reconcile...well, they might appreciate clean sheets.

"Up you hop," she told Suzie.

Sean appeared just as she was finishing stripping the bed.

"Find me a set of clean bedsheets, will you?" she asked.

She and Sean remade the bed in surprisingly companionable silence and then after hitting each room in the house with a generous spray of air freshener, they closed the windows and headed for the door— Suzie in tow.

"You're a miracle worker," Sean said.

Jess nodded, pleased with the changes they'd

wrought in such a short time. "It's not bad. Of course, we didn't do the bathrooms, and everything still needs a good airing out, but it's a start."

"You're taking Suzie with you?" Sean asked.

This is it.

Jess steeled herself. Whatever happened next, she wanted to be able to look back on it with a sense of pride and satisfaction, knowing she'd handled things appropriately.

"Yes, I'm going to take her."

"Can…can I come, too?" He was tentative, hesitant—not at all the Sean she'd grown used to.

He didn't call you for five days, a little voice reminded her.

He had no obligation to call you, either, another voice said. *Besides, isn't this what you wanted? One last night? A night to say farewell?*

She gave him a measured look up and down. "Well, you do smell better now."

"I might have a concussion," he said very seriously but with that mischievous glint in his eye. "I'll need to be monitored."

She rolled her eyes, but mostly to cover the effect that mischievous look had on her. Was she kidding herself? Could she really have one last hurrah with Sean and be okay with it…and then move on cleanly?

On the other hand, could she bring herself to turn him down and end things right here, right now?

It wasn't even a decision.

"All right. Come on. Out, out." She waved both
Sean and Suzie out the door, making sure it locked
behind her.

CHAPTER THIRTEEN

ON THE DRIVE to her place, Sean closed his eyes but Jess could tell he wasn't asleep. He still clutched the no doubt warm-by-now ice pack to his face.

When they arrived home, he diligently helped her get Suzie settled into Rocco's old bed and kept the dog still while Jess double-checked her paws.

"Is she going to be okay?" Sean asked.

"She'll be fine."

"I feel so bad." He grasped Suzie's head in both hands. "I'm so sorry, Suzie. I'm really, really sorry."

"What actually happened?" Jess asked.

"She knocked over some beer bottles with her tail and they smashed," he said, his attention still on the dog, scratching her behind the ears. "Then she walked on the glass. She was on her way to comfort Rob after *he* walked on the glass. It was…dumb."

"And why did Rob hit you?" Jess couldn't contain her curiosity.

He looked away. "Nothing important. A brother thing. A misunderstanding," he mumbled. "It was just…everything. It got out of hand."

"You can say that again." Jess got to her feet and headed to the kitchen to wash her hands. "As a doctor,

I probably wouldn't recommend this, but I'm going to have a glass of wine—do you want one?"

A shudder went through Sean's body and he groaned. "No. No more alcohol until at least Christmas."

"Right."

Jess poured herself a glass of white wine and grabbed a container of homemade vegetable soup from the freezer and popped it in the microwave to defrost. She hadn't eaten, and from the trash she'd picked up at Rob and Hailey's, it seemed Sean likely hadn't eaten anything even vaguely nutritious for several days.

Then she leaned against the kitchen counter to take a moment to gather her thoughts.

Now that all the dramas with Rob and Hailey and Suzie were done—for now anyway—she needed a moment to work out how she wanted to handle this situation with Sean.

Having him in her home again after believing that he might have left town felt strange—parallel universe strange. She was definitely still angry with him, but wasn't sure she had the right to be. Besides, if this was going to be their last night together, wouldn't she prefer to remember it as a pleasant one? Perhaps it was better to just sweep everything under the rug and pretend it didn't exist. This wasn't a *real* relationship. It wasn't as if they needed to have things sorted out.

Yes. That's how she'd play it.

Shutting away strong feelings was nothing new to her. Compartmentalizing emotions like anger and longing and betrayal and putting them away in a box at the back of her mind was an old trick she'd mastered years ago.

Sucking in a deep breath, Jess pushed herself off the counter and began preparing their meal. "Would you like something to eat?" she called out.

"Anything but pizza or ribs," Sean called back.

"Homemade veggie soup sound good to you?"

"Yes-s-s-s. Vitamins. Please," he groaned, confirming her suspicions about his diet these past few days.

Jess served up the soup and some fresh bread and they ate silently, Sean scarfing down his food and going back for seconds.

He leaned back in his chair and stifled a burp. "Thank you. You're a lifesaver."

"You're welcome."

"I don't suppose you could save my life a little further and find me some painkillers?"

"Sure."

Jess produced some pills and a replacement ice pack made out of a package of frozen peas wrapped in a towel. "Here. It's worth continuing icing it, to help with the swelling."

Sean took both the pills and the cold pack gratefully and grabbed Jess's hand as she turned to walk away, bringing it to his mouth to press his lips to her knuckles. He looked up at her and smiled a twisted smile from behind the pack of peas. "You are too good to be true."

"I know," she said simply. And that was her problem. Because what was happening *wasn't* true. Wasn't honest. She wanted to yell at Sean, she wanted him to apologize for hurting her, the way he'd apologized to Suzie.

If she thought throwing kibble at Mark was a turning point, then she was wrong. She hadn't really learned anything.

Was she destined to never be able to have a healthy relationship? One where she knew how to compromise without losing her identity in the process? One where she came first in the eyes of her significant other? Where she didn't play second fiddle to someone, or something else—whether it was a mistress, a vampire-wannabe fan, or a dirty house?

The thought brought a surprising sting of tears to her eyes. She tried to turn away, and free herself from Sean's grasp.

"What's wrong?" he asked, pulling on her hand before she could get away.

"Nothing." She plastered a smile on her face. There was no point getting into all that when he most likely wasn't even going to be around tomorrow.

"You sure?"

"Looking at your face is making my eyes water in sympathy."

Lame excuse, but Sean seemed to go with it.

He removed the cold pack and did an exaggerated preen. "I think it makes me look tough."

She managed a short laugh. "I wouldn't go making it a permanent feature. You're too pretty. Your fans wouldn't like it."

"I don't care what my fans think."

She couldn't help her scoffing noise at that. "Sean, let's not make this night a total lie." The words were out before she could call them back.

"What do you mean by that?"

"Nothing. Forget it."

"No." He pushed back his chair and stood up, standing face-to-face with her. "What's going on?"

Jess had taken off her shoes and in bare feet she had to look up at him. His green—and bloodshot—eyes were troubled.

"I just..." Should she give in to the impulse to share her confused mess of thoughts?

"I'm sorry I'm such a doofus," he said.

"Huh?" Jess's thoughts were so focused on her own turmoil she didn't think to wonder what might be going on inside Sean.

"I've made a mess of your night. Did you have plans?"

Plans? Yeah, right. "It's okay."

"But it's not. What's going on in that brain of yours, Jess?"

"It doesn't matter, really, does it?"

"Of course it does."

She shook her head. "No, Sean, it doesn't. Our time together is almost over, now that Rob and Hailey are back, and none of it makes any difference."

He was silent for a moment. Then he raised his hand to her face and stroked her cheek with his thumb. "I missed you," he said.

No, Jess silently pleaded. *Don't go getting sweet*

and romantic on me. The only way she could cope with this was to focus on getting her one last night. The night she deserved.

Through pure force of will, she arranged her face in what she hoped was a seductive look.

"You missed me? Just how much?" As she spoke, she traced her hand over his hip to the front of his jeans, pressing her palm against him there.

Sean's breath caught. "Oh, a lot, baby. A lot."

He covered her hand with his own, pressing more firmly.

Then, abruptly, his hand lifted and he stepped away from her touch.

SEAN DREW A deep breath and let it out slowly. The painkillers had helped, but his head still pounded. The soup had settled his stomach somewhat, but it still swayed inside him from time to time like a child's balloon buffeted by a gentle breeze.

Despite his physical discomfort, his desire for Jess was instantly fanned to a hot ache at the feel of her hand on him.

And the realization of exactly how much he'd missed her these past few days echoed inside him. He'd missed her every single day, and yet he'd made no attempt to call her or see her.

Rob had accused him of running from every emotional entanglement he'd ever found himself in. Of ignoring things when they got deep or difficult.

He'd accused Rob of hiding from the situation with Hailey, and Rob had fired the accusation right back.

Perhaps it was a Paterson family trait. As a child, Sean had absolutely no memories of his parents arguing. However he did remember steely silences and extended absences—Tori at the tennis club for the weekend, Stephen at the golf club.

When his parents had reacted so strongly to his dropping out of university, to his decision to write and draw comics instead of analyze spreadsheets, his immediate reaction had been to run away. He'd left home and only ever came back when it was easier to give in than fight. Like the wedding.

When he and Jess had driven home from the convention on the weekend, he'd been aware of just how much her presence that day had meant to him. He'd also been aware of how quickly he'd grown to appreciate her company. How comfortable he was with her.

Then there was how much he wanted—needed— her approval, her support, her encouragement.

It was too much.

He *shouldn't* need her. He had his agent; he had Rob. He had *Twitter*.

His stomach did a loop, but this time it had little to do with his hangover.

Could it be true? Had he been hiding from Jess just as much as Rob had been hiding from Hailey?

Jess was standing there, looking at him. Her expression was fragile; he could tell he'd hurt her feelings by rejecting her touch. There was a pain in his chest from causing that hurt. That was the last thing he wanted to do. She was so kind, so sweet, so caring. She didn't understand the mess that was him—a mess that was way more difficult to clean up than a few broken bottles and some scattered pizza boxes.

"I've got so much going on in my life," he began. He wasn't sure exactly what he was trying to say.

Jess bit her lip. "I know."

"We said this thing between us was only going to be until Rob and Hailey got back."

"Yes, we did."

"And they're back."

"Yes, they are."

She kept agreeing with him. He wanted her to say something else—tell him she wanted to extend the deadline, tell him she wanted more.

But she didn't.

Maybe he should leave. He could find a hotel room for the night.

He cleared his throat. "Right. I guess that's..." He couldn't bring himself to say the words. He'd tried a permanent relationship before. It hadn't worked—he hadn't been able to commit. He knew he couldn't risk hurting Jess that way.

Jess's expression shifted. She stepped closer.

"Don't think," she said, stroking her other hand across his bearded cheek.

He managed a smile, remembering how he'd said similar things to her in the past. "I thought that was my line?"

Her fingers threaded through his hair. "Not to-night."

"So, looks like it's my turn for a freak-out." It was a joke, but saying it made him feel incredibly vulnerable. She could have no idea of the turmoil inside him right now, but he felt stripped bare.

She gave him a searching look. "Oh, does the great Sean Paterson do freak-outs?" Her tone was light, but there was a thread of genuine curiosity there.

"Not in recent memory," he said. And maybe that was his problem. Rob was right—he'd never had to learn how to manage a relationship once it got past the superficial stuff. Whenever it had, he disappeared. He always had a good reason—a convention in the U.S., a book deadline, a new project to research. He always made sure he had an exit clause built in to all his relationships. Just like he had with Jess.

"You've had a big week," she murmured, giving him an excuse.

"Yeah."

Her fingers continued to stroke his hair and she stood tantalizingly close. Her smell of sweet citrus tempted him, the warmth of her body a seductive tease.

What he really wanted, if he was honest with himself—and at this point he wasn't entirely sure that he could be—was to wrap her in his arms and tumble them both to the sofa. And he wanted Jess to continue stroking his hair, and murmuring comforting things in his ear until they fell asleep, tangled together. He was tired. And confused. And parts of his body really hurt.

"Oh, Jess," he began.

"What?"

How could he tell her how he was feeling when he didn't even understand it himself?

"I wish I was different. I wish I could..." *Be the kind of man you deserve.*

But that wasn't what their agreement had been about. He'd said, *Let's have some fun.* And that's what he'd delivered. That was what he needed to continue to deliver.

He couldn't expect to change the terms so late in the game. Especially not now that Rob and Hailey were back and things were at an end.

Besides, how hard was it to make love to a beautiful woman? Jess desired him and he wanted her. He might have a black eye and the hangover from hell, but he'd survived worse.

He was going to give Jess—and himself—one last night to remember.

SEAN'S EXPRESSION DARKENED as he slid one hand around her waist. But this time the darkness wasn't troubling. It was the devilish, wicked look that Jess recalled in her steamiest dreams. The look of the man who'd seduced her at his brother's wedding with a glass of champagne, a clumsy dance and the promise of a ride in his hotted-up car.

A teenager in a grown-up's body.

And a complex, talented, hardworking adult.

Sean was nothing if not full of contradictions.

"So," he began, tightening his hold around her. "How have you been surviving without me?"

It was a loaded question for her, but Jess knew now

wasn't the time. There would never *be* a time. She put on her best flirting tone.

"I drank a lot of wine and I ran out of batteries."

Sean laughed. "Good girl."

"Always."

He arched an eyebrow. "You look like you could use some kissing, though. Those battery-operated things aren't that good at that, are they?"

Much more the confident, seductive Sean she'd grown to love.

She froze. The word echoed inside her mind.

Love.

Her face must have revealed the crack in her carefully plastered facade as Sean leaned in to study her, taking her chin in his fingers.

"No. Tell me it isn't your turn to freak out now."

Jess shook her head. Not a freak-out. Not really.

Of course she loved him. In some ways she'd known that for a while now. That was what this past week of missing him had been all about. She hadn't just missed the revival of her social life—and her sex life. She'd missed his company. His smell. His overly confident driving. The occasional sparkle of gold in those green eyes. The way one side of his mouth could twitch upward and have the same effect on her as a beaming smile from anybody else.

One last night, she reminded herself. That was what this was.

"I'm fine." She smiled. "But I'd be finer if you'd get those jeans off."

"Oh. It's like that, is it?"

Jess pushed away her realization. It was going to hurt, later. *Really, really hurt.* But for now, she had one more night with Sean. And it was going to be the last hurrah she'd dreamed of, back when this had been just a temporary affair.

She placed both hands flat on his chest and pushed him toward the wall behind them. "It can be," she said teasingly.

Sean paused for a moment, then cocked his head with a mischievous expression dancing in his eyes— only spoiled marginally by the left one being puffy and bloodshot.

Oh, she would miss that grin so much.

"I don't think so," he said. He spun her around and pressed her hard against the wall, trapping her with his body. "I much prefer it like this."

The growing ridge of him in his jeans pressed against her belly as he kissed her. He wasn't tentatively seducing her, like he had back in the car those weeks ago after the wedding. And he wasn't teasing her with gentle touches as he often liked to do, either.

No, this time his kiss demanded. And Jess responded, helpless to do anything but.

She groaned as he leaned more heavily into her, pressing her against the wall, searching her mouth with his tongue. Her hands were trapped between them, while his were pressed against the wall beside her head. The need to touch him warred with the need to simply surrender to his claiming.

Sean took the choice from her, tearing his mouth

from hers to utter, "Upstairs," in a ragged, breath-less voice.

Jess nodded, and moments later they were in her bedroom.

She bent over the bed to pull back the quilt. "Let me—" she began. Her words were cut off as her breath was pushed out of her. Sean's body bracketed her, pressing her facedown on the bed.

He swept her hair to one side and pressed an open-mouthed kiss to the nape of her neck, his hips mov-ing sensually against hers, leaving her in no doubt as to the power of his desire.

She murmured his name as he captured her ear-lobe in his mouth, his breath hot and loud.

"Jess," he whispered, his lips a tickling caress against her ear. "God help me. I can't get enough of you, Jess."

Once again her hands were trapped and she burned with the need to touch him, to feel her skin against his, to run her fingers across his body.

She struggled beneath him. "Let me up," she said.

He laughed. "I don't think so."

"Sean."

"Oh, I love it when you use your schoolteacher voice. Do it again."

Jess made a tsking noise, but she felt a bubble of laughter in her throat. She loved his playfulness, too.

"You're rolling your eyes at me, aren't you?" he said. "I can't see it, but I bet you are."

"Se-an," she said again, this time deliberately play-ing up the scolding tone.

He lowered his mouth to her ear again. "You make me so hot, Miss Alexander."

At that, Jess could no longer keep up the pretense of the role-playing and she simply groaned.

"God, I love it when you make that noise," he said.

His lips marked a trail down her neck to where her shirt covered her. She felt him grab the collar between his teeth and growl, shaking his head from side to side like a dog with a bone.

This time she did laugh. "One of the benefits of letting me up would be that I would be able to take my shirt off."

"I guess," he said. "Although I do like having you under me like this."

"But how much better would it be if we were both naked?"

There was a moment of stillness and then a chill of cold air as he pounced from her.

"Good thinking. Come on, hurry up."

Jess rolled over and watched as Sean stood and stripped off his sweatshirt, ruffling his hair, and began to work on the fastening of his jeans.

"Whoa," she said.

Each time they'd made love there'd been an element of franticness about it. Not just from Sean, but from her as well—desperate to touch him, to taste him, to feel him inside her. Tonight Jess was going to take her time.

Sean stilled, his fingers about to undo his zipper, and gave her a curious look. "Whoa?" he echoed.

"Yeah, whoa." Jess pushed herself up until she sat

on the edge of the bed, facing him. "Come here." She began slowly unbuttoning her shirt.

His eyes widened and his mouth twitched. "Oh, really?"

"Yes, really." She shrugged the shirt off her shoulders, revealing her plain cotton bra. It could have been the finest silk for the look of hunger that flared in Sean's eyes.

She undid her trousers and lifted her bottom to peel them off, before sitting down on the edge of the bed again, opening her legs and gesturing for him to stand between them.

He opened his mouth, but for once no smart-aleck comment came out of it. Instead he stepped over to stand in front of her, bottom lip caught under his front teeth.

Jess started by taking his hands in hers. She squeezed them before she let go and ran her fingers up the outsides of his arms. His crisp hair and smooth skin was a sensual delight.

She traced the diagonal slash of his biceps before working her way to his shoulders, pressing a firm touch along the ridge of his collarbone.

When her fingers dipped to run down the center of his chest, Sean sucked in a harsh breath.

"Are you sure you know what you're doing, Miss Alexander?" he said.

"Trust me."

His stomach was flat and a dusting of dark hair led down from his navel. Above it, a streak of his skin was bright pink.

"What did you do to yourself?" she asked, skimming her fingertips gently over the hot skin.

"Burned myself with a coffee," he said. "It hasn't been a good day."

"Poor baby." Jess pressed a gentle kiss to his belly. "Let's see if we can make it all better."

He put a hand on her shoulder to steady himself as she undid his zipper, pushed his jeans down his thighs and freed him from his boxer briefs.

She leaned forward. He was hot and hard against her tongue, and he tasted of soap and defiantly aroused male.

"Jess," he groaned. His free hand tangled in her hair, pulling gently.

Jess looked up and met his eyes, the gold completely gone, the mossy green dark and captivating. Jess soaked in the taste and feel of him with her mouth and hands—his hot skin, hard thighs and panting breaths that made his entire body quiver.

A few moments later he pulled away and, after quickly ridding himself of his jeans and briefs, was pressing her back on the bed, climbing over her, kissing her with all the heat and passion she could desire. His clever hands reached behind her to undo her bra and the press of her aching breasts against his hard chest forced another groan from her.

"I love that," he said, rising up on his elbows to look down at her.

"So you've said."

He shook his head gently. "Your noises, yes. But

I meant this." He lowered just enough to brush his chest against her hardened nipples. "I love it when we're naked together. Our skin touching."

Jess wished he'd stop saying things like that.

"Me, too," she whispered. If her words caught a little he didn't notice, intent on fastening his lips around her puckered nipple and sucking hard.

She arched into him, another moan torn from her as Sean's fingers stroked down her belly and between her legs to rid her of her underwear. She knew he'd find her ready for him—it never took much more than a glance and that twitching grin of his—no matter what the circumstances or public nature of their environment. On the occasions that he'd winked at her she'd practically swooned.

"Sean, please." She squirmed under his knowing touch as he wrought exactly the response he wanted from her.

He swallowed her pleas with another mind-blowing kiss, his lips and tongue demanding a response just as his fingers were.

Jess managed to twist her head away long enough to make her own demand.

"Now. Please. Now."

He reached for a condom and once he had it out of the package, Jess took it from him in trembling fingers and rolled it over his length, taking the opportunity to measure him in her fist. He hissed at her touch, putting a hand over hers to halt her.

"Oh, baby, I love you touching me. But I'm going go over the edge if I don't get inside you soon."

"Yes."

And then he was over her, nudging inside her before filling her with one expert thrust.

The noises of pleasure and need that they both made were captured in another searing kiss, Sean's tongue moving in her mouth with the same rhythm as his body stroked into hers.

Jess ran her hands over his hot, damp back, curving around his muscled buttocks, pulling him into her, harder, deeper.

He pushed himself up onto his hands, giving him more power, and Jess gasped as he stroked at just the right angle inside her.

She was desperate to call out her newly realized love, to tell him she'd fallen for him in exactly the way she wasn't supposed to, to make him understand just how much this meant. The temptation to confess was almost overwhelming; the ache of knowing she couldn't was a sharp pain in her chest.

This was her final night, her chance to say goodbye. It was supposed to have been a night that would wrap everything neatly in a bow, not leave her devastated by loss.

After tonight, Sean would walk out of her life and their time together would be over.

Oh, God, she wanted to tell him so much.

Instead she gasped his name as he drove her over the edge, the peak of pleasure going on and on until she thought she might die from it.

Then, with a growl that would have been appropriate from one of the werewolf creatures in his books, Sean came, his body trembling and his breath rasping.

He called her name and then collapsed in her arms.

CHAPTER FOURTEEN

THE ELECTRONIC BEEPING was incredibly annoying. And it wouldn't stop.

Jess opened one eye.

It was still dark and the noise definitely wasn't her alarm.

Beside her, Sean slept heavily, his breathing slow and even, clearly not at all bothered by the sound.

He was still here?

They must have both fallen asleep after their love-making. That hadn't been Jess's intention—she didn't want a painful farewell breakfast. But her own exhaustion and the painkillers Sean had taken were likely to blame.

The beeping stopped and the sudden silence was almost deafening.

But then the beeping started again a moment later.

Jess groaned her annoyance and sat up, blinking as she tried to make sense of things with her sleep-fuzzed brain.

The noise was coming from the other side of the bed, slightly muffled.

She leaned over Sean, trying not to disturb him, and she spotted a faint glow beside the bed.

Sean's cell phone was ringing from the pocket of his jeans, which were crumpled on the floor.

And the caller was not giving up. Each time the call broke off, they simply dialed again.

Unless the phone was broken or something.

Jess picked up Sean's jeans and slumped back against the pillows, searching in the pockets until the noisy thing emerged.

Sean shuffled in his sleep beside her.

The name on the phone was simply Anne.

Once again, the call ended but before Jess could work out a way to silence the thing, it rang again.

This time Sean did stir.

"Wassup?" he mumbled.

"Your phone. It won't stop ringing. How do I turn it off?"

"Here." Sean's hand emerged from under the quilt and he took the phone from her. He muttered a curse when he looked at the screen and quickly sat up in bed. He scrubbed a hand over his face, wincing when he touched his bruised cheek.

"Is something wrong?" Jess asked.

"Yeah. I'm about to get my ass handed to me on a platter," he said under his breath.

He answered the call. "Anne. Hi."

The woman on the other end of the call was shouting so loudly Jess could hear her. It was hard to make out words other than the obvious and frequent swearing, but whoever she was Sean was clearly her least favorite person in the world at the moment.

He threw back the covers and stood, wobbling for

a second once he was on his feet. He gave Jess a tight smile and pointed to the door before walking out.

She could hear him, pacing up and down the hallway, occasionally trying to get a word in, not succeeding particularly well.

Jess fell back against the pillows.

She tried not to think about what would happen next and failed—she couldn't help jumping forward to the moment when Sean would leave. Was this going to be it? Woken by an angry phone call, he'd realize that he needed to get on the road?

She snuggled back into bed, finding herself drifting over to Sean's side, where the covers were all warm and smelled like him.

How long would she wait before she washed the bed linen? Actually, maybe she should do it now. Get up and strip the bed and get the sheets in the washer so that when Sean left there'd be nothing of him left behind. If she was going to cope with the pain of his departure, she had to make a clean break.

She sat up, genuinely wondering if she should remake the bed before common sense intervened.

It's the middle of the night.

Don't be so pathetic.

Sighing in frustration at herself, Jess rolled onto her back and stared up at the ceiling, listening to Sean's end of the conversation—if only as a way to ignore the thoughts swirling in her head.

Sean's voice, sheepish at first, had increased in volume and now he was shouting, too. Asking for more time. Demanding "they" listen to his opinion. Swearing about contract terminology that Jess didn't understand.

The conversation ended abruptly.

There was a loud, vicious curse and then a thud that made her wince.

A moment later Sean returned to the bedroom, cradling his fist.

"Did you hurt yourself?" she asked as she sat up. The look on Sean's face made her already-anxious belly twist harder.

"Not really." He shrugged. "Sorry 'bout your wall, though. I'll pay for the plaster to be fixed."

"Right."

He let out a long breath and then sat down heavily on the bed, his back to her.

He practically quivered with emotion and Jess's own turmoil took a backseat in the light of his distress. Having only overheard Sean's side of the conversation, she was still none the wiser as to what the phone call had been about.

"Do you want to talk?"

He was silent for so long Jess wondered if he'd heard her, but then he twisted around and leaned against the headboard, legs stretched out in front of him, seemingly oblivious to his nakedness and the chill in the air.

"It was my agent. I thought she was calling to ream me out for missing meetings about the screenplay this week. It wasn't that." He sucked in a sharp breath. "The movie has been indefinitely postponed," he said, staring bleakly straight ahead.

"Can they do that?"

"Yes, they can. Apparently it happens all the time. The contract..." he trailed off.

"But it's your story."

"I know."

Jess wasn't sure whether to reach out and comfort him or not. She settled for resting her hand on his thigh.

"So can you just find someone else to make it? If these guys don't want to?"

"Nope. They own the rights now. They just get to sit on it until they decide they want to go ahead."

"Why...?" Jess wasn't sure if she should ask.

"I don't know why."

His earlier anger had faded and been replaced with a defeat Jess had never expected to see in him. What had happened to the supremely confident Sean Paterson?

"There will be other options," Jess said. She had no idea whether there would be or not, but it couldn't be as simple as that, could it? There had to be a way around it.

Sean just shook his head.

Jess was at a loss. "Oh, Sean."

Sean swore under his breath and then scrubbed his face with his hands. He looked completely devastated—on the verge of tears.

Jess fought warring reactions.

This was what Sean looked like when he lost something vitally important.

He was distraught. It wasn't even close to the reaction he'd had when they'd talked about this being their last night together. When he'd told her he had so much going on in his life.

Too much to fit her in.

Disappointment, frustration, anger. At him, and at herself—she'd gone and made herself vulnerable again, despite all her efforts to never let that happen.

And yet…

She couldn't help the urge to comfort him—it was stronger than all her other emotions.

Jess tugged on the covers and wrapped them around Sean, pulling on his arm until he shuffled down and his head rested on her shoulder. At first he lay stiffly against her, but slowly he began to loosen up.

"I hate this," he said in a quiet voice. "I hate it when other people tell me what I can and can't do."

"Did they give you a reason?"

"Apparently there's an actor they want for the role, but he's not available. Then when he's available, the director isn't. They might need to find either a new lead or a new director."

"But that's just scheduling stuff. Surely they can work that out?"

Sean snorted derisively. "You'd think. But then it doesn't fit in the producer's schedule."

"So they have to find some new people who are available. Which means—"

"Which means it could still start next month, or it could be a year away. Or more. Or never."

They fell silent for a while. Jess wondered what it

would be like to be in Sean's position. To have a huge project that you'd been working on for years fall into a heap due to other people's activities.

And then she realized she kind of did know what that felt like. Her project had been a marriage not a movie, but she'd failed, too. Or at least she'd felt like she had.

There were no words. Instead she hugged him tighter.

Sean let her hold him, but all too soon he drew away from her, turning to lie on his back, one arm thrown over his eyes. "This blows," he finally said, all exasperated frustration. The tears, if they'd been there, had faded.

"I know."

"It was going to be so important."

"Yeah, but you've got the werewolf book nearly finished. That's important, too."

"It's not the same." In the dim light, Jess could see his bottom lip sticking out. On such a masculine face, the expression was almost funny. *Almost*.

"Why?"

"The movie was... It was just *important*."

"I know. But now you've got more time to write the werewolf book."

"I don't *want* to write the werewolf book."

Jess restrained an urge to roll her eyes. "You will. Once all this fades."

"But...I wanted to show off."

"To who?"

"To my fans, my parents, the world. You."

She couldn't help the little jolt of joy that went through her when he included *her* in his list. But she still didn't quite understand the problem.

Jess propped herself up on an elbow, frowning. "But why do you need to do that? You're already so successful."

"I just do." He sounded petulant, like a toddler who'd had his favorite toy taken away.

"You want to show off?"

"I want something to show what I've achieved."

"To your parents," Jess guessed. As flattered as she was at being included in the list, she was pretty sure that Sean was talking mostly about Stephen and Tori Paterson. She recalled their visit to the bookstore, when Sean had confessed that no one in his family except Rob really cared about his success.

"Yeah."

"You'll find another way."

"No. I won't. The movie was perfect. And now it's ruined."

His pouting was becoming less amusing by the minute and Jess found herself getting irritated. Sure, he'd suffered a setback and was allowed to be hurt by that, but this tantrum was not how their last night together should end. Not with him behaving like a spoiled child and her having to cajole him. She might be older than him, but she wasn't his mother.

"That's pretty childish, Sean."

SEAN'S BRAIN WAS racing a mile a minute, and Jess's comment stung. He opened his mouth to reply but nothing came out—there was too much else going on in his head for him to form a proper response.

All his plans had suddenly been upended.

The movie was meant to be the achievement that would finally make his family sit up and take notice—realize that he had not only turned his "silly comic books" into a career, but that it eclipsed any kind of achievement he could have made as an accountant.

But now there was no movie.

No shining achievement to hold up to prove his worth. If only he could be like Rob. Rob had an accounting career, a marriage and soon, most likely, a child. Proof positive of a successful life.

What did Sean have? A ridiculously expensive car and a collection of books that his family didn't care about and would never get around to reading anyway. And no movie.

If only he could be like Rob.

But he couldn't. A life like that wasn't for him—at least not for a long time into the future. There were so many reasons.

He'd never felt comfortable staying in one place.

At least, not until these past couple of weeks in Melbourne, a little voice inside whispered.

He'd never wanted to think further ahead than his next deadline.

Except recently he'd been thinking about what it might be like to have a dog. A house, even.

He'd never found a woman who didn't bore him after he'd seduced her.

Not until he'd met Jess, who made him bring his A-game every time. He wasn't even close to bored with her. Couldn't imagine a time when he would be. She was all hard angles and soft edges that combined into a fascinating puzzle he wanted to spend a long time trying to solve.

He sat up, suddenly, staring at Jess, who was looking at him with a distinct frown.

What he wanted and what he needed had been right there in front of him and he hadn't even seen it. All the movie drama faded in an instant as the realization sank in.

"Let's make a go of this, Jess." Yes, he'd tried and failed at a relationship before, but hadn't life as a writer taught him that after a knockdown, he needed to step back, brush himself off and try again? He'd never have had a single book published if he'd let failure or rejection hold him back. Surely he could apply that lesson here?

Jess blinked. "Huh?"

"I mean you and me. We could have something, don't you think?"

She reached for the bedside lamp and switched it on.

"What are you talking about?" she asked.

He squinted at her in the sudden light before grabbing her hand and squeezing it tight.

Yes, this was perfect. Jess. He could have a life with her. He really could. Just a few hours ago he'd been hoping she'd want more than this one last night together. He realized now just how strong that hope had been. His critics said that his books took too long to reveal the true evil at work within each plot. That Sebastian's investigative skills sometimes left a lot to be desired. Perhaps they had a point. Perhaps Sebastian's process mimicked Sean's own: clearly in this case he'd been a little slow to connect the dots.

Now he just had to convince Jess.

He took both her hands in his. "I've never felt like this before. I really like hanging out with you. I miss you when you're not there." Even as he was saying the words he realized the truth of them. This was what he wanted. Jess. A home. He was *ready.*

"You mean...*you and me?* For more than right now?"

Did he imagine the hopeful tone in her voice?

"That's exactly what I mean."

She was silent for a while and then, when she spoke, her voice wasn't the enthusiastic agreement he'd been expecting.

"You haven't called me for *five days,* Sean." Her voice was brittle. "And if Suzie hadn't been hurt, when would I have seen you?"

Sean opened his mouth and closed it again. She had a point. "Fair enough. I know—that was pretty pathetic. We spent so much time together and then I just disappeared." If he could take back his actions over the past five days, he would. Not the spending time with Rob—that had been great. But the way they'd spent it. He hadn't really helped Rob deal with his problems at all. He had merely helped him run away from them.

Jess clearly didn't think that was enough. "You disappeared after we'd had a fight. After Rob and Hailey returned. I thought you were gone, had left town."

He'd forgotten about the fight after the convention. It hadn't really been a fight, though, had it? More of a disagreement. "I wouldn't have left without saying goodbye." Surely she didn't think that little of him.

"How was I to know?"

He'd helped Rob run away from his problems, but perhaps the running away hadn't just been for Rob's benefit. Maybe he'd needed some space, too—to work out the things that were tumbling around in his mind.

"I apologize. I am so sorry," he said. He raised one of her hands to his mouth and kissed her knuckles. "It was dumb. I got caught up with Rob. If it means anything, I had absolutely no idea it had been five days. Which isn't an excuse, I know. But..."

"But?"

"But maybe the time was a good thing. I think it's helped me get some things straight in my head. Like wanting to be with you. I mean, it's been such a mess, everything going around in my head—me trying to work out what to do with my life. But it's just kind of all come together now." He hoped that didn't sound too pathetic. It was the truth.

"And what does this have to do with the movie?"

"What?"

Jess's eyes narrowed. "Earlier tonight this was going to be our last time together. Now you want more. Something changed in the meantime—the movie. So I want to know why."

Sean fought for the right words. How could he explain? "It's, like... I was thinking about Rob."

Jess's eyebrow arched. "Rob?"

"Yeah. And he has Hailey and a home and a job. And I'm never going to be an accountant. I mean, I love writing too much—even if I made no money from it, I'd still do it. So there's no way I'm ever going to take my place at Paterson Associates, no matter what my mother and father think. But maybe I can have some of what Rob has. Some stability. A home. You."

Sean's chest swelled. He was proud of his declaration, proud of finding the right words for once. It was perfect, really. It would once and for all prove to his brother and his parents that he didn't run away from everything. Jess was older than him, too, so if an older woman could take him seriously as a romantic partner, surely that *had* to prove that he was grown-up, capable of sustaining a relationship.

But Jess wasn't smiling. "So now you don't have a movie to show off to your parents, you're looking for something to replace that?"

Crap. Clearly he hadn't done as good a job of explaining as he'd thought.

He grasped Jess's hands more tightly.

"It's not like that at all. I mean, that's what I *started* thinking, but then..." His imaginings began running away with him and he found himself babbling. "I was thinking how much I want to change my life. I could stay put in Melbourne—most of the time, anyway. We could get a house, or I could live here with you, of course. I like this place. And we could get a dog! Whatever kind you want, although I admit I'd probably like a golden retriever because I've grown kind of fond of Suzie. And when I have to go to L.A., if the movie ever does get the green light again, there'll be lots of meetings. But when I'm not doing that, or attending conventions, I could be here. With you."

There was a pause. Jess shook off his hands and pulled the quilt snugly around her. Sean's gut tightened. He'd never made this kind of offer before, never revealed so much of himself to another person. He was as raw and exposed as he'd ever been.

"So I'd be your stopgap," she said, not looking at him. "Wait here for you to be done with other stuff."

Her tone was bitter, and in what should have been a rosy glow from the lamp, her expression was icy.

What was going on? Sean hadn't had a conversation like this before, but surely this wasn't how it was supposed to go? He hadn't necessarily expected Jess to fall at his feet with gratitude, but he'd thought she'd be receptive to the idea.

A cold dread began trickling in—maybe he was way off base.

"No, no, not like that," he said. But before he could explain more, she cut him off.

"Yes, it's exactly like that. That's precisely what you're proposing."

He blew out a breath in frustration. He knew he wasn't expressing himself properly. The writer, lost for words yet again. Jess was the only one who caused that.

"Jess, what I'm saying is you'd be my base," he said, trying to find a different way to explain himself. "I could come and go from here, but I'd always come back. To you."

"Lucky me," she said bitterly.

Sean felt the entire conversation slipping out of his control and a panic rose inside him. "I don't know what I've done wrong! I'm trying to suggest we have a proper relationship!"

"No, you're trying to suggest that I accept playing second best to everything else you have going on in your life, Sean. You're saying that when you're not doing other stuff, I'm okay to hang out with."

He scrubbed a hand over his face. Why was she interpreting things so literally? "No, that's not what I'm saying."

"Yes, it is."

"What do you want me to say, Jess? I'm trying my best here. You know commitment isn't something I've had a lot of practice with. I want to give it a go. With you."

"Maybe I don't want to be the one you practice on, Sean."

The chill in her voice was making his earlier anger return. Frustration swelled his chest and he flexed his aching fingers. "I let you practice on me! Remember our first date? We said it was a practice run."

Her cold anger slipped and she suddenly looked

incredibly sad. Disappointed. She shook her head. "Oh, Sean."

For the first time since they'd met, Sean felt the gap in their ages. Her resigned sigh reminded him of his mother: her *oh, Sean* uttered after whatever it was he'd done to embarrass or disappoint her.

"Don't do that," he said, surprised at the angry growl in his voice.

"What?"

"Be all superior and condescending."

Her smile was fragile and her eyes shone. "I'm not. Really I'm not. I'm just…"

She left her statement hanging, unwilling or unable to finish it.

In his life, Sean had had a lot of memorable moments in bed. This would be another, only not quite the way he would have wished it.

He searched for the next logical step in their conversation. Did he try again? He wasn't going to beg. Did he just accept that she didn't want him? Instinct told him that wasn't true. He'd laid himself bare and she'd thrown it back in his face. It hurt. Deeply. So much so that he couldn't begin to comprehend it; instead he let his frustration take the fore.

He threw up his hands. "I don't know what you want from me here."

"Something you can't give me," she said softly.

That only served to increase his anger. "How do you know that? You won't even try! You're afraid, Jess. Too scared to take a risk, too timid to try something new."

"It's not new, Sean. It's dressed up in different clothes, but it's very old and way too familiar and I'm not doing it again."

So this was about her ex-husband somehow? "I wouldn't cheat on you."

She winced. "Sean. You don't understand, it's—"

That condescending tone was back and he hated it with a passion. He wasn't going to hang around for any more. So much for not running away. So much for trying to have a normal life. Clearly he just wasn't built for it.

"Forget it," he said. He threw the covers off and jumped out of bed, pulling his jeans on and searching for his shirt.

Jess just sat, silently, watching him.

"Well, I guess this is it," he said, once he was dressed.

She managed a little smile that made his chest ache. *Great, another part of his body that hurt.*

"Bye, Sean."

If he'd been waiting for her to stop him, to say something more, it didn't come. He hesitated at the door, just in case, but she remained silent.

He spun on his heel and was outside and on the street in no time, walking so fast his breath caught and his head ached. When he didn't see the familiar sight of Dezzie parked outside a momentary panic clenched his belly until he remembered they'd left the car at Jess's surgery. He walked to the nearby main road and was able to hail a passing taxi. Thankfully, just a few minutes later he was blessedly sliding in behind Dezzie's wheel.

He breathed deep, waiting for the usual sense of peace and serenity to wash over him as it always did once he was back inside his beloved car.

It didn't come.

The smell of the leather, the comforting rumble of her engine, none of it helped.

You just right royally screwed up something really, really important. Something really special.

And the most frustrating thing was, he wasn't even sure *how*.

He drove for a while, following roads blindly before he realized what a stupid idea that was. Yet another stupid idea in a night of whoppers.

He steered the car in the direction of the bay, finding a deserted beachside car park and pulling up in a dark corner.

He grabbed the sleeping bag he kept in the trunk and wrapped himself inside it before stretching out as best he could in the backseat of the car. It wouldn't be the first night Dezzie had provided him with a bed.

It likely wouldn't be the last.

Yeah.

This was the way he rolled. Nothing to tie him down. Just like Sebastian, he was a man of the road, a drifter. Wherever he found himself was where he was meant to be. For Sebastian, that meant fighting whatever demons lurked in the darkness. For Sean it meant making the most of his current situation until it wasn't fun anymore.

And Melbourne—Jess—all of it? It had suddenly become no fun at all.

A lot of men would be jealous of his lifestyle: travel, women, no commitments except his next book deadline. And that would be enough. It had been enough for the past few years—there was no reason to change now.

It would be enough.

It would have to be.

CHAPTER FIFTEEN

SEAN WASN'T SURE what kind of reaction to expect when he knocked on Rob and Hailey's door a few hours later.

He'd managed maybe an hour of broken sleep, and then the growing hum of morning peak-hour traffic on Beach Road had made further attempts impossible.

Of course, he could have gone to a hotel, or even hit the highway and headed to Sydney and hunkered down in one his usual hangouts there, but instead he found himself outside the brick-veneer house that had been his home for the last little while.

"Sean!"

Damn. He'd really wanted Rob to answer the door.

But then, to his immense surprise, Hailey—the same Hailey that had told him to "not be there" when she got home—gave him a hug and pulled back with a beaming smile. "Come in."

The house was in an even better state than he and Jess had left it the night before—almost fully restored to its usual perfection. A twinge in his chest reminded him of how Jess had helped out, bringing her usual pragmatism and efficiency to deal with the mess he and Rob had made. He was going to miss that about her. For a man who lived a lot of his life in a world filled with vampires and the supernatural, her common sense and practicality was wonderfully grounding.

Hell, that barely scratched the surface of the things he was going to miss about her.

"Would you like a coffee?" Hailey's brightness was almost too much for him to deal with.

"Sure."

She led him into the kitchen, chattering as she went.

"Rob's just finishing in the shower. He's been cleaning the bathrooms this morning and between that and mopping the floors and, and, well, *other stuff,* he got a bit sweaty."

She giggled, and Sean shook his head.

Good for you, Rob. He didn't want to know the details.

Hailey continued to chatter about inconsequential things as Sean sank down into a chair with a groan. He felt like an old man. His face still hurt from Rob's punch. His knuckles hurt from hitting Jess's wall. His back ached from sleeping crookedly in the backseat of his car. And he felt an overall uneasiness, as if he'd forgotten something very important. Or lost it.

Hailey put a steaming cup of coffee in front of him, and Sean could have kissed her. From the first sip it began to revive him, like Frankenstein's monster jolted with electricity.

"Uh, Hailey?" Sean dared to ask when he'd downed almost half the scalding beverage.

"Yeah?"

"Don't take this the wrong way, but why are you being so nice to me?"

She laughed. "Oh, yeah. I guess after yesterday you'd be wondering that."

"You told me never to come back here."

"Well, of course you had to get your stuff."

He nodded. "Right. So you're just thrilled that I'm going to be out of your life once and for all very soon, then." Seemed like a common reaction that women were having to him today.

She tsked. "No, silly. Rob told me what really happened. How you tried to get him to talk to me. You told him that he should listen to my point of view. And that he punched you when you insisted. And how you helped him and Suzie when they got hurt."

"Ah." The story was a little bit embellished, but if it meant a happier relationship with his sister-in-law, Sean could only be thankful to Rob for twisting the truth slightly.

"And he also told me that when he got home from Rome, the house was in perfect condition. That he was as responsible for it being such a hellhole as you were."

Thank God they'd come over and cleaned up before Hailey had seen what it had *really* looked like.

Sean shifted awkwardly under Hailey's beaming gaze. "Yeah. Well, you know. Rob's never been much for housekeeping."

"Tell me about it!" Hailey looked down and brushed nonexistent dust from the tabletop. "When the baby comes, we're getting a cleaner."

It took a moment for her words to sink in.

"Baby? That's great, Hailey. Congratulations."

She flushed, and Sean thought she'd never been prettier, not even in her wedding finery.

"Thanks. How does it feel knowing you're going to be an uncle?"

Sean sat back in his chair. He hadn't thought about that. "Wow." He liked the idea. He could be the cool uncle who brought expensive toys and T-shirts from foreign countries.

The cool uncle who could draw funny pictures and tell good stories, but didn't really know what was going on in the kid's life, because he was never around.

The cool uncle who was fun to play with for a while, but whose presence at birthday parties and Christmases would never really be missed.

The ache in Sean's chest intensified. He rubbed at his breastbone with his fist—the uninjured one—as if he could somehow soothe the pain away. It didn't help.

"Hey!" Rob appeared, looking freshly scrubbed, clean shaven and just as happy as he'd been at the wedding.

Despite his own situation, Sean couldn't help but smile. "Hey, yourself. Just heard the news from Hailey. Congratulations."

"Yeah." Rob walked over to his wife and pressed

a kiss to the top of her head before heading to make himself a coffee. "You were right. If I'd just listened to her, we'd probably still be in Rome right now."

"We can always go back," Hailey said.

"True. We can put the baby in one of those back-pack things you wear on your front and see the sights." Rob gestured to his chest, patting an imaginary baby in a sling.

The image struck Sean at his heart.

His younger brother had a house, a dog, a wife and was going to be a father.

And last night *he* had slept in his car.

All that pride he'd had in his nomadic lifestyle, in staying on the move? It all seemed pointless now. He'd been so determined to escape his parents' dire predictions of failure that he'd ended up fulfilling their very worst expectations. Yes, he had a lot of money in the bank, but what did that mean, really?

He'd determined that he only stuck around some-where until the fun ran out. But right now, *here* was no fun, and yet Sean couldn't think of anywhere else he wanted to be.

Man, was that ever a depressing thought.

"You still look like shit," Rob said mildly as he sat down at the table with them.

"I know."

He grimaced. "Sorry about the shiner, again."

Sean shrugged. "It's okay."

"Does it hurt?"

"Yeah."

"You want an ice pack or something?" Hailey asked.

"Thanks, but I think it's too late for that."

"I can get you some painkillers," Rob offered.

"*Those* I could definitely use. As strong as you've got. I'd really like to sleep for the rest of the day. The rest of the week, if possible."

Rob disappeared and returned a moment later, shaking a white plastic bottle. "I've still got these from when I had my wisdom teeth out. They knocked me out completely."

"Good."

Sean reached for them, but Rob pulled them away at the last minute.

"Really not in the mood for games, man," Sean growled. He twitched his fingers in a "give them here" gesture.

Rob shook his head, holding the pills behind him. "What happened with Jess?"

"What?"

"You heard me."

"What do you mean, what happened with Jess?" Hailey asked.

"Sean and Jess have been, *you know*," Rob said.

"No!"

Sean hesitated before answering. He and Jess had never explicitly discussed whether their affair was a secret, but Sean had been pretty sure she didn't want Rob and Hailey to know about it. When they'd come back here after the convention—it felt like years ago now—she'd been pretty cagey around Rob and he'd followed her lead, playing it straight.

"You're not as dumb as you look, then," Sean said.

"Ha, ha, funny man. Spill."

"How did you know?" Sean was curious.

"I might have been out of it with jet lag when you two were here on the weekend, but even a corpse would have picked up on the glow between you. And then at the clinic yesterday…well, it was pretty obvious. So, how did it all happen? We don't need the gory details," he added quickly, "I'm just keen to know how mild-mannered Jess brought the great Sean-O to his knees."

It was that obvious?

"Hang on! What do you mean? You and *Jess?*" Hailey looked outraged.

"They're both adults, Hailey," Rob said.

"But Jess is my friend! My boss!"

"And I'm sure she's grown-up enough to separate whatever's happening between her and Sean from the relationship she has with you," Rob said soothingly. "That is unless sparkles here really screwed things up. What's going on?" he demanded again.

Sean sat at the end of the table, Rob and Hailey either side of him, both eagerly awaiting the great Jess and Sean love story. He could tell Hailey's renewed enthusiasm for him had dimmed a little at this revelation, but her curiosity was winning over her disdain.

Sean slumped back in his chair. "I really screwed things up."

"What happened?" Hailey demanded.

She had a right to know, Sean figured. Jess was her friend and, more important, her boss. If what had happened between him and Jess affected Hailey…

Not that he thought it would. He didn't think Jess would let something like that happen, but then again, his understanding of Jess had proved woefully lacking recently.

"We had a *thing*," he began weakly.

"Like a fling?" Hailey asked.

"Did you guys hook up at the wedding?" Rob asked.

"At the wedding?" Hailey's tone rose.

"Or was it later?"

"Whoa." Sean held up his hands. "I'm not playing twenty questions with you guys."

"Okay, we'll shut up," Rob said.

"But—" Hailey interjected.

"We'll shut up," he repeated firmly.

"Fine." Sean took another revivifying gulp of coffee. "Yes, at the wedding. It was just going to be a one-night deal but then…" He couldn't admit to the episode of rushing Suzie to see Jess after she'd eaten the headache pills. It was cowardly of him, but Suzie was fine and they didn't need to know. "Then we ran into each other again."

"Go on."

"We decided to hang out, for as long as I was house-sitting." It had seemed so simple, at the start. "We just did stuff together, went out. It was nice."

"Can't help noticing you're using past tense there, buddy," Rob said.

"It got…complicated."

"Like how?" Hailey asked.

Sean gave Hailey a warning look and she pinched her lips together with her fingers.

"Just, complicated. She got so burned by that ex of hers."

Hailey nodded in vehement agreement, but kept her mouth shut.

"She won't trust anyone. And I guess I'm not all that good at..." He searched for the right words.

"Being in love with someone," Rob supplied.

"No, I..." Sean trailed off. He knew that was what Jess had been waiting for him to say last night. That he was in love with her. But he hadn't been able to bring himself to admit it. Not even to himself.

Idiot. What is this if it's not love?

He loved Jessica Alexander. Yes. A thrill of nerves went through him at the thought, but it wasn't anxiety. More the excitement of something fuzzy becoming clear, the joy of certainty. He'd already known—somewhere deep inside himself.

But the thrill was short-lived, doused by the icy fact that even though he did love her, he'd lost her.

"Yeah," he said eventually. "Being in love with someone. With Jess." That's definitely what it was. Only love would hurt this much.

"Did you tell her that?" Hailey just couldn't help herself.

"No." *Damn.* Maybe *he* was the coward, not her.

"Chicks need to hear it, man," Rob said. He gave Sean a wry look. "A wise man told me, not that long ago, that women like to talk about that kind of stuff."

"I guess." Yet he'd said just about everything but

that to Jess! She should have known—she should have been able to put it together from what he *had* said. Sean huffed in frustration. "I told her I wouldn't cheat on her."

"You didn't!" Hailey gaped at him, and Rob just shook his head ruefully.

"Well, that's what the stupid ex did," Sean said, feeling defensive. "I was trying to let her know I wasn't like him."

"What *else* did you say?" Hailey demanded.

Sean thought about what he'd said. He cringed when he remembered confessing his thoughts about showing off how grown-up he was to his parents. "Do you think Mom and Dad would like Jess?" Sean asked.

Rob looked confused. "Why? What has that got to do with anything?"

Sean groaned as realization sank in. "You are so right." Stephen and Tori's opinion of Jess meant nothing. Their opinion of him meant nothing, too. He'd survived practically his entire life without their approval. *No, not just survived, thrived.* He'd been more successful than they could imagine. Jess had accused him of being childish—and she was absolutely right. He was still pouting like a kid whose parents hadn't come to watch the ball game. And he was twenty-eight years old.

Time to get over it.

"I might have said that having a relationship with her would prove to Mom and Dad that I was a success," Sean sheepishly admitted.

"Whoa. Harsh." Rob sucked in a breath through his teeth. "Mate, you've gotta get over that."

"What?"

"This thing in your head between you and Mom and Dad. I know they haven't been very supportive—"

Sean snorted at the understatement.

"I know," Rob said. "But if you're waiting for them to come around, you'll be waiting for a long time. You've already proven it—you're a success. There are practically people waiting in line to tell you that. You're holding out for the ones who won't—which, quite frankly, is stupid. You're an adult. You need to grow up, man."

Sean felt anger rise at Rob's words. How dare his little brother tell him to grow up? But the anger was muted with the uncomfortable realization that his statement exactly echoed Jess's accusation of him being childish. Were they both right? Was Sean holding out for something that wouldn't come, out of some misplaced resentment?

"It's just—" he began, preparing to defend himself. But then the words failed as truth hit. "You're right. What Mom and Dad think doesn't really matter." Part of him would always care what his parents thought—he wasn't foolish enough to believe that in some way he'd ever stop wanting their approval. But living his life in order to gain it was giving them the exact control over his destiny he'd fought so hard to avoid. It was time to really start living his life on his own terms.

Rob nodded. "Can I tell you a secret? I *like* being an accountant."

The brothers shared a smile.

"You're both idiots," Hailey said bluntly. "But back to Jess. What did you say next?"

Sean cleared his throat and returned to the matter at hand. His chest ached when he remembered Jess's expression as she'd sat in bed, looking at him—so sad, so hurt, so determined.

"I said that she'd be my home base," he recalled. "That when I had stuff to do, I'd go do it, and then I'd come back and spend time with her. Which is true."

"Well, that sounds okay to me," Rob said, frowning.

"Jeez, *men!*" Hailey threw up her hands.

"What's wrong with that?" Rob asked.

Hailey rounded on Sean. "What do you think Mark did?"

Sean bristled at her tone. "I told you—he cheated on her."

"We know that. And each time he cheated on her, what did he do?"

Sean was getting frustrated. "I don't know! I wasn't there to see it when he walked in the door!"

And then it dawned on him.

"O-o-o-oh."

He came back. That's exactly what Mark did. He went off with other women, and then came back to Jess. She was his standby, his option when nothing better was on offer. And, in his clumsy way, that was more or less what Sean had offered her last night.

"Right," Hailey said, nodding, a pleased expression on her face.

"What?" Rob asked. "I don't get it."

"I'll explain it to you later, darling," Hailey said.

"But that wasn't what I meant," Sean said. The way he'd said it had made it sound like that; he could see it now. Jess had seen a halfhearted offer: be here for me when I don't have anywhere more important to be, anything more important to do, anyone more important to see.

He'd been halfhearted because he'd been too scared to offer more. Scared of rejection—of failing, just like his parents predicted. He'd striven hard to ensure he never failed at anything, ever. Since relationships were hard, it was just better not to try.

But he was going to have to get used to it. He'd failed with Jess. And he'd failed at getting his movie on the screen—even if the reasons were totally out of his control.

He groaned as the memory of the phone call with his agent crashed over him again—he'd forgotten all about it.

"I have to call my agent," he said. She'd said something about getting his ass to L.A. this week to make up for the meetings he'd missed. To see if there was any chance of getting things back on track. And now seemed as good a time as any to hop on a plane, he guessed—it wasn't as though there was any reason to stick around here.

"No, you have to call Jess," Rob said.

The very idea called out to something deep inside him. Yes. He knew he needed to talk to her.

But he couldn't.

He'd completely blown it—and he'd spend the rest of his life regretting that fact.

Sean shook his head. "Nah. The best thing I can do for Jess is to leave her the hell alone. She doesn't need me screwing up her life. She'll find someone new soon enough." And she would. He remembered thinking that when he was driving home from the convention. How one day Rob and Hailey would be telling him about her new man. The thought made the coffee in his otherwise empty stomach curdle.

"You said you loved her," Rob said. "You can't just give up on that."

"Does she love you?" Hailey asked.

Sean shrugged. He wasn't sure of anything anymore.

"Mate, you've got to give it another try," Rob said.

"I don't think so."

"Hey, who was the one convincing me to call Hailey every day this week?"

"I still can't believe you didn't call me," Hailey said.

Rob gave Hailey a sheepish look before turning back to Sean. "What can it hurt?" he urged. "If it's all a mess right now, the least you can do is try to clean it up. Maybe you just need to explain yourself better. Make her understand that she's really important to you."

"The *most* important," Sean said thoughtfully.

Could he do that? He'd accused Jess of being a coward but it was clear now that the yellow streak ran both ways. It wasn't something he was used to thinking about himself. *Sean Paterson a coward?*

"Or you can just run away again," Rob said with a shrug. "It's up to you."

Rob was clearly on a roll. Perhaps slugging his older brother had given him an overinflated sense of self-importance.

"Hey, watch it," Sean said, half joking, half not. "Just because you got a good one in yesterday—" he pointed to his shiner "—doesn't mean I can't take you down."

Rob put out his hands, palms up. "If it'd help, you're welcome to take a crack. But I think you've got more important things to do. Like not running away from one of the best things to ever happen to you."

Sean sighed. Rob was right. Again. It was starting to become annoying.

"Maybe," he said hesitantly.

"Maybe?"

"Yeah. Yes. Okay. You're right." Sean leaned his head back and stared at the ceiling. He'd had plenty of rejections as an author. Some of those had really hurt—although it was nothing like the pain of losing Jess.

He'd be kicking himself for the rest of his life if he didn't at least try.

"Finally," Hailey said, rolling her eyes. "So, what are you going to do to get her back?

Good question. What would Sebastian Douglas

do? Despite the wild imaginings of his fans in some of the more outlandish fan fiction Sean had been told about, Sebastian wasn't a romantic hero. He was an action hero, a man who'd rush in, sword drawn and guns blazing.

Sean wasn't good with either swords or guns, but he did have his own weapon: words. Even if they had been failing him more often than he was used to recently.

"Jess doesn't have Twitter, does she?" he asked. He could create an account for her and send her messages—get his fans to send her messages. An outpouring of love notes from a thousand strangers.

"Nope. And it's not really her thing," Hailey said.

Damn. She was right. And besides, Jess wouldn't care what a thousand strangers said—only what *he* said.

"I could write her a letter...."

This time Rob poured cold water on the idea. "Bzzt. Wrong answer. You need to go talk to her."

His brother was right, too. Now wasn't the time to hide behind a computer screen or a pen and paper.

"I need to clean up first."

"Yes, you certainly do." Hailey wrinkled her nose.

"And maybe get some sleep. So you look more like your normal pretty self instead of a reanimated corpse from that zombie show you made me watch," Rob said.

"Thanks, asshole," Sean said fondly.

"You're welcome, jerk."

"I will never understand brothers," Hailey said.

Then she cocked her head to one side. "I wonder if we're going to have a boy or a girl?"

Rob's expression became dreamy as he clearly began imagining either playing football with a mini version of himself, or buying teddy bears for a mini Hailey.

Sean decided that was the right moment to leave. He took the pills from Rob's hand and headed for the bathroom. He'd shower, shave, take the pills, grab a few hours' sleep, and then he'd be clearheaded. He'd go see Jess and talk to her—make her see reason. See if he could convince her to give him one more chance.

In his writer's mind, Sebastian Douglas threw a cigarette to the floor and ground it out with his heel. He straightened his fedora, gave Sean a short salute and wished him luck.

CHAPTER SIXTEEN

JESS HAD ALWAYS prided herself on giving her patients the absolute best care she was capable of. But today she wasn't so sure she was living up to that standard.

She'd barely slept after Sean had left and as a result her responses were sluggish and her brain on go-slow.

After she'd asked one patient's owner the same question about vaccinations three times, Andrea had asked if she was okay. Jess had said she thought she might be coming down with the flu. Hailey would have noticed something was up straightaway, but she'd called that morning with a giggle in her voice to say that she wouldn't be in—perhaps not for the rest of her interrupted vacation.

At the moment Jess was stumbling over writing up simple notes in a patient file.

This was why she wasn't ready to date.

Because she wasn't ready to deal with the consequences.

She'd gone and fallen in love with the first guy to be nice to her. A guy who'd offered to keep up their little tryst when he didn't have more pressing matters to attend to. A guy who wanted to try out having a relationship so he could prove to his parents that he was an adult. A guy who didn't see anything wrong with either of those two things.

And, the rub of it was, she'd been tempted to accept.

Oh, yeah, being Sean Paterson's second-best option had been mighty appealing.

But then the core of her, the strong part, the part that had finally confronted Mark and asked for a divorce—the part that had thrown a bag of kibble at him and had been growing within her these past few weeks—had decided it wasn't enough.

Sean was wonderful. She loved him. But for her own sanity she couldn't accept his measly offer.

It was hard enough breaking it off with him now, after just a few weeks together. If they spent months—years—together in what was Sean's idea of a "relationship" and Jess was forced to do the same thing then, she wasn't sure she'd survive.

It was better to stay safe. Alone, but safe from this kind of pain.

The purpose of dating Sean had been to get ready for the dating world again. Interestingly, it had had the opposite effect. Jess was pretty sure now that it simply wasn't for her. She'd get herself another dog, maybe a cat or two, work hard at the clinic, volunteer at the shelter, go out with friends, and that would be enough. She had a nice home, a decent car, enough money for an occasional vacation.

That was a pretty good life, by many standards. It would do.

Thankfully the clinic's schedule wasn't too hectic

today and by early afternoon they only had two patients left to see.

"Will I call them and send them to the animal hospital in Caulfield?" Andrea suggested. "That way you can head home and get some rest."

Jess had never closed the clinic early in her life, not even when she really *did* have the flu. But it was probably in the animals' best interests.

"Yeah, sure. Let's see if you can reach them."

A half hour later, the place was cleaned up, the computer sorted out and they were ready to finish for the day.

Jess was in the consulting room when she heard the door open and close. The bell had a weird, tinny sound since Sean had crushed it against the wall when he'd staggered in with Suzie in his arms.

Damn him for invading her thoughts every minute!

She'd replace the bell so she'd never have to think about that moment again. She was going to get rid of everything in her life that reminded her of Sean. She'd also have to replace the door, her bed, her couch, and if Rob and Hailey could just move house, that'd be great. Pity she couldn't just replace her brain.

"Uh, Jess? There's someone here to see you."

Jess's stomach dropped and her pulse sped up, just on the off chance it was Sean. Idiot. It was probably a walk-in patient.

Andrea stepped aside, and Jess put a hand on the table to steady herself.

"Hi, Jess."

He looked better than the last time she'd seen him.

Washed, hair spiked, clean shaven. Apart from his eye, which had begun to bloom colors that marred his otherwise smoothly tanned complexion.

"I'll just be out the front," Andrea said, making a discreet exit.

She sucked in a breath to try to calm her racing heart. Why had he felt the need to come and see her? She would have been so much better off if he'd just left things the way they were.

"How are you?" he asked.

He stepped into the room and closed the door behind him.

Jess eyed the door, panic rising inside her. Why was he here? What on earth needed to be said that hadn't already been said last night?

"Did you get any sleep?"

Damn that sleek confidence of his! He was as poised and self-assured as always, while she felt—and knew she looked—shaky and brittle.

She realized she hadn't said anything since he'd appeared. That wasn't the way to handle this. She had to call upon that inner strength she knew was there. Show him that she was fine.

"I slept very well, thank you," she said, pretty sure he could tell she was lying through her teeth. Andrea had no doubt bought the "flu" story in part because Jess looked so sickly.

But he didn't so much as blink at the blatant falsehood. "I didn't. I slept in Dezzie down at the beach." He put a hand to his back and stretched with an exaggerated grimace. "I think my days of sleeping in the car are behind me. I've got a cricked back this morning."

She couldn't put up with the pretense of polite conversation any longer. Mostly because she wasn't sure how long she was going to be able to hold herself together.

"There was no need for you to come here, Sean."

He stepped forward, reaching a hand out to her. "No. I did such a crappy job of explaining myself last night, Jess. I need to apologize for that, if nothing else."

"You were very clear." Jess stepped behind the stainless steel examination bench, needing a barrier between them. She held on to it tightly, below Sean's line of sight. She didn't want him to see her white knuckles. Or the fact that she needed to hold on to it to steady herself. He'd made her a second-rate offer and she'd turned him down. That was all there was to it. So she loved him. That was her problem.

"I was dumb."

"It's fine. We both knew what this was, right from the start. It perhaps didn't turn out the way we expected because of Rob and Hailey coming back early, but that's just how it is."

He cocked his head on one side. "What do you think might have happened if Rob and Hailey hadn't come back early? What would we be doing now, do you think?"

Jess didn't want to wonder about that. Would she be anticipating yet another of Sean's mystery dates? Blindly fooling herself that she could be casual and temporary when she knew her feelings for him had grown well beyond that?

But Rob and Hailey *had* come back early. The agreement she'd had with Sean had to end—regardless of any inappropriate feelings she might have developed. That was it.

"Sean, it's fine," she said again. "There's no point going into what-ifs, because what's done is done."

"But…" He trailed off with a sharp breath, suddenly looking uncertain and vulnerable. It was a side of him she rarely saw. A side of him she loved, just as much as the cocky Sean, and jokey Sean, and serious Sean.

A sudden thought about why he might be visiting struck. "Look, if you're coming to tell me that you're hanging around in Melbourne longer than you thought and want to continue with our little fling, I'm sorry but—" Her voice broke a little and she paused to take a breath. She hated herself for finding the idea tempting, but was proud enough not to give in. "I'm sorry, but I can't do that. As far as I'm concerned, our agreement has come to an end."

"Oh, Jess. I really screwed things up. Screwed you up."

She managed a mocking smile. "I was pretty screwed up without your help, thank you very much."

He rubbed a hand across his mouth, which Jess took as confirmation of her statement. His eyes were wide and very green. No gold flashes today.

"You have every right to be angry with me. I tried to explain how things unraveled in my head and I did a bad job. You called me childish and you were right. Striving to gain my parents' approval is just ridiculous—and suggesting that having a relationship with you was a way to go about that was...well, idiotic. I know they love me, even if they don't approve of what I do. Being an adult isn't about living my life the way they expect me to, it's about accepting that they will never approve and being okay with that. I'm not saying I've suddenly been able to do that, but I guess I've realized that's what I need to work toward."

"I'm glad you can see things that way." And she was. The issue of Sean's insecurity around his parents was something she was pleased he'd been able to recognize. And hopefully work to remedy.

There was a beat of silence.

"I'm flying to L.A. Tonight at midnight."

Something inside Jess sank, at the same time as a wash of relief flooded through her. She wouldn't have to see him again—not anytime soon, anyway.

She wouldn't see him again—not anytime soon.

She absolutely was not going to cry.

"So you've come to say goodbye," she said, proud her voice stayed steady. If only her knees would do the same.

"No. I..." He threw up his hands. "Damn it, Jess. You're the only person in the world who makes me feel like I have the language skills of a chimpanzee. Words are my profession, but I lose them all when I'm with you."

She laughed, an empty sound. "Where's Sebastian Douglas when you need him?"

"Exactly."

Jess wondered if she'd look back on this moment and regret the way she handled it. Like with Mark—would she wish she'd yelled and thrown things? But yet again, like with her divorce, all she felt was tired, and hurt, and stupid. She'd fallen in love when that wasn't what was on the table. She'd been offered a position as second best, yet again. At least this time she hadn't taken it.

She wasn't exactly sure what Sean wanted. Forgiveness? Absolution? He was, at heart, a nice guy, and perhaps he felt bad for hurting her—she was sure it was obvious to him that he had.

Perhaps it would just be easier for them both if she gave him whatever he was looking for and let them both move on. Sean to Hollywood. Her to her newly dedicated monastic existence. She could start by heading to the shelter this afternoon and finding a kitten or a puppy to take home.

"Sean, really, it's fine. I'll be fine. It was nice of you to come here, but you didn't need to. I wish you the best of luck with the werewolf book and the movie—I'm sure everything will work out and it'll be on the screens in no time. I'll definitely go see it. And I'll finish reading all of your books." She tried for another laugh. "After all, I need to find out if Sebastian and Elvire ever get together."

"Oh, Jess. Just shut up."

In a flash he was around to her side of the table, peeling her fingers from the death grip they held on it.

And then his hands clasped her cheeks, tilting her head, bringing her lips to his.

His eyes were closed and his lips unrelenting as they moved against hers. Shocked, it took Jess a moment to react. Her first instinct was to pull away, but as if anticipating her, Sean dropped one hand from her face so he could wind his arm around her waist, holding her in place.

And then the impulsive, reckless Jess came out of hiding for just a moment.

Screw it.

Her tongue slid into his mouth, her breasts crushed against his chest.

Sean made a muttered sound of surprise, but adapted instantly, adjusting his stance to support them better, opening his mouth to deepen their connection.

One last kiss.

She'd miss this. She would miss it all—but kisses like this especially. Kisses that made her forget the world, lose all sense of place and time, lose herself. Kisses that forced her to surrender to the heat, passion and maleness of Sean.

Which was exactly what she couldn't afford to do.

She'd lost herself once before.

Couldn't let it happen again.

With that sobering thought, Jess pushed away, pressing her hands against Sean's chest until he let her go.

"What?" he said.

She tried to even out her breathing, to dull the loud

thud of her pulse in her ears. She needed to be rational again. Adventurous Jess needed to pull her head in.

"Sean, your kisses are amazing. That's not the problem."

"I love you, Jess."

He was a man stripped bare—she could see that. He was telling the truth—she could see that, too. Something deep inside her warmed and glowed with the knowledge. *Sean Paterson loved her.*

Her lips parted, but then she wasn't sure what to say. *I love you, too?* Because she did. Every tiny molecule inside her wanted to shout it aloud. But it wasn't enough.

The tiny warmth was extinguished quickly by the cold flood of reality.

Whether he loved her or not wasn't really the issue.

Mark had loved her, too.

"I got it all wrong last night," he said in a rush. "I shouldn't have said what I did—the way I did. You're important to me, Jess. The *most* important. Not just a stopgap between other stuff. You're my priority and the other things will just have to fit around us. I want us to try to build a life together." He gave her one of those heart-stopping, lopsided smiles. "I know I'll make mistakes along the way. I just hope you can be patient enough with me. And I know you have history that makes this a huge leap of faith. But I'm hoping that you can find the courage to do that, Jess, to take the leap with me."

He took one of her hands in his. "I realized I was

being a coward, not telling you how I feel about you. Feel my hand. Can you feel me shaking?"

She could, but only just, over the trembling of her own hand. *Sean Paterson loved her.* And she loved him.

It wasn't enough.

Sean's look turned pleading. "I did it. I found the courage to come and tell you. I'm scared of failing, Jess. I have all these stupid expectations about what I need to do to prove myself. You were right—it's childish to be an adult and still have the need to show off. I don't need to have a movie. I don't need to *be* Sebastian Douglas or live like him. I just need to write good books. And be with you."

"Sean..." Jess's throat ached; she could barely swallow for the huge lump there. She put a hand to her eyes, hoping to stem the flood of tears threatening to burst the fragile walls she'd put in place.

"I can't," she said eventually.

His eyes pleaded with her to reconsider. "But—"

She shook off his grip and held up a hand to stop him. Her courage was going to be completely used up in resisting him. She didn't have any left over to try anything else. Somehow, she had to explain, let him know why they couldn't do this. Why love wasn't enough.

"I'm too broken, Sean," she managed to say raggedly. "I don't know how to have a healthy relationship. I know that every time you go to a fan convention, I'm going to be wondering if you'll finally meet the Elvire that calls to the Sebastian Douglas inside you. When you go to L.A., I'm going to wonder if you'll meet exciting, adventurous people and decide a suburban vet is too boring for you."

"I wouldn't do that. That won't happen."

"You say that now."

"Jess, since I left home, I've been living a vagabond life. I've lived in L.A., surrounded by vapid actors and up-themselves writers. I've been to dozens of conventions and met a lot of Elvires. I've never fallen in love before. Never. Not till I met you. I watched Rob and I was dismissive of his choices, of his life—thought he was playing the 'good son' card. But now I know I was jealous. I want what he has. And I want it with you."

She wanted to believe him. Saw the earnestness in his eyes. Knew he was being honest.

But there was one problem.

Her.

Here he was, Sean Paterson, laying out his heart for her to take. All she had to do was step forward, close her eyes, *jump...*

Her breath caught in a sob.

She couldn't do it.

"I'm… I'm too damaged to trust you, Sean." *Oh, God, how much it hurt to say that.* "Not just *you,* I mean. Anyone. I'm just not capable of it. I can't…"

Sean's eyes shone with unshed tears. He slumped against the bench. "Jess. That's the one thing I can't help you with. I love you. I want to be with you. But if you can't find the courage to believe in me, in yourself…"

She swallowed hard. Would taking the risk be any more painful than this moment right now?

You'll never know.

"I'm sorry, Sean. I really am."

There was a long moment of silence. Jess held back her tears by pure force of will. She stood, trying to concentrate on the solid floor beneath her feet, because if she didn't, it would fall out from under her.

Sean finally pushed himself to standing and took a step toward the door. "I guess that's it then."

She guessed it was.

He stood for a moment, hand on the door. She knew he was trying to make eye contact, but she couldn't look at him. Couldn't meet his eyes and see evidence of her cowardice. It was enough to have had to admit it aloud.

"Bye, Jess," he said softly.

And then he was gone.

Jess let out a breath in a rush and leaned on the counter for support. Her legs were weak and unsteady beneath her, as if she'd run past the point of endurance.

"Are you okay?" Andrea appeared in the doorway.

Jess plastered on a smile. "I'm fine."

It was obvious Andrea didn't believe her, but that she wasn't quite sure what to do about it.

"Are you sure?"

"Sure."

"Well..." She hesitated, but then seemed to make up her mind. "I'll head off. Leave you in peace."

"Yes, yes. That would be great." Jess knew her

response didn't make much sense, but she was hoping that just by saying words she'd eventually get Andrea out of there.

"Okay. Well, see you Monday."

"Bye!" Jess said with brutal cheerfulness.

But thankfully Andrea decided it was best to leave Jess on her own.

As soon as she heard the bell clang and the door close, Jess slumped into the nearest chair. She prepared herself for sobs, but she was too frozen even for that.

She wasn't sure how long she sat there, staring into the distance, her mind a blank. She couldn't bring herself to think about what had just happened. About the turning point it would be in her life.

She'd had a chance at finding happiness again. A chance at love.

But the risk was too big. The possibility of getting hurt too great.

And as it turned out, she was a total and utter scaredy-cat.

Coward. So afraid of life and the world that you won't even try.

The look on Sean's face…

Think about something else.

Scaredy-cat.

Cat.

That's what she needed.

A pet.

She stood and searched for her purse, relishing the simple tasks of locking up the clinic and heading out to her car. Activity would stop her from thinking, and she badly needed to stop thinking.

Getting herself a new pet was a perfect way to distract herself over the weekend. A kitten would need a lot of attention. She'd have to buy toys and food and a bed. Perfect distraction activities.

If she was about to begin her new life as a confirmed spinster, she at least needed an animal to share that life with. A cute, fluffy, playful little kitten would be perfect.

She'd go to the shelter right away and get one.

CHAPTER SEVENTEEN

THE VOLUNTEERS AT the shelter were thrilled to see her. Which was nice. Except that Jess didn't want to be around humans. She just wanted to get in, get her kitten and get out before the fragile web that was holding her together gave way. So after brief hellos she headed straight for the admin office.

But it seemed that wasn't meant to be.

"Jess?" Chris, one of the volunteers, called out to her from reception as she looked at the list of cats they had available. As usual, there were plenty of adult cats. But Jess specifically wanted a kitten—and luckily according to the list there were four available.

"Yes, Chris?" she called back, distracted.

"I know you're not officially on the roster, but we could use you out here if you've got the time."

Jess sighed. She had the time—she had nothing but time. She put the clipboard down and headed out to the reception foyer. There she found Chris facing two high school girls in prim, private school uniforms. One of the girls held an animal travel case.

She'd left her own clinic because she wasn't feeling up to her usual professional standards—she certainly hadn't intended on ending up looking after any animals here. And yet...

"What happened?" Jess asked.

Chris gave the girls an encouraging smile. "Tammy, why don't you tell Jess what you told me?"

"We found this dog out in the parkland next to the shopping centre. Some boys were teasing it and we stopped them. It doesn't have a collar or a tattoo or anything and it looks pretty ugly. Missy ran home and got her cat's travel thingie. We only managed to get it in because its leg was hurt. It tried to bite us."

Jess stepped closer and it became clear that whatever was in the case was shivering violently. Much as she wanted to turn her back, go collect her kitten and get out of there, she knew she couldn't turn away from an animal in need.

"Why don't you girls come in to the clinic room? Let's set the dog down and see what we've got."

The girls nodded.

Jess preceded them into the room and gestured for them to put the case down on the floor.

Missy released the door, but nothing happened. So she loosed the fastenings around it, and lifted the removable lid. As soon she did, a blur of white, matted fur leaped up at her and began barking aggressively with wide, frightened eyes.

Missy staggered back, holding the case lid in front of her for protection.

The dog looked around wildly, assessing the danger in the room—four humans—and decided to up the volume of its barking. It was shaking violently.

"Oh, f—fudge," Chris said.

Jess was glad he remembered the girls. She wanted to swear, too. And why she'd thought coming to the shelter would be a good idea when she was feeling so emotionally fragile she'd never know.

"That's a really ugly dog," Tammy said.

"It's hurt," Missy, clearly more sympathetic, said.

Jess gave them both tight smiles. "Thank you so much for bringing her in. I think it would be best if we had as few people in the room right now as possible, so she's not too scared. Do you want to come back tomorrow to see how she's doing? See if you'd like to adopt her?"

Both girls shook their heads.

"I've already got two dogs," Tammy said.

"My parents won't let me have any more pets," Missy said sadly.

"Well, thank you both for rescuing her." The dog was still yapping and had retreated into the nearest corner. Jess needed to get her to calm down, if only so she could see what kind of injury they were dealing with. That was if the dog was going to let her anywhere near it.

Chris took over, gently ushering the two girls out of the room so Jess could concentrate.

Jess grabbed a lead and hung it in a loop and then crouched down beside the dog. Her goal was to catch the loop over the dog's head and pull to fasten it, just so she had a way of restraining her. This poor, bedraggled, hurt little thing looked a hundred times more scared than angry, but Jess knew never to underestimate an animal.

"Come on, sweetie," she murmured. "No one's going to hurt you now. I just need to put this lead on you to protect both of us."

The dog kept barking at her, high-pitched yelps that, had they been human, would have been screams.

Jess hated to think what had happened to bring the dog to this state. Dogs that were terrified of humans usually had good reason to be.

"Shhh."

Jess leaned a little closer and managed to hook the lead over the dog's head. As it tightened, the dog yelped louder and scrabbled around on the floor, urinating in pure fear.

"Come on, come over here," Jess coaxed, pulling the dog away from its mess. She sat down on the floor to give herself better leverage over the skittering animal and hopefully make herself look a little less threatening.

The dog shook her head and barked as Jess dragged it across the floor toward her.

It looked like a Maltese, maybe with some poodle and a few other variations in there.

Tammy was right. It was an ugly dog. Her ears, which should have been fluffy and floppy, stuck out at weird angles. Her face was thin and pointed in a way that didn't match with her more barrel-chested body. And then there was the panicked, aggressive barking. This wasn't a dog that was going to make it out of the shelter in the arms of a loving adoptive family.

But despite her likely fate, Jess couldn't do anything but try to fix her.

"What are we going to call you?" Jess wondered aloud, keeping her voice low and steady. She was taking her time shortening the lead, slowly bringing the dog closer and closer. "I can't just call you *girl*. What sort of name would you like?"

The dog was still barking, still shivering.

"We need to give you a nice little name. Something sweet, so that maybe someone will take you home. I know, how about Eddie? It can be short for Edwina. Because I have a feeling that once you get cleaned up, you're going to be a regal-looking girl and that's a royal-sounding name."

The dog was almost at Jess's knees. It stopped barking and looked up at her, still visibly shaking.

Jess held out a cautious hand. Eddie stopped barking long enough to sniff at it.

Jess risked stroking her head lightly.

Eddie didn't duck away.

She risked a firmer pat, a stroke all the way down the dog's body. Partly a pat, partly a clinical, assessing touch.

"Ooh, look at you," Jess praised. "You're really a sweet little thing aren't you?"

Eddie whimpered.

Jess was confident enough in Eddie's state to lift her up into her lap. She cradled the dog, giving her long, loving strokes. "There you go. Everything's okay. No one's going to hurt you now." Jess's own pain returned to the fore, knocking her breath from her for a moment. *Why couldn't someone make the same promises to her?* But life didn't work that way.

Eddie nestled into Jess's lap and, after a minute or two of Jess stroking her and murmuring comforting things, her frail little body finally stopped shaking.

"Wow, will you look at that." Chris had returned to the room, but he kept his distance, allowing Jess to continue to subdue the frightened animal. "I didn't think that would happen. I figured she'd be a goner for sure."

Some of the dogs that came into the shelter were so badly abused, so hurt and damaged that they simply couldn't be helped. They had to be put down almost immediately.

Jess was infinitely glad Eddie wouldn't be one of them. Maybe she actually had half a chance of finding a new home. Dim as those prospects might be.

"Eddie just needed a hug."

"Eddie, huh?" Chris smiled. "I like it. Is she hurt?"

"I'm not really sure. This right hind leg is looking a little strange—maybe a break that didn't heal properly. She was favoring it, so we might need to check that out. Her fur is really matted and pulling on her skin, too."

"Do you think she's ready for an exam?"

"Maybe. Just give us another minute or two."

Jess sat on the floor with Eddie in her lap for a while longer, talking nonsense in low, reassuring tones.

When Jess leaned over to hug the dog, Eddie licked her face.

"Did you see that?" Jess asked.

"Yep," Chris said, the same pleasure and wonder in his voice as Jess felt inside. Dogs were amazing creatures. They got hurt and they bounced back. So amazingly resilient. So unlike humans. So unlike *her*.

"I think she's ready."

With great care, Jess stood, keeping Eddie close, and then she settled her on the examination bench, maintaining contact. Eddie froze up for a moment, but as Jess continued her stroking, she relaxed again.

An hour later, a doped-up Eddie looked like a different dog.

Shaved of her matted hair, which only enhanced her weird sticking-out ears, she was even uglier than before. But she was washed, and the nasty gash on her leg they'd discovered was cleaned and bandaged. Jess's suspicions were confirmed—it was likely the leg had been broken at some earlier time and it had healed badly, making it stick out and therefore more prone to injury. They'd need an X-ray to be sure: this was a dog that was going to require a lot of veterinary attention in the immediate future. And with that fact, Eddie's chances of getting out of the shelter winked into nothingness.

Jess had administered a mild sedative to make the cleanup process easier on both the dog and the humans involved, but sleepy as she was, Eddie kept her eyes trained on Jess, watching her movements wherever she went in the room. She tolerated Chris, but it was obvious she didn't really trust him like she trusted Jess.

"Thanks, Jess," Chris said. "I know you didn't come here for this tonight, but I really appreciate your help."

Eddie was curled up in a dog bed on the floor while she recovered and Jess gave her a smile.

"No problem. I didn't have anything better to do." Jess hoped she sounded lighthearted and not as bleak as she felt inside about that fact.

Concentrating on Eddie for the past hour had been a blessing. For that short time Jess had been able to ignore the yawning emptiness inside her.

Despite herself, Jess couldn't help checking the time. Sean would be heading for the airport in an hour or so. Off to L.A. and out of her life. And she was letting him go.

It's for the best.

It didn't feel like it.

She might be able to push the pain away for moments at a time, like when she was concentrating on treating a dog, but it was still there, an ache in her gut, an almost overwhelming sense of loss. And it was all her doing. Sean had put it all on the table, laid himself bare to her—she was the one who wouldn't take the risk.

Chris gave her a smile. "Still, it's great of you to have done this. Why don't you get going? Did you still want to look at the cats?"

"Yeah, I guess." Jess shook herself out of her thoughts. She might as well get started on this new life of hers. Just her and some pets.

If only that didn't sound so terribly lonely.

"Okay, let's go down to the cattery. I'll leave Eddie in her bed for a while and then I'll come back and get her."

"Good."

Jess didn't want to look at Eddie again. She and Chris both knew Eddie wouldn't be making it out of here, and it was too sad. It was too much emotion on top of a day so full of emotion that it left her feeling punch-drunk.

Chris opened the door and gestured for Jess to go through first. As she stepped outside, Eddie whimpered and then let out a yelp. There was a scrambling noise as she got out of her bed and lurched across the floor, determined to follow Jess despite her drowsiness.

"Aw, Jess. I think you've made a friend for life."

Jess's chest ached as the determined little dog scrambled across the floor toward her—no doubt hurting her leg in the process. "She needs to lie down again. Maybe we need to give her another dose of sedative."

"Sure, I'll take care of it after I've shown you out." Chris began to close the door, shutting it behind them.

It was silent for a while, but then came the sound of heartbreaking whimpering.

"Isn't it amazing?" Chris said, his voice sad. "Dogs are so brave. Who knows what happened to Eddie, but clearly some asshole really hurt her. Neglected her. And yet she was willing to try again—to trust you." He paused, as if taking in the astonishing resilience of animals. "Do you think maybe they can smell whether someone is a good person or not? Do you think she just somehow knew?"

"I don't know. But if she can keep it up, maybe she's got half a chance of getting adopted."

"Maybe," Chris said doubtfully. "She grew to trust you, but that's no guarantee she'll trust anyone else. But we can hope." He sighed. "Well, let's get going."

Eddie's whining faded and once again there was silence. But Jess couldn't will her feet to move.

"Cats?" Chris asked, nudging her.

Still she couldn't move.

A sudden revelation washed over her: she didn't want a cat.

Jess swallowed hard and forced herself to face the truth. She wanted an ugly, injured dog that was going to require a huge amount of love and care and veterinary attention.

She wanted to give Eddie a second chance. The brave little dog deserved one.

"Chris? I think instead of a kitten I'll take Eddie with me."

"Uh-oh." Chris shook his head. "You sure? You know what you're getting into there?"

Jess opened the door and searched the room. The bed was empty. Eddie had retreated into the corner, shivering again. But as soon as Jess took a step inside the dog's head popped up and she stumbled to her feet. Eddie staggered over to Jess, and her little tail wagged. *You came back.*

It was the tail wag that clinched it.

Jess blinked back tears. "Yep, she's mine."

"Okay. Let me get a travel case. And let's give her another shot of sedative to make the ride home easier on her."

Eddie has no reason at all to trust you.

But she's willing to give you a chance. To show her that she can be loved. That you can be trusted.

Just like Sean had offered to her.

What he'd offered her wasn't second best, *it was a second chance.*

And if this hurt, abused, injured little dog could try, then why couldn't she?

Sean was right. This wasn't about him. He could only offer himself, his love and his attention. Finding the courage to try again? That was Jess's issue, wholly and solely.

Did she really want to live the rest of her life alone? Like Eddie, barking at anyone who came close, fearful that everyone she came in contact with would hurt her?

That wasn't the kind of person she wanted to be. She'd bungee jumped. Had wild times backpacking around Europe. Done exciting things. Been in love with someone enough to marry them. Yes, so things hadn't turned out the way she'd thought in that particular scenario. But if she let that one experience determine her whole life, what kind of coward was she, really?

Everything was a blur as she rushed Chris through organizing Eddie and raced to the car.

Sean would still be at Rob and Hailey's. If only she

could get there in time. Once he got to the airport it'd be impossible to find him.

She needed to see him before he left. Tell him she loved him. Tell him she wanted him to come home to her.

CHAPTER EIGHTEEN

DEZZIE WAS STILL parked out front of Rob and Hailey's when Jess pulled up.

That didn't necessarily mean anything—maybe they were just looking after Sean's car while he was away.

Eddie was in a travel case in the back of Jess's car. Thankfully the dog hadn't been too bothered by the car ride and seemed to be sleeping off the knockout shot. But Jess didn't want Eddie to wake up and find herself locked up and alone, so she opened the case and scooped up the drowsy dog. Eddie whimpered, licked Jess's face and then settled on to her shoulder like a sleeping child.

She ran up the pathway to the front door and knocked loudly.

What if you're too late?

Sean might have already left. And even if he hadn't, after their last conversation, he might have decided that she was too much trouble, too difficult for him to bother with. Why would he put up with her when he could have practically anyone he wanted?

"No, Jess." She said the words aloud to bring her raging thoughts to a halt. This was what had to stop.

This internal undermining of herself. Mark might have taught her the habit, but she was the one who was keeping it up.

No more.

"Jess?" Hailey answered the door, her eyes raking over Jess, no doubt taking in the fact that Jess still wore her navy work scrubs and held a bandaged dog in her arms. "Is everything okay?"

"Is Sean still here?"

"Yeah, but—"

"Jess?"

Sean's voice coming from within the house sent a wave of relief washing over her, so strong she felt her knees go watery.

At least he's still here. At least you get a chance to try.

"Sean?" She cuddled Eddie tighter in her arms.

A moment later he was at the door.

He was wearing that canvas jacket that seemed to be his favorite, and his hair was artfully spiked. His jeans fit him in a way that should have been illegal and his puzzled green eyes with their long lashes were swoon-worthy.

He was too good to be true.

Too young, too handsome.

But she wasn't going to think like that anymore.

He loved her. He'd said so. Of all the people in all the world, Sean Paterson had fallen in love with *her*.

He didn't quite know how to handle it.

Neither did she.

Somehow, they'd work it out together. Jess just had to find the courage to try.

"Jess? Is everything okay?" he asked.

"I…" Now that the moment was here, Jess was struck dumb. What could she possibly say to explain her own jumbled thoughts?

He gave Eddie a look. "I have to say, that is one very ugly dog."

"What's the story?" Hailey asked. Rob appeared behind her, putting one hand on his wife's shoulder.

Hailey's question gave Jess an idea, a place to start. She tilted her head to press it to Eddie. Eddie gave her a sleepy lick in return.

"This is Eddie," she said, her eyes trained on Sean. She couldn't work out what was going through his mind—his expression was carefully blank. So blank it gave Jess pause—what if she'd irreparably damaged this fragile thing between them?

So what?

Even if she had, even if Sean was going to tell her to go away and never come back, she had to try. That was what having courage was all about. In Sean's books, Sebastian was always charging into every situation without a second thought, but it was Rob, the guy who didn't really know how to fight, who was terrified of all the things that went bump in the night, who was the courageous one. He did what needed to be done, knowing that it might be more than he could handle.

Jess sent a weird prayer to the fictional Rob: *help me find the courage.*

"Eddie came into the shelter tonight," she continued, hearing the nervous waver in her own voice. But she kept eye contact with Sean, and thankfully he held her gaze. "She's been badly abused. One of her legs was broken and never healed properly. She's malnourished and has been completely neglected for a long time. She'll probably need surgery and it's still hard to know whether she'll be able to be socialized."

"Oh, poor thing," Hailey said, carefully reaching out a hand to Eddie's head so the dog could sniff her.

"That's a sad story," Sean said. He was still leaning against the doorjamb, a slight wariness in his stance. And who could blame him?

Jess forced herself to plow on.

"She's been so badly treated in her life, her first reaction to people was to bark and fight back. But as soon as I started petting her, as soon as I hugged her, she trusted me. She was so brave..." Jess's voice broke, but she sucked in a breath. She couldn't dissolve now. She needed to see this through. And then, if Sean didn't want her, she'd turn around and go home and she and Eddie would comfort each other.

Hailey crooned quietly to the dog. Eddie licked Hailey's hand and Hailey began stroking her.

"Hailey, would you mind taking her?" Jess asked as soon as she saw that Eddie was comfortable. "She seems to like you."

"Sure I can. Come here, baby."

Jess and Hailey took a moment to gently exchange Eddie. Eddie settled happily in Hailey's arms.

"That's a really ugly dog," Rob said.

"Oh, hush," Hailey said. "Don't you listen to him, Eddie. You're beautiful."

Rob and Hailey discreetly stepped inside with the dog, leaving Sean and a grateful Jess standing in the doorway.

Relieved of her bundle, Jess turned to face Sean, her hands by her sides.

This had to work.

"Sean, I'm so sorry. You were right. I was being a coward. And the person I need to learn to trust is myself, as much as you."

Sean held up his hands. "I still have to go to L.A., Jess. I still need to do my work."

"I know. And I'll be waiting right here for you when you get back."

Sean searched her eyes. "Are you sure? Can you really do it?"

"If I don't, what kind of life am I building for myself? One where I never trust anyone again out of fear? That's not who I want to be. I need to learn to live differently." The admission made her feel as if she'd torn her beating heart out of her chest and had put it on display to the world.

Sean didn't react the way she expected. He didn't drag her into his arms. Or fall to his knees with relief.

Instead, he eyed her suspiciously. "So, I'm just practice again?" His voice was raw. "I'm the young kid who'll help you get back on your feet. And once you're feeling confident again, you'll dump me and find someone new."

Jess's lungs had constricted to half their normal

size—she couldn't catch her breath. Tears burned her eyes.

She was getting it all wrong.

"I want *you*. For as long as you'll have me. I love you, Sean."

Jess watched the tendons in his neck work as he swallowed.

"I love you, too, but—" he began.

Jess stepped closed and put a finger to his mouth.

"We love each other. We're both not really sure how to make this work. You've never done it before. I've done it before—but I learned all the wrong habits. We can both teach each other. If we make an effort, if we talk to each other about how we're feeling...don't you think we owe it to ourselves to try?"

Sean tunneled his fingers through his hair. "Jess."

She watched the emotions play across his face. A few seconds passed, but it seemed an eternity, standing there, waiting to see if the man she loved still wanted her.

And then, the corner of Sean's mouth twitched. Just the tiniest bit.

Nothing less than pure joy, so sharp it hurt, flooded Jess's entire being. A hot, heavy tear spilled over and rolled down her cheek.

She'd dared and won. Survived the leap.

"Sean."

The breath whooshed out of her as he wrapped his arms around her and crushed her to his chest.

"No more freak-outs, okay?" he whispered in her ear.

She could feel the pounding of his heart against her breast, as rapid and frantic as her own.

"Promise," she managed to say as her breath caught in a sob.

He chuckled. "You know what? I think I'll kind of miss them."

Jess sniffed. "I won't."

And then he was kissing her, and she wondered how she'd ever thought she could live the rest of her life without this. She now knew that any risk was worth taking to feel this loved, this cherished.

"I love you, Sean," she said against his lips.

Sean settled his forehead against hers. "I love you, too, Jess."

"And I can't wait for us to start our life together."

Sean pulled back a little, his expression turning suddenly grim. "But...I still have to go to L.A. Now."

"I know. But you'll come back to me."

"I'll come back to you," he echoed softly, rubbing his nose against hers. "And I'm only gone for a week. We can survive a week, right?"

Jess didn't want to be apart for a minute, but she had to live in the real world. "We can survive it."

"And I'll call you every day."

"Uh, Sean?" Rob's voice called out before Sean could answer. "I'm sorry to interrupt, but if you don't get on your way to the airport, you're gonna miss your flight."

"I'll take you," Jess said urgently. "Please, let me take you."

Sean nodded. "Okay, just let me get my bags."

SEAN'S PHONE RANG just as they were pulling out from Rob and Hailey's street with Sean's bags loaded in Jess's car. Eddie was being looked after by Rob and Hailey until Jess got back—and Jess could already tell that Eddie and Hailey had bonded, and Eddie had even tentatively licked Rob. That was a good sign—maybe Eddie was going to be fine.

Sean took the call and it was clearly about the arrangements for his trip once he arrived in Los Angeles. He kept shooting Jess apologetic looks, but Jess just mouthed, "It's okay," and kept driving. It was logical: he needed to know where to head when he hit the ground on the other end of the flight, so he needed to take the call. Jess told herself to be patient, even if it was the last thing she wanted. They had so little time before he'd be on the plane....

The conversation kept him busy all the way out to the airport, through parking the car, locating a trolley and pushing his luggage into the departures hall. He hung up, but then there was no time to talk as he found the correct counter and checked in for his flight.

Before she knew it, they were both standing at the security checkpoint. She couldn't go any farther. It was time to say goodbye. And although Sean had said he'd come back to her, and although it was only going to be a week, Jess didn't want to let him go.

"I don't want you to go," she said. Looked like her courage to speak her mind, make herself vulnerable, hadn't been a fleeting thing. That was good.

He gave her a smile that set her tummy fluttering with nerves.

"I've still got a few minutes before I have to go through."

"I know."

"And I'm going to be back before you know it."

Jess wished it wasn't so noisy and busy around them. There were people everywhere, milling about. This felt like a conversation that needed to be private. She wished they were in her bedroom, lying in bed in the dark.

She wished that for lots of reasons.

Sean's eyes slid past her and locked on someone in the background.

"Rachel?" he said.

Jess turned around and saw a woman emerge from a nearby café. She nodded to Sean, a sheepish look on her face.

"Hi, Sean."

It took Jess a moment to recognize Sean's dedicated fan without the blond wig and vampire getup. But clearly Rachel had a thing for costumes. Today she wore a '40s man-styled pin-striped suit with an exaggeratedly large gold fob chain and a cravat at her neck. Her own blond hair was slicked back. She quickly shoved a cardboard sign behind her back.

Jess had forgotten all about her. Sean had been dismissive of Rachel's importance to him, but Jess wasn't so sure Rachel saw things the same way.

But he was hers now.

If Rachel wanted a fight, she was getting one. Jess

had let Mark cheat on her and she'd taken it as if it were a punishment she deserved. Never again.

"Hi, Rachel," Jess said. She stepped closer to Sean and made a show of taking his hand in hers. He returned her grasp with a quick squeeze.

Rachel gave Jess a quick "Hi," and then turned her attention back to Sean. "What are you doing here?" she asked.

"Heading over to the States for some meetings," Sean said breezily.

Rachel looked disappointed. "So I guess we won't be having that fan meet-up anytime soon."

Ah. Rachel and Sean hadn't been arranging a date. Jess felt some tight thing inside her release.

She wasn't going to make assumptions anymore, wasn't going to imagine the worst, right off. Sean deserved her trust; she was going to place her faith in him. It was the most terrifying thing ever. But she would do her best.

She tightened her grip on Sean's hand and in response he tugged on her grip to pull her closer, so she was pressed right up against his side.

He shook his head in answer to Rachel's comment. "Uh, no. Sorry. Watch for my updates on Twitter. Then you'll know what my movements are."

"Okay." Rachel shuffled and if Jess didn't know better, she would have said the girl looked awkward. Uncomfortable even.

Sean waved a hand at her costume. "I don't recognize the outfit."

Now Rachel definitely *did* look uncomfortable.

"Oh, it's… Well, it's from Stuart Ross's books. You know, the Dragon Tamer series?" She pulled the cardboard out from behind her back and showed it to them.

Welcome to Australia, Stuart Ross! From your number-one fan!

There were love hearts all around the edges.

"I thought you were *my* number-one fan," Sean said.

"I am! But I'm allowed to be the fan of more than one person," Rachel said defensively.

Jess choked back a laugh both at Sean's hurt expression and Rachel's defensiveness. For one, she was very glad that Rachel spread her adoration around.

"Is he flying in tonight?" Jess asked.

"Yes. In fact, I better get down to arrivals. I think his plane has just landed."

"He'll be a while getting through customs."

"Yeah, but I want to be right in front when he comes out."

"Good idea," Jess said.

Rachel started to walk away.

"I'll let you know via Twitter when I'm going to be back," Sean called after her.

Rachel gave a wave as she walked away, but didn't turn around. "Awesome." Her reply was only barely audible over the hubbub around them.

Sean turned to Jess with a pout that would have done a two-year-old proud. "That's pretty disappointing," he said.

Jess burst out laughing.

"What?"

His pout deepened and only made her laugh harder. "Jess?"

"Nothing." She wiped her eyes and sucked in a breath, trying to control her reaction.

Sean looked at his watch and Jess instantly sobered. They were on borrowed time. He had to walk through those doors in the next few minutes.

"I really should get going," he said.

"There's so much I still want to talk about," Jess said, beginning to feel frantic as the clock ticked down to the minute he would have to walk away.

"There's always the phone."

He was right. It wasn't as if he was disappearing into a black hole.

"And I could always get a Twitter account," Jess suggested with a shrug.

That made him laugh. "That would be fantastic. But it wouldn't be enough. I think we need more than a hundred and forty characters to say what we need to say."

"You're probably right."

"Although right now? Right now I only need ten." He stepped closer, wrapping his arms around her. He lowered his lips to her ear. *"I love you."*

Jess wondered how long it was going to take before hearing those words from Sean Paterson didn't make her feel as though a gilded cage inside her chest had burst open and doves had flown out trailing satin ribbons behind them. As corny and beautiful as that sounded.

"I love you," she said in return.

"I wish we had more time." Sean pulled back and she could see the longing in his eyes.

"We've got all the time in the world," Jess said with a smile.

The corner of Sean's mouth twitched up in the way that had bewitched her right from the moment he'd appeared in front of her holding a glass of champagne and sat down beside her to talk about cars.

"So we do," he said. "But no matter how much time we have, I'll never get enough of this."

And with that he closed the small gap between them, pressing her body against his. When his lips touched hers, Jess gripped his shoulders, her fingers digging into hard muscle. One of his hands slid around her, fanning out over her lower back, while the other tilted her head to his liking, allowing him to control the kiss.

At first he kept things light, nibbling at her lips with his own. Capturing each of her lips between his. Sucking on them. Then light swipes of his tongue.

Jess groaned and opened her mouth to him. He didn't wait for further invitation, delving into her with hot, wet passion.

Jess was oblivious to the other farewells taking place around them. For the first time in recent memory, she was too happy, too sure of herself, too confident in her decision to worry about anything else.

She was going to be waiting for Sean when he returned, and they'd take up again right here where they left off.

Well, perhaps not *right here* in the airport.

With that sobering thought, Jess managed to push against Sean's chest and lowered her chin to break from the kiss.

"What?" Sean asked raggedly. He didn't let her go one inch.

Jess bumped her forehead against his. "We're at the airport."

"Yeah, so we are." His breathing was rough.

"Probably should stop things there."

She felt his forehead wrinkle against hers as he quirked his eyebrows. "Why?"

"Oh, you know. Standards of public decency and all that," Jess joked.

"These people are so bored...they're all just waiting for a show."

"A song-and-dance number, maybe, but probably not what we've both got in our minds."

Sean gave a soft laugh. "Yeah, okay. Gotcha. There might be kids around."

"Exactly."

There was a pause and then Sean let out a long breath.

"I really don't want to go to L.A. anymore."

"Yes, you do. Go sort out Sebastian. Get the movie happening. Then come back home to me."

"Home to you," Sean echoed, a touch of wonder in his voice.

He slowly unwound from her, releasing his firm hold on her back, and grinned. "I like the sound of that."

"Me, too."

Jess swallowed hard as she watched Sean hitch his backpack a little higher on his shoulder and take a few steps toward the sliding doors that would take him out of her sight. A crowd of people suddenly surged around him, and Sean was carried through the doors faster than she would have liked.

"I'm coming home to you!" Sean called out before he was swallowed up, the opaque glass doors sliding shut and shielding him from view.

Jess blinked back tears, but for once they were tears of joy. She turned and headed for her car. She had to go pick up Eddie—they likely had a long night ahead of them once the sedatives wore off. And then she had to get her house ready. Her life ready.

Sean Paterson was moving in. And she couldn't wait.

EPILOGUE

Twelve months later

JESS'S FEET WERE twitching in their uncomfortable heels, and she hoped most people would mistake it as an urge to get up and mingle. Actually, it was an urge to get the hell out of there.

She really enjoyed spending time with Rob and Hailey. But the Paterson family *en masse* was a different story.

Today had been a huge day. Her feet were sore, the muscles of her face worn-out from smiling, and she'd been too busy posing for photos and talking to people to get the chance to eat or drink. More than anything she wanted to go home, soak in a hot bath and then enjoy some Thai takeout in front of the television. Snuggled up next to her family.

"Here, you look like you could use one of these."

A misted glass of champagne materialized in front of her eyes.

"Yes, please."

She took the glass gratefully, taking a sip of the cool, bubbly liquid, closing her eyes as she enjoyed the feel of it sliding down her throat.

"If you don't wipe that expression off your face in the next two seconds, I won't be responsible for my actions."

Sean's flirty comment made the champagne bubbles explode like fireworks in her belly.

"Promise?" Jess asked.

She opened her eyes just as Sean sat down beside her. He was as gorgeous as ever in a navy suit, snowy-white shirt and red tie.

Jess was quite proud of her own knee-length jersey wrap-dress in tomato-red. It was the coordinating four-inch heels that were the problem.

She deliberately arranged her face into a more mild expression. "There, is that better?"

He smiled at her. And her heart skipped. Like it always did.

"Better. But I want to see that other look back again when we get home." He leaned across to put a quick kiss on the tip of her nose.

"You're on."

Sean shifted his chair closer to hers and stretched his arm out behind her. They sat in silence for a while, observing the activity in the room.

"I think Caitlyn Louise's head has well and truly been wetted," Sean said.

"You think?" Jess asked sarcastically. "I've never seen such a huge christening celebration before."

Stephen and Tori Paterson had hired a function center for a reception after the church service. At least a hundred people were drinking champagne and eating finger sandwiches in honor of the baby girl who was currently taking a well-deserved nap in her father's arms.

There was even a two-tiered cake with matching pink-frosted cupcakes surrounding it.

"Well, being as she is the cutest baby in the entire universe, she does deserve it," Sean said indulgently.

He'd taken to *uncledom* with absolute glee. Baby Caitlyn Louise now owned more than a few toys that she would take several years to grow into. Like the remote-controlled car. And the authentic collector's edition *Star Wars* light sabers. Luckily her dad and uncle seemed willing to ensure those toys didn't go rusty from disuse.

"That goes without saying."

Sean leaned in and whispered in her ear, "Let's get out of here."

"We can't. They haven't cut the cake," Jess protested. But then she frowned. "I don't know what the etiquette is here. Do we need to wait for them to cut the cake?"

"We won't be cutting the cake," a stern female voice said from behind them. "It will be kept for Caitlyn's first birthday. But the cupcakes will be given out to all the guests shortly."

Tori Paterson appeared before them in her usual severe splendor. Her strawberry-blond hair was immaculately groomed, and her pastel blue suit entirely appropriate for the occasion.

Jess had spoken to Tori and Stephen Paterson on a few occasions, but she always found them more than a little intimidating. Besides, Sean rarely let any

conversation with them last much longer than pleas-
antries, so Jess hadn't had much opportunity to get
to know them.

"Hi, Mom. Nice party," Sean said. His voice was
pleasant, but he'd stiffened up in his chair and had
shifted his arm so it was around Jess's shoulders,
gripping a little too tight.

"Thank you, Sean. And I thought you did a very
nice job. You both looked very…*dignified* when you
stood up with Rob and Hailey as Caitlyn's godpar-
ents."

Sean bristled and Jess knew he'd heard veiled criticism in his mother's words. As if she was surprised
he'd managed to hold the baby without dropping
her. Though Jess wasn't sure that that was what Tori
meant. Maybe the woman was trying to be friendly,
to mend the gap between mother and son—she was
just going about it all wrong.

"Thanks, Tori," Jess rushed in before Sean could
say anything. "We were so honored that Rob and
Hailey chose us. And Caitlyn is just the most gorgeous baby ever."

Tori preened with grandmotherly pride. "She is,
isn't she? She's just like Sean was when he was her
age, a good sleeper, not fussy at all."

Jess elbowed Sean. "You hear that? You've been a
good sleeper all your life."

Sean managed half a smile. "Yeah, but I'm pretty
fussy now."

"Okay, well…" Tori smiled tightly. "I guess I'll

get back to circulating." She hesitated and Jess saw a crack in the imposing facade.

"How's Paterson Associates managing without Rob?" Jess asked quickly. Rob had taken a several-weeks-long service leave to be at home with Hailey and Caitlyn, and Jess wanted to give Tori a reason to keep talking. Maybe, if she did, she'd work out the right way to begin mending bridges with her son.

On the other side of the room, Jess noticed Hailey hoisting Caitlyn into her arms, cradling the little bundle and gazing down at her with absolute devotion. One day, long ago, Tori Paterson had loved Sean like that. Probably still did—she just didn't know how to show it.

These days, Jess was all for second chances.

But Sean's fingers dug into her shoulders, leaving her in no doubt that he wasn't pleased. He didn't want the mother-son conversation extended.

"Fine, fine," Tori said. "Of course Stephen is working too hard, but he'll do that no matter what I say." She pulled a handkerchief out from a pocket and began twisting it in her hands. Her gaze slid from Jess across to her son. "Rob tells me you've been working some long hours recently, too," she said quietly.

Jess did an inner fist-pump. *Good on you, Tori.*

Sean was silent for a moment. "Um. Yeah. I'm on a deadline for revisions on my latest novel. And there have been a few rewrites on the screenplay that I've had to oversee."

"Right. Good." Tori nodded, but didn't seem to know what to say next.

"The movie is coming along really well," Jess jumped in to say. "It's filming right now. We're actually having a little gathering at Rob and Hailey's place next weekend to watch the draft version of the trailer."

"Oh. That's exciting."

Jess decided to go all-in. She wasn't sure how Sean would react, but she was going to try anyway. "Would you and Stephen like to come?" she asked.

Tori was silent for a moment.

Sean's arm disappeared from around her and he sat up straight in his chair. "You don't have to. I know you're busy, and with Rob on leave, Dad's probably got too much going on. Besides, it's only a silly movie."

Jess hated hearing Sean denigrate his own success. The past year together had taught each of them a lot about trust and love and having faith. Sean's relationship with his parents, though, was still a minefield.

"Actually—we'd love to come."

Jess couldn't be one hundred percent sure, but she was positive she spotted tears in Tori's eyes. But they were gone in an instant.

"One of your father's clients has significant investments in the movie industry. Apparently it's quite risky, but that's what he likes about it. I can't see your father and I investing in anything like that. It's all just a bit unpredictable and shaky, isn't it? Why would you put money into fancy stories when you could buy mining shares?"

Jess could practically hear Sean's teeth grinding

together and she held back a sigh. *Well, it was a start.*
And if Tori and Stephen came to watch the movie
trailer and said anything other than how fantastic it
was, they'd have Jess to answer to.

"I'll have Rob and Hailey pass on the details for
next weekend," Jess said, standing up. "But if it's
okay, Sean and I were just talking about leaving.
We've got a dog at home that had surgery during the
week, and we need to check on her."

"Yes, we need to head home," Sean said, getting
to his feet beside her.

"Oh, your rescue puppy. How is the poor little
thing? Rob told me about her. She's had three lots of
surgery on her leg, is that right?"

Jess nodded. "Yes. But this last lot should fix
her up permanently. She's got much better mobil-
ity now." Eddie wasn't quite as ugly now that her
fur had grown back. And she was the cuddliest dog
Jess had ever known—her favorite place in the world
was curled up on the sofa snuggled between her and
Sean.

Jess had to admit that was one of her most favorite places, too.

"That's good to hear," Tori said. "Don't leave just
yet—let me go get you your cupcakes to take home."
With that she spun on her heel and headed across to
the other side of the room. But before she got to the
cake stand, someone interrupted her and a moment
later she was deep in conversation.

"Can we get out of here now?" Sean whined.

"We should say goodbye to Rob and Hailey at least," Jess said.

"Sure." Sean cricked his neck and peered around the room, spotting Rob at the other end. He waved frantically until Rob looked over and then Sean made elaborate hand gestures to explain that they were leaving. Rob gave them a thumbs-up before returning to his conversation.

"There. Done. Let's get out of here."

He took her hand and tugged on it, but Jess didn't move. He turned back to her with a frown. "What's up?"

Jess put a hand on her hip. "Maybe it's true. Familiarity *does* breed contempt."

"Huh?"

She put on a teasing tone. "Time was, you'd whisk me out of here with a promise of a ride in your fast car and potential shenanigans in the backseat. Now it's just 'let's get out of here.' Disappointing, Mr. Paterson. Disappointing."

In a flash that wicked grin was back. "I thought that shenanigans in the backseat was standard operating procedure these days."

"A girl likes to be wooed, Mr. Paterson."

"Wooed or seduced?"

Jess bit her lip and pretended to think on that. "Both. I'll take both, please."

"Done."

With a laugh Sean bundled her into his arms and pressed a kiss to her mouth. "And don't think I don't know what you just did with my mother," he leaned in to whisper into her ear.

"Just giving her a second chance. We all deserve one."

Sean made a mock growling noise before he sighed. "I guess so."

Jess kissed his cheek.

Sean stepped back, took her hand and began to lead them toward the exit. He looked back over his shoulder at her, his green eyes flashing with gold.

"Let's go for a drive."

"Just a drive?" Jess asked.

He grinned. "Oh, no. Way more than just a drive."

* * * * *